He Will Have the World

David-Jack Fletcher

SLASHIC HORROR
PRESS

ISBN-13: 978-1-7637256-8-3

This book is dedicated to everyone who has ever suffered the stigmas associated with mental health.

ONE

"I DON'T WANT YOU to go."

The words stabbed at my heart. I bit my lip to stop the tears. After everything... after what I did, he still wanted me—still loved me. I could hear the ache in his words, even as an airport announcer called for missing passengers. Through the chaos of the fellow travellers and the noises buzzing around my head, I could still hear it. He'd always been like that, helping me cut through the noise.

We both knew I didn't deserve it. Didn't deserve him.

Yet there he was.

Aiden waited for me to reply, and I held the phone away from my ear so he couldn't hear the heavy breathing. Or the tiny whimper as I replayed his words in my head. I watched a family pocketing their passports and wheeling their cabin luggage through the airport to a café. Four of them, a typical mother, father, and two kids—a boy and a girl, the regular nuclear family. The mother kept looking at her phone and then staring up at who I assumed was her husband. He was absorbed by the passports, nodding at her with disinterest.

My chest tightened as he tucked something into the back of his pants. *See something, say something. See something, say something—*

"Charlie?" Aiden's tinny voice echoed, and I brought the phone back.

The family continued on its way, and my eyes tracked them. The little boy was scanning the area. He looked scared. The girl looked over her shoulder at me. I waved, and she poked her tongue out. I narrowed my eyes at her, and she tugged at her dad's shirt, pointing at me. The father glared in my direction and ushered the family away.

I spun around to face outside, even though the plate-glass windows were black, like the world outside. Night was the worst, but it would have to do, and I searched the windows, staring beyond my bleak reflection—the messy hair, the stubble, the dirty, stained clothes. I had to do something, though; I had to avoid that little girl and her father. They were bad news, I could tell, and if they saw me staring, that would be it for me.

In the reflection, I saw them walking away, the father giving me the once-over as he did. Beyond them, the airport. It was too busy. My face was hot, the people were breathing all over me, and the noises—wheels on the floor, the hum of phones ringing, the crying of someone somewhere, machinery—made me want to puke.

"I'm here," I said, turning back to the family as they ambled away. Again, the father tucked something behind his back. I couldn't see what it was. I looked around for security. Nothing.

Only people off on holiday. The kid looked at me again and smiled, her lips stretching thin and wide, her eyes low and dark.

She's one of them.

"You can... come home." Aiden sounded a little scared as the words tumbled from him. As if he were afraid of what might happen if I did, in fact, go home.

"You know I can't." I ran a hand through my hair. I looked at my feet, the shoelaces hanging over the sides, then looked back up.

The family was gone; the girl vanished. I knew those eyes. I'd have recognised them anywhere.

"Aiden, a second ago I... saw something."

He sighed, letting the deep exhale sink into my ear. "Charlie, did you take your pills?"

"I didn't even say what I saw," I mumbled. "This is real, Aiden."

"Please come home," he said. His voice was calm, but it had that sharp undertone he was famous for.

Clutching at my own boarding pass, I swallowed, still searching for that little girl. She was in the airport somewhere, watching me. I could feel her eyes on me. Her father's too. The mother hadn't been classified. She might not know what'd happened to her family. She could be innocent—unaware.

I need more information.

"Charlie?" Aiden's voice was shaky now. "Charlie, what did you see?"

He doesn't believe me. He never believed me. That's why I—

"Talk to me."

"Nothing," I said. "It's nothing. I have to go."

Aiden tried to say something, but my finger was already on the red icon. I hung up, shoving the device into my pants pocket, and breathed through the chaos around me. My flight was boarding in twenty minutes, and I wasn't even at the gate.

The signs overhead directed me, and I followed them, and the girl followed me. They were leading me somewhere, and I reminded myself it wasn't to anywhere special. It was just to the gate, to a bunch of uncomfortable seats in a poorly air-conditioned space with a group of strangers.

Enemies.

I felt for my medication in my breast pocket and pushed the intrusion out of my mind. Not everyone was an enemy. Not everyone was bad. Not *everyone*.

Wheeling my bag to Gate 9A, I studied the faces of my fellow travellers. The flight looked to be sparse. I'd chosen this flight because it was the first one heading to Perth; it was just luck that it was low on bookings. The flight was leaving anyway; I might as well have been on it, and with fewer passengers, the chance of finding one of *them* was reduced.

Not impossible.

My psychologist told me a good way to remind myself that we were all human was to look into their eyes. 'Find the light in their eyes, and you'll know you're okay.' It was my advice to her, but she'd repeated it to me when I needed to hear it.

She hadn't been wrong so far.

The girl and her family weren't there. The evidence suggested she was, in fact, not following me. The evidence told me I was being unreasonable, that she was just a kid on her way to a theme park somewhere. She wasn't even on my flight. At least I hadn't seen her.

I was being symptomatic again. The feeling in the pit of my stomach wasn't so sure, though.

"Boarding pass, please," a woman asked, her hand extended.

I was at the front of the line, and didn't remember getting there. Autopilot had kicked in, and I made a mental note of it. I was supposed to stay present, to always know that I was still myself. I'd been too busy studying—twenty-three passengers, twenty-four including me. All the lights in their eyes were fine, even the guy with the hoodie in the middle of the Australian summer.

Handing my boarding pass to the flight attendant—Calista, by her name tag—I smiled. It was forced and empty, but she didn't notice. Her smile was genuine. She was happy, but why? I couldn't figure it out as I passed her, gripping my ticket tightly to my chest.

Someone behind me was laughing. I stopped and spun around, feeling drops of sweat slide down my face and neck. It wasn't the heat; it was the paranoia. I *knew* it was paranoia. People were allowed to laugh, to be happy and jovial. The sounds didn't mean they were laughing at me, yet my gut stirred.

"Are you right, mate?" Hoodie guy stood in front of me, his own cabin luggage just a Nike shoulder bag. There couldn't be much in it, and I remembered security had been very light earlier. Under the hoodie, I saw light brown hair. He was fair-skinned. Maybe he didn't want to get burned in the heat. Except we were inside, under the luminescence of the halogens.

He's one of—

I nodded to him, staring into his eyes. He looked away and scratched at his nose, watching me grab my pills from my breast pocket.

"Nervous flyer, huh?" he asked, and then he continued on his way.

"I don't like tight spaces," I replied, even though I was talking too low for him to hear me. "Claustrophobic, on top of everything else," I muttered to myself.

Other passengers moved straight past me, a few people giving sad smiles as they saw my sorry state—sweaty, pale—and I looked down at myself to see my polo shirt was creased and unkempt. My jeans had mud stains on them. Aiden had asked me to change, begged me in fact. As usual, I hadn't listened to him. I'd been listening to the voice inside me telling me he was trying to control me, trying to make me something I'm not.

Aiden was human; that much I knew. And I loved him.

That's why I was taking this flight to begin with.

Swallowing my pill, I resumed walking down the narrow air bridge. The walls grew thinner as I went, shrinking, shrinking as the door of the plane became more prominent.

I breathed through the nerves. That's all they were. I tried to convince myself of that, repeating the idea on a loop as a different flight attendant, a man this time, asked to see my boarding pass again. One person asking, I could understand.

But two?

Searching his eyes, I was a little at ease. I showed my pass.

"All the way in the back row, sir," he said, pointing me towards the aisle.

People were packing their luggage into the overhead compartments, and the route seemed so unclear. A straight line, yet not really. I began to see patterns, different pathways through the chaos, through the people and their junk, and the pressure in my head started to build.

My seat is way too far away. I should have booked my flight earlier. I should have asked for an aisle seat. For the exit row. I didn't request a specific meal. What entertainment do they have? Where's the toilet? Where's the fucking *toilet? How do I get off this thing?*

"Sir, please," the attendant said, smiling. He must have seen my chest puffing in and out, because he added, "Everything okay, sir?"

Sir, sir, sir. "Sure, I'm good." I headed down the aisle, taking a deep, deep breath and holding it as I shuffled towards my seat: 26C.

A woman with flowing black hair was struggling with her cabin luggage, and she muttered "Sorry" as she heaved it above her head. She looked at me like she expected something. Help, maybe?

No way. She's on her own.

I pushed past her, ignoring the passive-aggressive "Arsehole" from a nearby traveller, an old woman with shaking hands and grey hair wrapped in a tight weave.

Repeating my actions with four others, their eyes all filled with light, I made it to seat 26C. The row was empty—*thank fuck*—and I stuffed my bag above me and plunged into the seat.

The seatbelt was under my arse, and I pulled it free, strapped in, and shut my eyes.

THEY WANT YOU TO STRAP IN. THEY WANT YOU SHACKLED. THEY WANT YOU—

I took another pill, and the voice subsided. My psychologist had told me that times of stress can make it stronger, so I needed to practice my breathing. I trusted her. She believed me. She was human.

My neck sweat was seeping into my clothes as I sat there, letting the cabin's humidity engulf me. A quiet hum settled around me, a small vibration as the plane's engines idled. Humidity like that reminded me of Far North Queensland, where locals thought 46° Celsius was brisk but still chugged beer like water.

I could have used a drink. Alcohol and medication were never a good mix, and I was usually a stickler for rules. As I sat in the chair, surrounded by hums and vibrations and flight attendants checking the aisles for rubbish, all I wanted was some dark liquor—the darkest they had.

A man and a woman walked towards me, lugging their bags over their shoulders. He wore a Slazenger shirt; she wore a skin-tight Echt thing, as if she were on the way to the gym. My lip curled, and I raised a hand over my mouth, pretending to look away.

"You good, buddy?" The man saw me and raised an eyebrow.

I nodded. "Sure."

"You looking at my girlfriend?" he asked. His biceps inflated, and my lip curled further.

"No," I said. "I was just... looking around. In general."

He scowled at me, and his girlfriend put a hand on his wrist. Tugged him away. I took a breath and thought about another pill. Too many made me dizzy, and I needed to keep my head in the game. For better or worse, I was on this flight.

For better or worse, I would get to Perth.

As the cabin crew prepared the plane for take off, I fiddled with my seatbelt. The voice had subsided again, crawling back into the shadows of my mind. At times like that, when I was truly me, truly alone in my head, I could see so much more clearly.

Light in the eyes—what a joke.

In that moment, as the pilot's voice crackled through the chair speakers, I knew it was rubbish. I knew the whole thing about light and the stuff I *thought* I'd seen—all of it was rubbish. I was lucky not to be locked up.

I only had to maintain my sanity for six hours until we'd land at Perth airport. What I'd do there, I didn't know yet. With another slap to my breast pocket and the comfort of my rattling pills, I was confident I could do it. I could get away, go somewhere, and just *be* for a while. That's all I needed.

Even as the plane sped down the runway and my stomach lurched.

Even as I looked across the aisle to the other side of the plane, and saw *her*.

The little girl.

TWO

WHEN I BLINKED a few times and looked again, she was still there.

That wasn't supposed to happen, not on the pills. They were supposed to stop hallucinations. The girl wasn't on my flight, nor were her parents. Yet there she was, staring at me over her shoulder again, that small pink tongue sticking out.

The plane rocked as the wheels left the ground, and I gripped the arms of my chair. Squeezed until my knuckles were white. The girl didn't even notice the shaking or the change in cabin pressure that made my ears pop.

My brain seized for a moment, the feeling of being stabbed right through the head dulling my senses—but only for a second. I blinked through that, too, and then stopped opening my eyes. The girl wasn't real. She couldn't be real. I'd seen every passenger on the way to my seat, and she and her family weren't among them.

Why is she here now? What does she want?

As the plane ascended and the seatbelt sign flashed—*THEY WANT YOU SHACKLED*—I opened my eyes.

She was gone.

As she should be.

She was back there, in Sydney somewhere. She didn't exist here. Not anymore. Not really.

Taking a deep breath, I felt for my pills again. The urge to take another one was a little too strong, surpassed only by my desire for a scotch. My head was still ringing from the take off, and only a few drinks could make that go away.

I pressed the call attendant button and looked around. Passengers were stretching out in empty rows and exploring the in-flight entertainment menu. To my right, on the far side of the plane by the window, a lone woman gazed out into the darkness, or perhaps she stared at her own reflection in the bleak light of the cabin. She had curly, fiery red hair down to the middle of her back, and she played with the tips with long, pale fingers. Her eyes, faint in the reflection beyond her shoulders, were pale green.

They darted left and stared back at me. She tilted her head.

I tried to look away, but her smile caught the periphery of my vision.

The call attendant button was still lit, so I focused on the bright yellow light to avoid the woman's eyes boring into me. I saw the silhouette of a man walking toward me and slowly began to recognise his uniform. The shiny gold nametag on his left breast was blurry, but the letters slowly cleared as the man stepped forward—Eric.

When he leaned toward me, I smelled musk and soaked it into my nose. His arms, even beneath his shirt, were strong and meaty, and his belly hung over me slightly as he reached for the call attendant button to switch it off.

"Can I help you, sir?" His accent was Italian, and my skin buzzed at the way his words rolled around his tongue.

"Yeah," I said, nodding.

His eyes were brown, the same as his thick, manscaped beard. He smiled at me the way all customer service people do—that polite but disengaged formation of the lips where the façade of happiness doesn't reach the eyes—and waited for me to complete my request.

"Do you have scotch?" I asked.

He nodded and asked how I took it, winking a little. I didn't know if I'd imagined it. *Hoped* I hadn't. Between his meaty arms and full beard, the man was my vision of a god. Give me scotch, give me whatever you want. I'll take it any way I can get it.

Aiden. I miss him already. The thought came from nowhere, and my fingers strayed to my wedding ring, turned it around my finger.

The flight attendant noticed, cleared his throat, and asked again in that rich, smooth accent, "How would you like it?"

I caught the green-eyed woman looking at me, her whole body turned to face me, one leg dangling over the other at the knee. She leaned in, watching the encounter, and I squeezed my hands as I told the bear attendant that I'd like Coke and ice.

He ambled off with an "Of course, sir," and I found myself watching his arse as it bounced down the aisle.

"Trouble in paradise?" The green-eyed woman had a hand under her chin, a lazy smile directed at me as she spoke.

"What do you mean?" I asked.

She moved out of her chair and shuffled through the middle row of seats towards me. Plonked down next to me. "You're going to twist your ring finger right off if you keep doing that." She nodded at my fingers, which were still turning my wedding ring.

"Oh." I continued.

"I'm Rachel." She didn't give me a hand to shake but threw her head back, dug her fingers through her hair, and scratched at the back of her scalp. "We're in for a long flight. You have family in Perth?"

"Um... I, uh... "

She smiled again. "Relax, mate. I'm just making conversation." I must have reacted somehow, because she continued. "I'm a psychologist. I know when someone's nervous."

"I'm not nervous," I said, swallowing hard.

Rachel nodded and looked away with wide, disbelieving eyes.

"Here's your drink, sir," the bear attendant said, placing the scotch in my hand and turning on his heel.

I watched him leave again, and Rachel followed my gaze. "You have a wandering eye."

"I don't." I took a sip of my drink. It was cold and strong, exactly what I needed.

When I took the cup from my lips and looked at Rachel, she had one eyebrow raised. "Should you be drinking?"

"Excuse me?" I narrowed my eyes at her and leaned over. "What I do is none of your business."

She lifted her hands to her chest, palms outward, and frowned. "Sorry. I'm always in work mode. I see a person in clear distress, and I just can't help myself. I... I will leave you to it." Moving away, she turned back to me once more and said, "Sorry, Charlie."

I took another drink, angry at her bluntness, at her words—angry that she was right. Trouble in paradise? Well, there hadn't ever been a *paradise*, but for all intents and purposes, she was right. Aiden and I were over, even if I hadn't signed the paperwork yet. Even if he was begging for me to come home and telling me he loved me. It was over, and he'd been the one to file for divorce. I was used to mixed messages, but only from the voice in my head. I didn't need them from Aiden, too.

Another sip of scotch, and I knew she was right about that, as well. I shouldn't have been drinking. It was either that or take yet another pill, and I remembered what had happened last time I'd taken too many.

Shoving that thought down with a swig, letting the liquid burn and scratch at my throat, I looked over at Rachel, who faced away from me. Her eyes had been human, maybe a little *too* human.

Maybe a disguise. Did they do that? Studying her movements, the way her black pantsuit clung to her curves as she shifted from one butt cheek to the other, I couldn't see any sign that she wasn't what she claimed to be. Yet.

Sighing, I took the last swig of scotch and crushed the plastic cup in my hands.

WAIT, the voice in my head shouted. *HOW DOES SHE KNOW YOUR NAME?*

THREE

It was a good question, and I wished I'd thought of it.

A stranger on a plane knew my name. She knew quite a few things about me and claimed to be a psychologist. What did I know about her, though? What had she told me? Just her name—Rachel. Common enough. I hadn't seen her flinch the way people do when they lie.

I wasn't paying attention. That's why.

She was lying. She was a fucking liar. She was one of them, had to be. How did she know my name? Except her eyes were human. *What does that mean?*

TROUBLE IN PARADISE, TROUBLE IN PARADISE.

The voice was awake now, well and truly. I reached for the pills in my breast pocket, but stopped. Dulling the anxiety—the voice—now wasn't the best idea. It had warned me, helped me. It wanted the best for me. Not like Rachel. Not like Eric, whom I could see now in the middle section of the plane, fiddling with drinks and whatever else—chatting up the other flight attendants, who looked bored.

None of them wanted the best for me. They were just doing their jobs.

Except Rachel.

She wasn't doing anything. Just sitting there, staring into the black night outside…. Staring back at me in the mirrored reflection of the window.

What does she want?

A good question. What *did* she want?

My breath was caught in my lungs as I unbuckled the seat belt and headed to her. She watched me get closer, but didn't react. As if she had *expected* this to happen. Like she knew what was *about* to happen.

She's definitely one of them.

"How did you know my name?" I asked, standing above her in the aisle with a crooked posture and neck. The power dynamic wasn't what I expected, though. She was smaller than me; I towered over her, but she was powerful and calm. I was a sweaty mess who couldn't stand straight. My eyes were full of fear.

Hers were full of something I wanted to believe was compassion, but it was fake. It was all fake. She wanted something from me, and I had to find out what.

"I saw it on your boarding pass. I was behind you when we boarded," she said.

"Bullshit," I spat. "How did you know my name? What do you want from me?" I leaned down to her, our faces inches from each other.

Rachel recoiled a little and grimaced. "I'm sorry, Charlie. I didn't mean to scare you. I truly did see your boarding pass."

She's fucking lying.

It could have been true. I was holding it when I boarded. It was out there for all to see. Anyone watching could have seen it, could now know my name. My eyes darted around, searching for... anything. How many of them know who I am? What else do they know?

What else does she know?

"Charlie?" Rachel's voice was low and soothing. "I apologise. But you need to respect my space now."

I stepped back, took my face from hers, and scanned the area, unsure where to look. What to do. How to be. "I'm... " My breath came back in waves, heavy and hot, and I shook my head at the woman. "I'm sorry," I said.

She didn't seem worried or upset. Just a little annoyed. Her eyes, though. Still full of compassion, I believed that now. The voice was screaming at me now—*GRAB HER BY THE SCRUFF AND FORCE THE INFORMATION FROM HER.*

I shook my head at the thought of violence. *Ask her why she followed me. Ask what happened to the little girl, and what she knows about me. What she knows about me.*

I stepped away again, muttering my apologies, when a crackle came over the plane's speakers. My focus shot to the nearest screen, and I listened as words formed through the noise.

"Attention all passengers," it said. My eyes darted down the plane to see Eric speaking into the speakerphone. "We're heading into a storm. Nothing to worry about, but please return to your seats, fasten your seatbelts securely, and expect a little bit of turbulence."

Whenever someone said there was nothing to worry about, it always meant we should hold each other and wait for the end. At least, in my experience. I rushed back to my seat, for the moment forgetting about Rachel, and strapped myself in.

They want me chained.

"No," I replied to the voice. "*I* want to be chained."

Rachel must have heard me, because she had a half-smile tugging at one corner of her lips, but it was laced with concern.

"Leave me alone," I snapped at her, and knew I shouldn't have.

She looked away from me with a snarl, brushed a hand through her hair, and focused on breathing as the plane began to shake.

Turbulence. Just turbulence.

The cabin rocked left and right, and the pit of my stomach lurched again and again as the sudden raging storm outside struck the plane. Looking out the window, I saw lightning, like tendrils, racing across the sky, reaching for us—for me.

I gripped the arms of my chair, squeezed tight until I felt the bones in my fingers ache. The lightning came again, ripping through the black sky with a rumble of thunder I wasn't sure I was supposed to be able to hear.

The hairs on my arms and neck stood up, reacting to the change in temperature, to a sense of static seeping into the cabin from outside, and I dared to look away from the window—back to the seat in front of me.

To the right.

Down the aisle.

Others were doing the same, gripping each other for dear life as the flight attendants politely tried to reassure everyone before strapping themselves in. Eric stumbled in the aisle against the old lady—the one who'd muttered "Arsehole" at me earlier—whose hands still shook and trembled, though likely from fear this time.

Eric reached his seat just as the cabin lights flickered and plunged us into darkness.

Someone screamed—A kid. *The little girl? She was here?*—and I was thrust into silence. Just my own breathing, my own heart thumping against the lightning and thunder and spikes of rain stabbing at the window.

I'm going to die.

FOUR

The lights flickered back on.

"I'm okay," I whispered. "It's just turbulence." Deep breath, *one, two, three.* "Just—"

A crack of thunder struck outside, and the plane dove. It came again, like the tendrils of light were aiming for us, and the sudden lurch of my stomach told me we had descended.

The girl's face flashed at me in the darkness.

"All passengers, please be advised that we are experiencing an electrical storm—"

No shit.

Darkness again, and I stared at where the lights should have been—the flight attendant's voice vanished.

The girl was gone, too.

She was never here. But she was. Wasn't she?

I knew she wasn't, couldn't be. My pills weren't working.

"... tighten seatbelts... "

I stopped listening as Eric continued. I couldn't hear anything; my ears flooded with blood, adrenaline, and panic.

My heart was almost melting into my ribcage. I couldn't even reach my pills. They seemed so far away, bouncing against the turbulence in my breast pocket, but light-years from my hands.

I'll never see Aiden again.

The voice was getting louder, screaming at me that we were closing in on the end, that I needed to live for *its* sake. The lights flashed again, and the voice cried out for my death. Warning me, guiding me to the end of my life. It needed me and I needed it. The plane shook again, my stomach finally spilling its contents into my lap and the seat in front of me. I screamed.

Bile and vomit spat from my mouth as I let the scream tear through as much of the plane as it could. In the corner of my eye, I saw Rachel watching me again. I didn't care. I didn't have time to care. It was me and the voice, screaming together, dying together, and that was all that mattered.

My lungs ached from the force of my fear. My eyes watered. I squeezed them shut until I saw static—through the lids, a crack of lightning and thunder flashed red. It was close—so close.

The seatbelt squeezed my waist. It scraped against me, cut into me as I struggled to breathe. I didn't need the voice to tell me to get up. I figured that out on my own, unbuckling and throwing the leather belt away into the empty seat next to me.

Heaving again but managing to breathe through my stomach's desire to purge, I grabbed at the headrest of the chair in front of me, pulled myself up. The plane shook again, and I stumbled into the aisle as the lights flickered in red, directing me to the thin path.

I stumbled in the aisle as the plane took a dive. I heard someone praying. Someone else was crying. Rachel held onto her necklace, silent and breathing steadily. The voice in my head pounded at my skull, daring me to yell and scream, but I couldn't. Not again. If I opened my mouth, I'd spew. My guts would spill to the floor.

A green light flashed somewhere down the aisle, and as the plane was knocked around by the heavens again, I tumbled forward. Looking up, I saw the light—a beacon.

The toilet.

The tiny, cramped space was my salvation. In that moment, it was everything. I raced down the aisle, ignoring the prayers and the whimpers and the weeping mantra of "I don't want to die" on repeat from the bitch with the hair weave.

I pushed the door open, threw myself inside, and locked myself in.

A bang on the door told me Eric, or someone, had seen me. Not Eric. A woman. She was yelling at me to get back to my seat, but I put my hands over my ears and rocked back and forth, letting the voice stifle all the noise and chaos on the other side.

YOU'RE STILL GOING TO DIE.

"I'm... not... ." Tears rolled into my mouth as I begged the voice to be wrong, challenged it once more. It had been right so far, but this couldn't be the end. Aiden was waiting for me; I needed to see him again. I needed to apologise.

As I rocked again and again, the pills in my breast pocket rattled. I grabbed at them as the plane trembled once more, lightning crashing into the side. Screams filled the plane again. I twisted the top off my pill bottle and threw back as many as I could.

Crunching them in my teeth made the voice fall into the background.

"—ascending above the storm—"

Eric's voice cut through the noise, the way Aiden's always did, and it didn't make sense. Above the storm, how high were we going? How high *could* we go?

Throwing back a few more, I swallowed them straight down, ignoring the continued *bang bang* on the door. Unlatching the lock, I let the door swing in. The flight attendant banged on my chest.

"Sir!" she cried, steadying herself as the turbulence struck again. "Get back to your seat!"

I nodded in a daze as the pills began to work.

"Now!" she yelled.

Her face told me she was upset, her eyes confirming she was human. The voice echoed in the background, begging me to turn around. I ignored it as the lights flickered again and the lightning struck the plane's wing.

Eric was saying something, but his voice—trembling, shaking—was drowned out by the storm. A wave of deep blue passed by the windows as I fought my way back to my seat, thrusting my pill bottle back into my breast pocket. Lunging into the seat, I pushed my head back, noting the flight attendant had followed me. She sat across from me in the aisle, staring at me with angry, desperate eyes.

LOOK, the voice said. *SEE.*

I turned away from her to where the voice was guiding me.

The lights were on again, dim, flickering on and off.

Wiping vomit and spit from my lips with the back of my hand, I tried to calm myself. The plane was heading upwards, and I could feel my body sinking into the chair, the back of my head firm against the fabric.

WATCH, it hissed.

There was nothing to watch; nobody was moving. The passengers were still, almost lifeless, but I watched anyway. My eyes scanned left to right, up the aisle, down the aisle, over to Rachel, who was sitting still. Her eyes were shut, her fingers white from gripping her chair arms, her necklace abandoned.

Back to the aisle, to the front of the plane.

I spotted the old woman's hairdo, the stupid fucking weave, and focused on that. Watched it shake about through the ongoing turbulence.

Another crack.

A beam of lightning struck the side of the plane. I resisted the urge to scream, listened to the voice again. *WATCH. NOW.*

The lightning hit again. I felt the side of the plane vibrate, almost recoil, and snapped my eyes to the sight. Through the window, in the dark, I saw it. Between the rain and the clouds and the emptiness of the night sky... .

I *saw* it.

It wasn't one of *them*. It was something else.

KEEP WATCHING.

Despite my best efforts to look away, to cover my eyes and beg for this all to be another nightmare, I couldn't look away. The voice had commanded, and I obeyed.

It was there—a shape.

Carried to the plane by the lightning.

I kept staring, wiped at the window to clear the fog, to see the shape—semi-transparent, its form changing and evolving like a blob of jelly rolling downhill. It was feeling at the side of the plane, rubbing against it, spreading along the outside, just by the wing.

See something, say something. See something, say something. My mind raced with the thought, over and over and over and—

I pointed at the shape, but the flight attendant wasn't watching. Her eyes were closed, perhaps retreating to happier times. Her family?

Another crack of thunder.

Lightning smacked against the plane again, and I watched, unblinking, as the shape was thrust inside.

The voice shouted at me, begged me to scream, to say something, to warn someone, but I simply stared. The shape floated above the seats—above the passengers—and then shot across the aisle to the old woman.

Her weave disappeared for a second—just a second—as she dipped her head from the force of the shape colliding with her. And then she was back, but as I stared on, I saw the shape melting into her hair.

Into *her*.

FIVE

Just like that, the turbulence stopped.

The lights came back on, and the screams, moans, and calls for mothers stopped, replaced by relieved whispers and unsettled laughter. The crew made an announcement, but my ears were tuned out. My eyes were fixated on the woman, her beehive hair unmoving.

A flashing light above my head caught my attention—the seat-belt sign.

I began to move my eyes around the cabin, to scan the other passengers as they smiled and swapped stories about their near-death experiences 40,000 feet in the air, even though they all had the same stories.

My attention jumped to Rachel, who was already watching me. I smiled and nodded. She searched my face, then unbuckled and made the awkward trip through the rows of seats until she was by my side.

"Are you okay?" she asked, a gentle hand on my shoulder.

Even with her looming above me, her shadow drenching my body into nothingness, I avoided her.

"Charlie?" She wasn't going away. Instead, she leaned back on the chair opposite me, filling the aisle. "We almost died."

Sucking my bottom lip inward and biting down, I nodded. But my eyes were still drawn to the beehive in the distance. The old woman wasn't moving. She wasn't engaging with anyone about the turbulence or how she thought she was about to die or meet God or whatever. She just sat there.

"Charlie." Rachel was forceful now.

"What do you want from me?" I asked.

"I want you to tell me you're okay," she replied, squeezing my shoulder.

Finally looking at her, I drew my eyebrows low. "Why do you even care? Go back to your own seat and leave me alone."

Her eyes told me she was human, but I trusted the voice in my head. The one that was whispering to me now, telling me she couldn't be trusted. She was one of *them*.

But then... What is the old lady? She's something different.

Rachel was still standing there, rubbing at her face and spinning her hair around her fingers. "I noticed you got up during the storm. You looked like you were having a panic attack and I—"

"I'm fine. I have a psychologist at home I can talk to, so you can find someone else to play doctor-patient with."

The corner of her mouth twitched, and I saw something different in her eyes. A flash of anger. She moved back to her seat. I breathed out, slow and steady, and unbuckled my own seatbelt.

Beehive woman was still unmoving.

SHE'S DEAD. SHE'S DEAD. THAT THING WENT IN HER AND—

"Shut up," I whispered.

The voice stopped for a moment, but I knew it would be back. It always came back. It had helped me during the storm, had guided me to watch the lightning, but right now, I needed to be alone. I needed to have all my wits about me to find out what was happening.

Moving down the aisle toward the old lady, I gulped, hands shaking. A chill ran through my whole body, the whispering growing louder again.

"I said *shut up*," I muttered. A passenger, the young woman with her boyfriend, noticed me and grimaced. "Not you," I said, and I kept walking.

Beehive woman was two rows ahead. I quickened my pace, stormed up to her as my heart beat faster, faster. Placing my hand on her shoulder, I towered above her, taking in her form.

"I saw what happened," I spat, and I took a step back.

The old woman shot me a look, her lips turned up in a scowl. "Get your hands off me, arsehole."

She was pale—paler than before—and the skin under her eyes sagged. I winced at the sight, but I couldn't be sure it wasn't regular old age. "Are you okay?" I asked. I tried to sound concerned, but my voice cracked.

"Why shouldn't I be?" The woman swatted me away, but her movements were strange. The way her arthritic hands swiped at the air was almost like she didn't know how to do it—flailing back and forth without purpose.

Her hand flopped to her lap, and the woman's head began to lower.

"I saw what happened," I pressed on. "What are you?"

She snapped her head in my direction, eyes so fierce they could burn into my soul. "What did you say?"

"I said,"—I stepped closer to her, raising my voice—"*What. Are. You?*"

I felt the attention on me now. Crew, passengers, all of them. Hearing my voice, hearing the concern and the fear and the accusation.

The old lady smirked, and that's when I saw it. A small spot in her eyes, vacant and dark, drawing me in. It lasted all of a millisecond, but it was there.

I TOLD YOU! the voice screamed.

Stepping back, I bumped into a crew member, whose frustration was visible beneath his polite words. "Please move back to your seat, sir."

I spun to face him, saw Eric, his hands on my arms to guide me away from the old woman. Except she wasn't an old woman anymore, the blue in her eyes, the blue inside her.

"She's not human." I pointed at the old woman.

She stared me down with a pitying glare.

"Okay, sir, we can talk about that when you're in your own seat," Eric said, and he gave the old woman an *'I'm so sorry'* frown.

I jerked my arms to make Eric let me go and pushed him away. He fell backward through the aisle as a rush of hushed whispers washed through the plane: onlookers, passengers, wondering about the fuss.

Turning to face the old woman again, her skin paler than it had been only minutes earlier, I pointed at her and raised my voice. "You are not human!"

I knew what I looked like. Even as I did it, I knew. Nobody believed me; nobody would ever believe me. It didn't change the fact that she wasn't human. She was something else now. I'd seen it, and these people needed to know they were in danger.

Are they in danger?

"This WOMAN is not HUMAN!" I shouted.

Eric was on his feet again, another crew member by his side. "Okay, sir, please stop making a scene. This lady doesn't need—"

"She's not one of us, can't you see it?" I said to him, begging him to look at her. "See her eyes, see the blue!"

Eric glanced at the old woman. "Her eyes are brown, sir."

"It's in the pupils; her pupils are blue. It's INSIDE HER!"

I could feel the eyes on me, the stares, and the pity as a tangible force inside the cabin pressing against me as the voice continued to rise in my head.

"Sir," Eric said, his voice firm, "I am going to ask one more time. Go back to your seat."

My heart was on fire as I looked back at the old woman, her arms crossed as she stared at me. The veins around her eyes were visible now, but she smiled.

"Look at her," I pleaded. "Just look."

NOBODY'S LOOKING, the voice said.

It was right. Nobody looked. Their eyes were on me. On me! Of course, they were. I was the problem. I was the one making a fuss when I should have been in my seat, watching in-flight entertainment and chewing on stale airplane food.

YOU HAVE TO SHOW THEM.

"Sir," Eric said again.

"Okay, I'm going."

SHOW THEM. SHOW THEM SHOW THEM NOW!

I turned to move, but the voice was raging in me now. I felt it in my fingers; the voice was in my nerves. I doubled back and grabbed at the old woman, shaking her by the shoulders as she wailed and cried and begged to be left alone.

"Tell them the truth!" I screamed in her face, flinging spittle onto her cheeks and lips. "Tell them!"

Eric and the other crewman were on me now, pulling at me, tugging at my elbows. I grabbed the woman's shirt, scrunched it between my fingers, but she slapped at my face again and again until the pain seared through me, and I let go.

"Fuck you!" I screamed. "*Fuck you!*"

I fell away, carried down the aisle by Eric and whoever else was with him. I fought and leaned back into them, putting my weight against Eric's body, but he was stronger than he looked.

"She's not human," I said to him. "Please, just look at her."

He ignored me, as I suspected he might. Instead, he shoved me harder until I fell into one of the chairs. The pill bottle tumbled from my breast pocket, the lid falling apart and the medicine spilling across the carpet.

I raced to collect the pills, but Eric pushed me out of the way.

"What are these?" he asked, picking up the empty bottle.

"I need them," I said. "Please, I need my pills."

"Clon..."

"CLONAZEPAM! Okay?" I slumped into my seat. The old woman had turned into the aisle, still staring at me with that fucking smirk. "Look at her!" I pointed.

Eric didn't look. Neither did the other one. Her name tag read "Calista." She was the inexplicably happy flight attendant who had checked my boarding pass as I got on the plane. Human, right? I think so. If I remember correctly.

"What are they for?" Eric asked.

I looked at him, silently begging him to leave me alone. The other passengers were watching. Rachel was watching. Waiting for an answer.

"Please, folks," Eric said, turning to face the growing crowd. "We don't need an audience."

Slowly, the passengers dispersed, turning back to their screens or whatever they were doing before I caused a fuss. All but Rachel, who watched on with concern as Eric held the pill bottle to my face.

"What is Clonazepam for?" he asked again, his voice softer now.

"It's an anti-anxiety medication," I mumbled. "Also used to treat OCD and psychosis, and a bunch of other things."

He leaned in and kneeled before me. "Sir," he whispered, "are you going to be okay?"

I looked at him, at his wide eyes that were so beautiful like Aiden's, and my breath caught. Tears began to form, and my cheeks felt hot and flushed. "She's not human."

The two flight attendants exchanged a glance, and Eric continued. "Take another pill. I'm going to ask you to sit here for the remainder of the flight. Any more disturbances, and I will have to call the police at our destination." He handed me the bottle and turned. Paused. "I'm sorry." And walked away.

Holding the bottle in my hand, trembling, I took another pill from the bottle.

WAIT, the voice purred. *WAIT.*

With my fingers at my lips, I did as I was instructed. Dropped the pill back into the plastic container and waited. Tears flowed down my cheeks, embarrassment washing over me as I continued to stare towards the old woman.

She fixed her hair for a moment and then stood. Shuffled down the aisle towards the bathroom. I watched as the OCCUPIED light went on and focused on my breathing. The voice was telling me to wait, but I couldn't. I couldn't hold back the shame and embarrassment. Burying my hands in my face, I wept.

"Don't be too hard on yourself," Rachel said.

I took my hands from my face and shook my head at her, my vision blurry like my mind. Psychosis aside, I knew what I'd seen. I didn't know how I was the only one, or why. Or why nobody would look at the old lady, just to make sure.

It was her skin. Pale. Growing paler by the moment. Sagging at the eyes. Those eyes. Big brown things staring at me.

"Sometimes medication is a weird balance," Rachel continued.

"I'm not crazy," I said, and another round of tears poured out. "Just go look at her."

Rachel sighed. "I can't. She's in the bathroom." Twirling her hair between her fingers again, she added, "Move over."

"What?" I asked.

"Shift over, I'm sitting with you."

I did as I was instructed, and Rachel sat next to me. I didn't know why she was talking to me, but I was grateful. She was the only one not staring and whispering about me. Despite how I'd treated her earlier, she was the only one willing to be with me.

"Talk to me, Charlie," she said. "Tell me what's going on."

I couldn't bring myself to look in her eyes. Not yet. They'd been human before, but I wasn't sure I could trust myself. And what if I did look and I'd been wrong? What if her eyes were... Then I truly would be alone in this. Whatever this was. I couldn't be alone right now. Looking down at my pill bottle, I told her.

The lightning.

The *thing* coming onto the plane.

Entering the old woman.

All of it.

"Wow." The single word said it all. She didn't believe me. I didn't need to see her face to know that. "Wow," she said again.

"I know what you're about to say," I replied. "Have another pill."

Rachel reached over to me, put a finger under my chin, and guided my face to hers. "No," she said. "I believe you."

"You do? Why?"

She swallowed hard and lowered her voice. Our eyes met, and in that moment, I didn't care what she was, because she said, "I saw it too."

SIX

"YOU DID?"

She was lying. She had to be lying. If she'd seen it, why wasn't she freaked out? Why wasn't she yelling it to the crew like I did? Why would she sit there in silence and just let whatever that thing was take the old lady?

"I saw... something." Rachel was squinting now, like she was trying to remember a distant memory. Trying to make sense of what she'd seen. "It was like a... I don't know." She shrugged. "A creature, but without a face."

"Yes!" I jumped in my seat and nodded. "It was like a blob, but there was life in it."

Rachel agreed with her eyes, and suddenly, I felt I could trust her. Even though she was lying, she was all I had. And it occurred to me, I was all she had, too.

"What is it?" she asked.

I scoffed, lost for words.

"What does it want?" She wasn't asking me. She was filling the silence, brainstorming. "Why did it enter the old woman?"

"Why didn't you help me?" I asked.

Rachel grabbed at her hair again, then caressed her necklace. "Nobody would believe me. Just like nobody believed you."

It was true. I knew it was true. It didn't matter anyway. She was here now, helping me, talking to me.

"She's been in the bathroom for a while now," I said, nodding towards the green OCCUPIED sign. "Is that normal?"

Rachel raised an eyebrow.

"I'm not familiar with how long women take in the toilet. Men are fast. It's easy," I said.

"It's not normal," Rachel replied. "You should check on her."

I laughed a little. The young lady and her boyfriend turned their heads to me, and I scowled at them. The guy's gaze lingered longer than it should have, but he turned away and wrapped an arm around his girlfriend.

"I'm serious," Rachel said. "You should go check on her. Knock on the door or something. Make sure she's okay."

SHE'S BAITING YOU.

I sighed to silence the voice, but it repeated the sentiment. It didn't make sense for me to go. Not after everything. Eric wouldn't let me anyway. I peered down the aisle to see food and drink carts making their rounds.

"You go," I said. "She's a woman, you're a woman... You go."

Rachel thought for a moment and nodded, slipped into the aisle and headed for the bathroom. Looking back at me, she knocked on the door, pressed her ear to it, and frowned. Shrugged at me as if to say "Nothing," and then headed back to me.

"I couldn't hear anything in there," she said. "But she's definitely in there."

"Maybe... I should try?" I asked, searching Rachel's eyes for an answer.

"You should," Rachel confirmed.

"Maybe after we eat," I said.

Rachel looked disappointed but didn't force the matter. Instead, she returned to her seat, fading into the window by wrapping a blanket around herself.

"Something to eat, sir?" Eric smiled, but I could tell it was fake. He hated me, and why shouldn't he? I was an arsehole passenger making all sorts of trouble.

"Is that old lady... Is she okay?" I asked.

Eric sighed, and his shoulders slumped. "Sir, please. Whatever is happening with that passenger is none of your concern. Now, do you want something to eat or not?"

"It's just that she's been in the toilet for a while, and she didn't look well." I motioned to the OCCUPIED sign, but Eric didn't look.

"Nothing to eat then?" He started to move the cart away.

"I am a bit hungry," I said.

He reached into the cart, pulled out a tray, gathered some items, and thrust it into my hands. Without a word, he headed off with the cart.

"I'm also thirsty," I called after him. He didn't stop.

Lowering the tray table, I set down the food and began to unpack whatever it was I'd been given. The packaging said it was chicken, but the mess inside told me it was anything but. Still, I picked at it with the fork and swirled the thick brown liquid around until I was ready to taste.

To my surprise, it was good. Chicken korma, and it was fresh. It just looked like shit. I glanced over at Rachel, who had a bottle of water but wasn't eating, and shrugged. In that moment, I didn't care. I just focused on eating.

THAT'S RIGHT, the voice said. *JUST EAT. YOU NEED YOUR STRENGTH.*

I hated it when the voice did that, when it tried to goad me, like it had been all day. I couldn't deny its purpose, though. It was the voice that had told me to watch, to see. The voice had guided me to the knowledge that there was something on the plane with us.

Something.

What?

Alien?

Demon?

An unknown species?

WHAT ELSE CAN IT BE? the voice asked. *IT'S HERE TO DESTROY US.*

I dropped the fork and swallowed my food. The voice was right. It was always right. That thing, the entity inside the woman, was here to destroy us. What other purpose could it have?

"What happens when we land?" Rachel was beside me again. I hadn't even heard her approach.

"What do you mean?" I asked.

She nodded toward the bathroom, the OCCUPIED light still a firm green. "If something really is inside her, what does it want? And what happens when we land?"

"It's here to destroy us," I whispered. My tray of food swayed and smooshed, spilling onto the carpet as I climbed over Rachel to get to the aisle.

"Where are you going?" she asked.

I didn't answer. Didn't need to.

The bathroom wasn't far. It was never far on a plane. I knocked on the door, gently at first. Pressed my ear to it, but all I heard was the hum of the plane. I knocked again.

"Sir!" Eric snapped at me. "What is it now?"

I knocked on the door again. "She's still in there," I said. "She's... Something's wrong."

"Didn't I tell you to stay in your seat?" Eric asked. "Go!"

"But she—"

"I know, she's not human. Very good. Now go." Eric pointed down the aisle, fed up with my bullshit. I probably would have been, too, if I hadn't seen the blue light.

Rachel looked on, shaking her head in disbelief.

"Wait," I said. "You have a duty of care to your passengers." Eric frowned. "And I'm telling you I think this woman is in distress in there."

Calista stepped up to us, a hand on her hip, inquisitive. Eric moved away a little to give her room.

"What are you going to do about it?" I asked.

Calista, with a gentle smile, placed a hand on my shoulder. "Sir, everything will be alright. Nobody is saying we don't care about the woman. We just don't think it's appropriate for *you* to be taking the lead on this one. If you can go back to your seat, the crew will sort it out."

SHE'S IN ON IT.

"In on what?" I asked the voice.

"Pardon?" Calista still smiled that gentle smile.

I shook my head and moved away from the toilet. "She's in trouble," I said, storming back to my seat. "Do something about it."

As I walked down the aisle, I saw anger on the other passengers' faces. I wanted to believe it was anger at the crew for not helping the old woman, but I knew it was anger at me. Have they all been overtaken?

I'm the weirdo. I'm causing a scene. Again. Fuck.

This is what Aiden always warned me about: minding my own business, not getting involved. It didn't matter if our neighbours were *them* or if the postal delivery person was one of *them,* too. A random person in traffic, the kids across the street. It didn't matter. Let them be *them*, and I can be me. That's what Aiden said.

The voice said something else, though, and it was always hard to drown it out. Impossible, even. That's why I had these stupid pills that weren't even working.

AND WHY AREN'T THEY WORKING? the voice asked. *YOU NEED ME.*

I took my seat, knowing the voice was right. Aiden had a point, too, but the voice was always there for me. It never went to work, it never stayed late, it never went to sleep to leave me alone. Aiden did, and now he was at home. He'd left me to do this by myself.

Again.

Yet it was Aiden who kept me grounded. When I went off the rails or picked up a knife in the middle of the night, he never cowered. He never hesitated. He always told me he loved me, cherished me, and wanted to be with me.

YET HERE YOU ARE. ALONE.

The voice wanted something from me. It wanted a distance between me and Aiden, and it had succeeded so far. Why? To lead me here to this plane, to this flight, so I could witness this thing stow away inside the old woman?

That was it.

That was exactly why it had done it. The voice was protecting Aiden from this. The voice must have known I was the only one who could stop it.

Yes, it said.

"Yes," I said.

YOU HAVE TO.

"I'm the only one who can."

Rachel asked me who I was talking to, but I ignored her. She grabbed at me as I stood once more, and I waved her off like swatting at a fly.

"Stay here," I said to her, knowing she was going to anyway. Eric saw me approach, and I balled my fists, raising them to chest height.

"For the love of—"

"Stay out of my way, Eric!" I yelled.

I felt the eyes on me again, but with the voice telling me I had to do this, and knowing I was the only one who could, I didn't care. Their pity, their rage—it all fuelled me. I reached the bathroom door again and banged as hard as I could with my fists.

"Hey!" I screamed through the door.

Eric came at me, and I punched him in the face. My knuckles ached from the effort, and I heard bone crack. I couldn't tell if it was me or him, but I turned to the door and banged again.

"Get out here!" I cried. "Open up!"

"Hey, man," someone said from behind me. "Chill out, dude."

It was the guy who'd stopped me as we came onto the plane. The guy in the hoodie, despite the summer weather. He wasn't to be trusted, either, and I ignored him as he stepped closer, his hands up in a keep calm gesture.

I banged again. Again.

No sound came from behind the door.

I banged again. Harder and harder until my fists bled. Even as Eric and Calista and Hoodie Guy grabbed my arms and shoulders, I banged on that fucking door until the wood splintered.

The door buckled, and I kicked as hard as I could as the three people tore me away against my will. I kicked again, and the door creaked open, the lock brutalised. The OCCUPIED sign flashed off, and everything stopped.

Eric and his helpers dropped me to the floor, and I stayed there, lifted myself to my elbows to see.

"I'm so sorry, ma'am." Eric bumbled his way to the door, slid it open, and stopped. "Ma'am?"

He looked back at me, suspicion drawn across his face, and then stepped into the toilet. I heard him say "Ma'am" again, and I rose to my feet, pushing past Calista and Hoodie Guy. From behind, I grabbed Eric's shoulder and forced him back.

Eric obliged and stood next to Calista with a hand over his mouth.

"Fuck," I said, and turned to face the passengers. "I told you! Didn't I fucking tell you?"

They stared at me; every eye on the plane was looking right at me.

"You didn't listen and now... Now she's dead."

SEVEN

She was slumped over, her arms dangling by her sides, chin on her chest, and panties around her ankles. What struck me as I took in the sight and stench of her death and piss was the contorted expression on her face.

Her mouth was twisted into a shape I'd never seen, teeth exposed and collapsing around each other. Her eyes were wide open, and somehow, even in death, she pleaded with me as I looked into them. Staring down at her, my heart ached at the thought, *I could have stopped this.*

YOU ARE USELESS, CHARLIE.

The voice was laughing at me. It did that sometimes when it wanted control. Now wasn't the time to let it behind the steering wheel, and as it receded to the background, I stepped closer to the woman. Kneeled before her.

"What do you mean she's dead?" Calista asked in a hushed whisper.

Keeping my eyes on the old woman, I said, "I told you she wasn't right."

"No," Eric spat, "you told us she wasn't human."

"It doesn't matter now." I stared into her eyes, waiting. I hadn't seen the creature shift out of her. *Maybe it died with her.*

"You need to get away from her," Calista said from behind me. Her hand came down on my shoulder and gave a gentle squeeze. "We have to secure the area."

I didn't argue with her. There was no point. Kneeling next to a dead body wasn't going to achieve anything, so I stood and stepped away.

"I'm sorry," I said, turning to Eric. "For... making a scene."

"Sir"—his voice was cold, but a hint of fear carried through—"it's time to go back to your seat." Turning his attention to the passenger manifest, a few sheets of paper on a clipboard, he began scanning names and muttering to himself about no doctors being on board. After a minute, he threw the clipboard down and sighed.

"What?" I asked. "What is it?"

He flashed a glance at me, brows narrow and angry.

I held my hands up defensively. "I know, go back to my seat. Sorry."

GO BACK TO YOUR SEAT, CHARLIE. BE A GOOD BOY.

I sighed and looked at the old woman one last time as I began to head back to my seat. Calista was leaning over the body, her hand poised over the eyes. She looked over her shoulder at me and gave a sad smile.

"She can't cross over if her eyes are open," she said.

Nodding, I watched as her fingertips pressed down on the eyelids.

After she folded down the lids and sealed away the pleading expression, Calista took her hand back and wiped it on her uniform. A light grey streak was left behind. She looked at her fingers and frowned.

Before she could speak, the old woman collapsed. Her body fell away into millions of particles on the toilet floor, dust swirling through the air as she came apart. Calista screamed and fell backward into me as I watched the woman's head, shoulders, and torso crash to the floor like a broken statue.

"What the—" I couldn't finish the sentence, didn't know how. I just stared on as the body crumbled, her thighs collapsing on either side of the toilet, spilling into the soiled bowl, until all that was left were her lower legs, stained panties stretched thin between them.

Calista turned away, vomit drooling from her lips as she raced for the comfort of Eric's arms, weeping, "Horrible, horrible" over and over. She wasn't wrong. My own stomach churned, the korma threatening to mix with the old woman's dusty remains.

Pushing me out of the way, Eric had palmed Calista off to Hoodie Guy, who was still awkwardly hanging around. He stroked at Calista's hair, soothing her, and led her away from the scene, his own expression betraying the shock he felt.

"What is happening he—" Eric stopped when he saw the remains. He blinked a few times, looking between the mess of collapsed body parts and me. Searching my face for answers to questions he hadn't even formed.

I shrugged. "I told you she wasn't human."

"This isn't... It's not possible," Eric mumbled, breathing hard. He cleared his throat and held a hand to his neck to calm himself. "Okay, I have to seal off this bathroom."

THIS IS IT, CHARLIE. THIS IS YOUR WAY IN.

I knew what the voice meant, and didn't debate with it. The creature had done this to the old lady. It didn't take a genius to see that, though I was the only one putting that piece of the puzzle together. The voice was right. This was my way in. If I wanted to find that thing, to see where it went after devouring the old lady, I had to stay involved.

CONTAIN THE CRAZY. BREATHE. BE NORMAL. DON'T LET THEM SEE THE REAL YOU.

"Let me help," I said, taking the voice's advice and thumbing over my shoulder to Calista. "She's not ready for this."

Eric shook his head, but I could tell it was just for show. The only other flight attendant was out of commission for the moment, given the fact that an entire person had just collapsed into dust in front of them.

"Just... don't get in the way," Eric said.

"I won't." I smiled, and Eric winced.

CLEAN UP ON AISLE THREE.

"Stop," I whispered to the voice.

Eric looked at me. "What?" He was stopped, one foot mid-air, holding onto the outer wall of the toilet. "Stop? Why?"

"Uh... " I searched for a reason, anything to prevent him from thinking I was crazy. Again. "You're going to step on her. Just be careful." He seemed to accept that response, and I reminded myself I needed to stop replying to the voice. Not out loud anyway.

As Eric went to get some kind of tape to seal the door shut, I told him I'd make sure nobody came by to use the facilities and would scoop the remains of the old woman into a few garbage bags.

The plane turned, and I fell on my knees, my hands planted in the dust. The remaining legs crumbled in front of me, falling away like sand. It was unceremonious, the way her form just disappeared. All that remained now were her socks, shoes, and underwear.

I felt something sharp scrape my fingers and dug out the object—the old woman's hair clip. I paused, turning the item in my hands. In that moment, with my hands covered in her remains, holding her discarded hair clip, a tear slipped from my eye.

I tried to warn them, but as usual, I couldn't communicate the way everyone else did. Aiden would usually hold my hand and help me breathe or guide me through what I needed to say. He wasn't here now, and part of me wanted to scream at his absence.

"What's that?" Eric asked.

Wiping my tear away with the back of my hand, I showed him the hair clip. "Nothing, really. I just wondered what to do with it."

"Bag it," he said, his voice cold once more. "It's all evidence now."

"So you believe me?" I asked, putting the hair clip into a garbage bag.

Eric handed me a dustpan and brush and looked away. "No, sir, I don't."

"You can call me Charlie," I replied. "'Sir' is getting a bit old at this point."

"Charlie," Eric said, kneeling behind me, "I don't know what happened here, but she was a person. A *human being*."

NO. NO. NO. WE KNOW WHAT WE SAW, CHARLIE. HE CAN'T TAKE THAT FROM US. NOBODY CAN.

"You're right," I said, and Eric thought I was talking to him.

The problem now was that I was cleaning up the ashes of the old woman, scooping her into garbage bags like waste, and there was no sign of the monster. I wondered if it had crystallised inside her and turned her insides to dust.

Even so, the remains of the jelly-like orb would be around somewhere.

I moved her clothes to the side to fold up later and scooped more of her into the bag, siphoning out earrings and a locket. Inside was a picture of what I imagined as the old lady in her younger years with the love of her life. He was probably dead, too.

"Are you almost done?" Eric asked from behind me, fidgeting with a roll of tape.

"Nearly." I scooped again.

I shifted my body up to look in the toilet bowl. Part of me hoped the entity would be in there, hiding or whatever. It was a translucent blob, though. There wasn't really anywhere it could hide.

EXCEPT INSIDE PEOPLE.

Swallowing hard, I stood and left the bathroom, smatterings of the old woman's dust still lingering on the floor. Eric pointed, and I thrust the dustpan and brush at his chest. Standing at the entrance to the aisle, I scanned.

YES, CHARLIE. LOOK. SEE. FIND IT.

There was nowhere for it to hide. Even inside another passenger, it wasn't really hidden—not from me. I would find the fucking thing. Before it got me.

I scanned the passengers. I remembered there were twenty-four of them, including me. Plus two crew. I knew it wasn't inside me, and the old woman was dead, which meant there were twenty-four suspects. Looking around, I was drawn to the people I'd interacted with.

There was the woman with long, jet-black hair, avoiding my gaze and staring at the screen in front of her.

There was the guy and his girlfriend, making out like the plane was their bedroom.

There was Rachel, watching me with concern as she played with her necklace again.

Among them, scattered through the plane, were randoms I hadn't paid attention to. Loners listening to music, a father and daughter with their eyes closed, friends wearing sports uniforms, and chatting away. Nothing out of the ordinary.

And that's what scared me.

Even after I announced someone was dead, people went back to their lives. Back to their mundane fucking existences, like nothing had happened. The apathy was palpable, and I felt the weight of it in my blood.

I looked around again, taking everyone in.

There was Hoodie Guy, right at the front, comforting Calista.

Calista.

The only one who'd been alone in the toilet with the old woman's corpse.

She was still weeping into his chest, his hands still stroking her hair. I walked toward them, sensing myself detaching, sensing the voice taking over. I tried to stop my legs, tried to stop my mouth from opening.

It's inside her, the voice warned me.

"It's inside you," I said, pointing at the flight attendant.

Calista turned to me, her face puffy, her eyes barely open. Tears ran down her face. "Wh-what?"

SHE'S PLAYING YOU!

"Don't play me for a fucking fool," I spat. "That *thing* is inside you. What do you want with us? Why did you kill the old woman?"

Eric came to Calista's side, sitting next to her and Hoodie Guy. "That's enough, Charlie. Can't you see she's traumatised?"

"Oh, I do see," I said, my words seething, my teeth grinding. I thrust my finger to her face and shouted, "I see you! What do you want?"

"Hey, man," Hoodie Guy said. "Chill the fuck out. Take another pill or something."

TAKE ANOTHER PILL, TAKE ANOTHER PILL.

"Chill out?" I laughed. "*Chill out?*" I turned to the rest of the passengers and raised my voice. "We're being invaded! There is something on board with us! A stowaway! It's inside her!" My finger shook as it waved in Calista's face.

SO MUCH FOR STAYING INVOLVED, the voice said with a deep sigh. *YOU JUST HAD TO STAY COOL, CHARLIE.*

Hoodie Guy pushed me in the shoulder. "Shut up, man. You're freaking everyone out."

I waved my arms to the whole plane. "Really? Because nobody *fucking cares*!"

A few people had looked up, but most had their headphones on, trying to sleep, or avoided me the way people avoided the homeless on the street.

Hoodie Guy didn't care, either. Just cared that I was upsetting poor little Calista, the vessel for whatever that thing was. He pushed me again, and I stumbled backwards. The other passengers took note, leaning forward in their seats, arching their necks to see the new fuss. Caused by me, just like the last one.

"You don't understand," I said to Hoodie Guy.

"No," he spat back. "*You* don't understand. Leave the woman alone. In fact, leave *everyone* alone."

For a second, I thought I should. I should leave them to be devoured by the creature, turned to dust like the old woman. For a second, I wanted that to happen. Until I remembered Aiden, my beacon of light and hope and all that was good about my life.

He wouldn't want that. He wouldn't want any of it.

I saw Rachel rushing through the aisle towards me, coming to my aid. I thought, *Finally*, and breathed out a little. She would tell them I wasn't making it up, that she'd seen it too.

"Leave him be," she said. "He's not done anything wrong."

"I'm just trying to help," I added.

She stood next to me with her arms folded and nodded. "And it looks like you could use it."

"We don't want your help," Eric said. "I will handle this."

"How?" I asked. "Tell me that. How will you *handle* this?"

"Sir," Eric replied, thin-lipped. "*I will handle this.* That's all you need to know."

We stared at each other for a few seconds, both breathing heavily through our noses. His eyes were human, but that didn't mean he couldn't be an arsehole.

"Okay," I said finally. Even though nothing was okay.

Hoodie Guy stepped to me again, fists ready, but I could tell in his stance he wasn't going to do anything. It was just a threat, and for now, I'd heed it. I needed time to figure out what to do. How to get the entity out of Calista.

"I'll go sit down and leave you all be," I said. Then to Rachel: "Come on. Let's go."

I felt their eyes on me, everyone I was turning away from. A few passengers clapped, and others talked quietly amongst themselves, but the general vibe was that they wanted me gone. I breathed through the urge to tell them all to fuck off and die and got to my feet.

I walked to Calista and put a hand out to her. "I'm sorry," I said.

She took my hand and shook it once. "It's okay," she replied. "We're all scared and confused."

She looked up at me and smiled as she let go of my hand. Then I saw it in her eyes.

The hole in her pupil.

SESSION #1

St Vincent's Hospital, Psych. Ward
23 May 2025
Patient: Charles M. Reed
Referring Psychologist: Dr R Schwarz
Consulting Psychiatrist: Dr J Mathis

THERE ARE A RARE few patients in my care who display such commitment to their delusions. Upon meeting Charles (who prefers to be known as Charlie) for the first time, I was astonished to learn he believes me to be a fictional—or rather, mythological—creature. I was called to St Vincent's, where I operate as a consulting psychiatrist, to see a patient who was known to be violent, has demonstrated serious mistrust and paranoia, and who also presents with possible dissociative identities.

From what I read in his patient file, his "other" identity refuses to be named, and Charlie himself is not able to tell anyone who this other person is. They seem to co-exist within the one mind at all times, which fascinates me. So, despite my already heavy caseload, I reversed my initial rejection of the addition and agreed to see the patient immediately.

The session is detailed below, according to my audio recording:

Charlie was curled in a ball in the corner of the room when I arrived, refusing to acknowledge my presence. I recognised these behaviours as classic symptoms of heightened fear and anxiety. Not unusual, per se. What was unusual, however, was that Charlie was concerned about my eyes.

"Hello, Charlie," I said, standing by the doorway. "My name is Doctor Mathis. You can call me James, if you like."

Charlie did not respond, as I had suspected would be the case. I stepped into the room and instructed the attending nurse to close the door behind me. Despite the patient's history of violence, both to himself and to others, I believed privacy to be of the utmost importance. Charlie had also already been sedated enough that he was likely incapable of doing much else than simply talking with me. The history of violence itself was strange, to say the least, as patients displaying dissociative identities are very rarely violent at all. Unlike the tropes in films, the reality is quite different. However, knowing the violent past did enable me to frame the session in a particular way, which I would use to my advantage, as it indicated I was not dealing with a typical case.

"Would you like to talk with me, Charlie?" I asked.

"It's the eyes," he whispered, avoiding my face. "It's always the eyes."

He tucked his head under his arms and rocked back and forth. I moved a little closer, crouched before him, careful not to touch him at all. He was jumpy; anyone could see that. I'd read on his chart that he'd been treated with a course of antipsychotics but was not responding to treatment. It should be known that the antipsychotics were not for his suspected D.I.D., but for other presenting symptoms. D.I.D. is not treated with such medications but through talk therapy. With the amount of medication he was on, he shouldn't have been jumpy. He should barely have been awake.

"Charlie, what about the eyes?" I asked.

Slowly, ever so slowly, he looked up at me and searched my face as if analysing all the minute details, from my crooked, pointed nose to my sharp eyebrows and my round chin.

"You're one of them," he said, and put his head back under his arms.

"One of whom, Charlie?"

He didn't reply, and it was clear he did not trust me. Paranoid delusions tied to dissociative identity disorder are hard to crack. This was my job, though, and I was second to none.

"You believe the eyes are a window to the soul?" I asked.

A small laugh. Not one of pleasure. One of ridicule. "They aren't right. The eyes are never perfect. You know that."

The session continued in this vein for some time, me crouching, him rocking back and forth, until he showed an odd willingness to talk to me. I believed him to simply want to be released, as is often the case, so I trusted his words were not entirely truthful when he told me I was a doppelgänger. I wasn't familiar with that word beyond what I'd read or seen in pop culture, and when I pressed him for more information, all he would say was, "You know what you are."

"What exactly am I, Charlie?" I asked. I needed to keep him talking, to get him to open up to me more. So I continued, "A doppelgänger? What is that?"

He looked at me, right into my eyes. There was fear in his expression, but also a desire to be heard. That was what I needed to grab onto. That was my entry point to his innermost thoughts. That was how I would help this troubled man.

"I don't know where you come from," Charlie said, still scrutinising my eyes. "I just know there are more and more every day."

"What do you think… we… want?" I asked. There was no point trying to convince him I was, in fact, not a doppelgänger. He had made his mind up about that before I even entered the room.

"You want everything," he replied.

"Is Aiden a doppelgänger?" I asked.

Charlie shook his head. "Aiden… I love him. He's human. For now."

"These doppelgängers aren't human?"

Another shake. "Imitations. Almost perfect copies. But the eyes… "

It was a fascinating, challenging case. Charlie believed with all his heart that I was, and many other people were, a mythical entity. Our motives were unclear, our desires unknown, but we were, without a doubt in his mind, out to destroy him.

"When you say they want everything," I pressed on, "what do you mean?"

He bit at a nail, the sharp sound echoing through the otherwise empty room. He was debating whether to tell me what he knew. Perhaps he thought I'd go back to Doppelgänger HQ and alert them to our biggest threat's knowledge. I waited in silence, my face as soft as I could manage. Non-threatening.

"You want the world," Charlie told me. "They all do."

He unfolded himself from the corner and moved towards me until our faces were an inch apart. I didn't feel threatened. I was the prey, sure, but he was not the predator the patient files had written him to be. He was a scared, confused young man.

Charlie's paranoia was yet to be overcome—it would take many, many sessions for that—but he had opened up to me. I suspected Dr. Schwarz had let him down, betrayed his trust in some way. Some such impetus had led him here in the first place.

"What will they do with the world?" I asked, and Charlie rested on his laurels.

He shrugged. "I don't know, Doc, you tell me."

A smirk. Just a small thing, but it was there. His demeanour began to change, his shoulders dropped a little, and his face relaxed. His breathing was calmer, shallower. The micro-expressions I'd been trained to look for were transforming before my eyes, too.

"Charlie?" I asked.

The man before me shook his head. "Nah, he got bored. I'm here now."

I remember thinking how fascinating it was to watch this man, so fragile and scared and rocking back and forth in the corner, change into someone entirely different in a matter of seconds.

"Do you have a name?" I asked. I put my hand out, ready to shake. "I'm Doctor James Mathis."

To my surprise, he shook it. "Good to meet ya, mate."

His vocabulary, tone, and cadence were all different. I'd been doing this long enough to know when someone was pretending. When they stumbled on their supposed character, their actions and movements were reminiscent of their actual persona. It was far too common, but also a symptom of psychological distress. This man, however, was not faking. That much became clear as the session continued.

"What is your name?" I asked.

"Just call me Other Charlie." He shrugged. "I don't care, Jamie boy. What's a name for someone who doesn't exist?"

"You don't exist?"

Other Charlie giggled, a half-hum, half-laugh, without opening his mouth. "That's a tricky one. I'm here, aren't I? Except, when Charlie first wakes up, I'm gone again. I'd like to stick around eventually."

"And do you think I'm a doppelgänger?" I asked. My question here was intended to establish a baseline. If the original Charlie was alone in his delusion, then

Other Charlie might represent a saner alternative, the part of Charlie's mind that wanted to remain stable.

"'Course you are," he replied. "And I'm gonna make sure you never get Charlie. He's taken."

"Taken?"

"He's mine." Other Charlie grinned. "He might be in charge out here in the world. But in here,"—he tapped his forehead—"I own him."

"What does Charlie think about that?" I wondered.

Another shrug. It was lazy and half-hearted, with only one shoulder really making the effort. "Who cares? I give him his body; he does what I want every now and then. I ain't concerned with what he thinks."

It was clear to me now that this second Charlie, who I was convinced had a name and just didn't want to share it, was behind some of Charlie's actions. The delusion, though? I needed more time to work on that. Other Charlie would surely get in the way of progress, so my first course of action would be to manage this other identity. Repress it, if not eradicate it entirely. From the short time I spent with Other Charlie, it seemed he was a strong identity. Wilful. Perhaps even the cause of the doppelgänger delusion. It was interesting to me how the original identity could be coerced into actions and beliefs by a secondary identity they themselves created.

"May I speak to Charlie again?" I asked.

"Not today, Doc," he replied. "We don't trust you."

There was something in the response, in the formation of the words, that told me he was done with me. That he had allowed Charlie to talk to me, and that his game—whatever that might be—was over for now.

It was also clear to me that I'd taken too long to realise we were in a game. And that he'd won.

<u>Recommendation</u>: Increase medication for anxiety and psychosis, and maintain daily therapy, under my guidance, to treat his dissociative identity. Reduce stimulation.

EIGHT

"YOU THINK IT'S IN the flight attendant now?" Rachel put a hand to her chest and gasped. "What are we going to do?"

I stared at her, eyes narrowed. "What do you mean, 'we'? You haven't done a thing to help me."

"I was at your side, Charlie." Rachel sighed and looked away as I mumbled that she could have done more. *Should* have done more. "I'm sorry," she said.

That was it. No promise to help me next time. No commitment to be there for me when the passengers and crew turned on me again. Just a half-hearted apology.

She knows something.

I blinked the voice away, but it was right. She was acting strange, even for someone I didn't know. I thought I could trust her. That's why I'd come back to my seat after Calista showed me her eyes and the weird spot missing from them. I'd thought Rachel might know how to handle it, what to do.

If she did, she wasn't sharing.

"Aiden would know what to do," I whispered.

Rachel turned back to me and searched my eyes. "What would he do then?"

I shrugged, and my hand went to my breast pocket. Rachel put her hand on mine and shook her head. "I need them," I said.

"No," she said, "you don't. When you take the pills, you don't calm down. I've seen you. They agitate you. We need you clearheaded for whatever is coming next."

She's watching you. She's watching us.

"You've seen me?" I asked.

She nodded. "I saw you during the turbulence. The pills didn't help then. I saw you with the old woman. They *certainly* didn't help then. What happens if you don't take them?"

I tried not to think about it and put my hand back down.

Don't listen to her, Charlie. She's one of them.

"I can't trust you," I said. Rachel's face told me she thought I was talking to her, and I didn't correct the misunderstanding. I couldn't trust the voice, and I couldn't trust her.

I was alone.

Calista was up there making drinks for people as though an old woman hadn't just crumbled into dust before her eyes. Smiling at passengers who were also keen to forget what Eric had started telling people was a minor medical emergency.

"Is she... dead? That man said—" one of the passengers asked.

Eric waved them off and poured her a scotch. "We're having some trouble determining what's wrong, but she is very sick."

Crowd control. I'd seen it way too many times before, though usually the crowd was being controlled because of something I'd done. Not because of a demon or alien or whatever that thing was inside Calista.

People needed to know the truth, but my approach earlier had been messy. I didn't need the voice in my head to tell me that. As I watched Calista pouring juice and handing out biscuits, her movements looked odd. Her arms grabbed at the snacks like pincers, and her torso twisted almost robotically, as though she wasn't sure how her body moved.

It's getting used to her, I thought, and the voice agreed.

Calista moved down the aisle, and her smile faltered for just a moment. Her face dropped, a flash of fear, and then the smile returned. I watched her movements become more and more human, more and more fluid, as they should be.

But her skin...

Something was different. It was hard to gauge, because I didn't know her and hadn't spent a great deal of time looking at her. Still, a strange hue appeared in her cheeks.

"Look at her," Rachel said, nodding towards Calista. "Something's not right."

Flicking my eyes to Rachel, I pursed my lips. "You should go back to your own seat." I climbed over her.

She mumbled something as my back end brushed against her knees, but I didn't catch it. I was too focused on Calista, the empty spot in her eyes, like a gateway to a soul that was no longer there.

"Excuse me," I said to her as I approached.

Her eyes locked onto mine; her smile was wide and toothy. Painted on, almost.

"I... Are you okay?" I asked.

Calista nodded, one slow motion up and down, and resumed serving one of the passengers.

"It's just—"

Calista tilted her head as she stared at me. *Into* me. Through me. "I... am... fine, thank you. Please, sir, if you can return to your seat, we shall all be eternally grateful." Her words were so slow, like she had to process each one on its own and wasn't sure how to form a sentence.

I waited a moment, startled by the exchange. I looked over my shoulder at Rachel, who hadn't returned to her own seat. She watched, her face twisted into worry.

What would Aiden do?

The voice was soft, and I wondered if it was my own thoughts or if the voice was trying to manipulate me. Trying to get me to pay attention when screaming in my ear didn't work.

"He wouldn't give up," I said.

"No, he wooooouldnnnn't," Calista said.

I froze.

"Aiiiden wod huv kept tryinnnguh," she continued. "R-right un-til theee... end."

She's in our head, Charlie. Get her out of our head!

Calista stepped around the cart, sliding past a row of passengers until she was standing in front of me. The passengers cocked their heads, eyeing me with curiosity. Nobody was looking at Calista. She wasn't the one causing trouble. She was just the poor flight attendant dealing with the crazy guy from 26C.

"What do you mean, '*would have?*'" I asked.

A slight tug at the corner of her lip, and Calista tilted her head again.

"What do you mean?" I asked, my voice rising.

Her eyes flashed anger and in the same instant, my skin broke into sweat. My heart pulsed in my ears, and my breath caught. Her words, her nonsensical words, drew me to action.

I gripped her shoulders and shook as hard as I could, begging her to tell me what she meant. What did she know about Aiden? Was he okay? Why did she say that? Why wouldn't she stop smiling as I shook and shook and shook?

One of the passengers I didn't recognise stood up in their chair and yelled at me to stop. To leave the poor woman alone. I shook again, Calista's head wobbling back and forth like jelly, but her eyes never left mine. Her smile never faded, not even for one second.

"What *are* you?" I begged, and the passengers came to her aid.

"I said," a woman said, tugging at my arms, "leave her alone."

I barely registered her, but the woman's hands were pulling at my arms as she called for help. Hoodie Guy was in the distance somewhere, careening down the aisle, and some other guy—bald with neck tattoos—was at my side with fists aimed at my head.

"You get one chance, mate," he said.

Hoodie Guy was on me now, too, as Calista rattled in my grip. I knew what I was doing was madness. I knew how I looked. I felt like a villain, my hands reaching for the woman's neck, screaming for her to tell me what she was, why she was here, and what happened to Aiden.

In the next second, a fist collided with the side of my face. I went down hard, smashed into an empty seat, my head slamming into the metal of the chair's arm. Calista was knocked off balance, but my grip released.

"I gave you a chance," Neck Tattoo Guy said. "Now fucking stay down."

Stay down, stay down. STAY down, stay DOWN. The voice was laughing at me, cooing with glee as the man stood over me.

I tried to stand, clammy hands searching for something to hold. I drew my knees up into a kneeling position, sweat streaming down my brow. I moved to get to my feet, but the guy hit me again, the punch echoing through my skull.

"I said stay down, didn't I?" He was laughing at me, too.

The voice swooned at the violence, and my body started to shake. He thought I was the bad guy. They all did. Calista, in the corner of my eye, was still smiling, but her face was drawn. The cheeks pulled in, gaunt.

"Can't you see?" I said, ignoring the pounding in my head. "She"—I coughed and turned around, back pressed hard against the seat—"isn't human."

Hoodie Guy was by her side now, a protective arm around her. If he wasn't careful, he'd be next. The creature would devour Calista and jump into him. It wanted all of us. If I didn't stop it, whatever it was, it would succeed.

"It's happening again," I said, rubbing my face. Neck Tattoo Guy kneeled in front of me, fists still at the ready. His smile was wry and arrogant, ever the hero for taking me down. "Please, just look at her."

He did, and he looked right back at me. "I just see a woman. We *all* just see a woman. Because that's what she is."

Shaking my head, I searched for Rachel, the only other person who'd seen what I saw. The only hope I had. She was nowhere to be seen. Probably sitting in her seat, staring into the black night sky.

"Rachel!" I called. "Help me!"

A crowd had gathered now, staring over the backs of their seats, leaning over them, gawking at me. I called again to no avail. She was abandoning me. I didn't know what else I'd expected, but all I had was her.

RACHEL RACHEL, WHERE ARE YOU? sHe ISn'T CoMinG, CHARLIE. IT'S JUsT You AnD Me.

I reached for my pills again, but stopped. Out of nowhere, Aiden's voice drowned out all the others—the one in my head and the voices of the passengers—and said, "Being on pills doesn't mean you're crazy."

The words were ricocheting around my mind when Eric forced his way through the crowd. "I've spoken to the captain and the co-pilot," he said, "and I've been instructed to restrain passenger 26C until landing."

"What?" I raced to stand. "You can't restrain me."

Eric nodded. "You have attacked people, sir. You are a danger to yourself and others." He stepped forward and, without being asked, Hoodie Guy and Neck Tattoo Guy came to his aid. Like the nurses at the hospital, glaring me into a corner until the brown leather straps were all over me.

"No," I begged, shaking my head. "It's real, it's real! Rachel!"

Frowning, mustering all the false care he could, Eric advanced on me. I moved backward, bumped into another passenger, the woman who'd wrangled with me earlier. Arms folded, she blocked my path. I tried to push past, but someone grabbed my wrist. Neck Tattoo Guy twisted my arm by the wrist until it formed a sharp V, and I cried in pain.

"Get back to your seat," he whispered in my ear.

I did as he asked, crying to be set free, shouting that I couldn't bear the leather restraints again.

"We don't have leather straps," Eric said, taking some tie-down ocky straps from behind his back. "We use these to hold our supplies in place."

The trio of men and the woman herded me to my seat, pushed me down into it hard, and held me in place as I screamed and kicked and begged. The straps were tied firmly around my wrists, one on each armrest.

"Please," I said through clenched teeth, jerking and writhing in my chair, "let me out. She isn't right."

Once I was restrained and staring over at Rachel, who frowned and looked away, the group dispersed. The excitement was over; there was nothing to stay for.

Eric waited, then let out a heavy breath. "I want to help you, Charlie. But you can't attack people. I have to ask Calista if she wants to press charges."

PRESS CHARGES. NO NO NO NO—

"I'm sorry," I said. "I know what I saw. You know what happened, too." Eric's eyebrow raised. "You saw the old woman. She crumbled into *fucking dust*, and you're playing it off like she's still in there having a medical fit. She's dead, Eric. Something is going on here. There's something on the plane, and Calista knows what it is."

Eric stepped back, raised his hands in an '*I don't care anymore*' gesture, and walked away.

I fought against the restraints, the thick wire rope grating against my skin. There was nothing I could do now. Everyone was at the mercy of that thing, and it would take us all.

One by one.

NINE

2 DAYS EARLIER

AIDEN BEAMED AT ME over the dinner table, a glass raised and twinkling in the candlelight. I picked up my glass too, the red wine swirling a little. The stem was cold, but the light was warm, and the steam rising from my plate was somehow sensual.

"Welcome home," he said, his voice soft and low.

I smiled back, but it was hollow. My eyes were drawn downward as I sipped at the wine. The doctors had all said not to consume alcohol, that it would interfere with my new medication, but a few sips would surely be okay. They must have meant I shouldn't drink too much. In any case, Aiden had been briefed since I was released into his care like a fucking child. And he was letting me drink it, so I was safe.

"I've missed you." Aiden pressed on in that way that he did. He was perceptive and gentle and always forging ahead with me like I wasn't some used-up, forgotten piece of shit—like I wasn't the worst thing to have ever happened to him.

"I missed you, too." I sipped again, mindful that the glass was steaming up from the heat of the food below. I looked at the plate. Didn't recognise anything on it. It looked like everything else I'd ever eaten. All the same, my stomach trembled.

Aiden giggled. "Someone's hungry."

"You did all this for me?" I asked, meeting his eyes for the first time that night.

He nodded. "Of course."

His eyes twinkled in the candlelight, and I saw something in them I hadn't seen before.. Whatever it was, I couldn't recognise it. The doctors had said my medication would take some adjusting to, and when I'd asked what that meant, they gave me vague answers I couldn't remember.

"I'm... sorry," I mumbled. I picked up my fork. Prodded at the food Aiden had painstakingly made for me, which I knew I wasn't going to eat. Despite my hunger, I couldn't. I just... couldn't.

"You don't need to apologise," Aiden replied with that same softness.

A tear jerked at my eyes, and I breathed in deeply.

"I told you I'm here for the long haul. Whatever challenges you face, we face them together," he said. "Okay?"

I looked at him again. His stubble was a little longer than I remembered, forming a brown beard that made him look even sexier than he was two weeks earlier. It matched his hazel eyes. I couldn't help but smile when he scratched under his chin, pouting as he did so. The same pout he made when he shaved.

"Okay," I replied.

Minutes passed in silence as Aiden sliced through his food, chewed it down, and sipped at the merlot. I watched him eat, and he pointed his fork at my plate to encourage me to eat. Instead, I refused the doctor's orders and drank more wine.

"Can I ask… " Aiden started, wiping at his mouth with a cloth napkin, "What was it like in there?"

The wine glass was empty, and the bottle was too far away for me to reach. So, I slid it away. It was so fragile, that stem. One snap and I could stab Aiden in the throat and just leave it there, plugging the hole.

"It was nice," I said. "You'd have seen it if you visited." Aiden cleared his throat, and I held up a hand to silence what I knew would be the truth. "I know, the doctors said I wasn't stable enough for that. And yet"—I looked around our house and spread my arms—"here I am. Home at last."

"Do you feel ready?" Aiden asked, reaching for his own glass again.

I sighed. "I don't know. I didn't think I was bad enough to be hospitalised in the first place. So maybe I'm not the best judge of character."

YOU AREN'T.

The voice was supposed to be gone. I got a buzz at its return, though, and gave a small smile. Aiden eyed me and smiled as well. Asked me what was up.

"Nothing," I said. "You want to know what it was like in the hospital? White walls. White uniforms. White sheets. White pills. It was boring, except for the thirty minutes a day I wasn't in therapy and could watch TV. Just reruns of old shows like *Bewitched* and *I Dream of Jeannie*. You know, nothing that could spark someone off, even though magic and genies aren't real, and people in that place are already questioning their own reality."

I stabbed at the food, now cooling.

"If it helped, that's what matters," Aiden said. "Aren't you going to eat?"

HE COOKED FOR HOURS TO MAKE THIS SLOP. HE'D HAVE BEEN BETTER OFF ORDERING TAKEOUT AND PLATING IT LIKE YOUR MUMMY USED TO DO, the voice snickered in my ear. We both knew my mother had never, not once, done that.

"I'm not hungry," I lied. I couldn't stomach whatever it was. I couldn't stomach Aiden's face, either, so sexy and gorgeous, kind and gentle, with his eyes so full of love. For me. For me, of all people. Fucking idiot.

"Do you want to go lie down?" he asked, forever sympathetic. "We could cuddle."

The thought made my skin crawl, and I reached for the empty wine glass. No stabbing tonight. It was just there, and I needed something to occupy my fingers. It wasn't Aiden that made my skin crawl. It was me. It was the thought that after everything I'd done—the many, many stints in psych wards—that he still wanted to cuddle and kiss and make love.

To me.

"Charlie?" He noticed I was staring at the empty glass.

I didn't know how long I'd been away or how far I'd drifted. I drew my lips in, sucked on the lower one, and nodded. "Sure, if you can stomach me."

He moved around the table and kneeled next to me. "Come on, Charlie," he whispered, caressing my cheek. "I love you more than I know how to say. Nothing will change that. And I mean *nothing*."

Taking me by the hand, he led me to our bedroom. It was so colourful with deep purple bedding, a brown throw rug, and a mix of art on the walls. It took a second for my eyes to adjust after being so used to seeing white.

White everywhere.

He guided me to the bed and slowly began to unbutton my shirt as he shimmied out of his own clothes. My heart started racing at the thought—the promise—of what was to come. My mind flashed to the wine glass.

The potential of the stem to slice through skin.

I leaned into him. "I'm sorry," I said again.

Aiden hushed me with a kiss, and we lay down to rest on the mattress, his body on top of me, his mouth breathing hard, searching me, yearning for me. My hands started to shake. My cock was hard and throbbing in my jeans, and I felt my body freeze.

"I can't do this," I said. "Not tonight."

My husband rolled off me without another word. He rested on his elbow and traced a finger down my chest, circling my nipple and threading its way down to my belly button. "It's okay, Charlie," he said, breathy. "I don't want to pressure you."

He loved me, though it was inconceivable. The voice was giggling somewhere inside me, telling me I was worthless and that the hospital was the best place for me. Among all the static in my head and the swelling of my cock and the hormones I was fighting was the wine glass, sitting empty on the table.

Just waiting to be thrown, smashed, and broken.

Waiting for me.

Aiden lifted the blankets and slid into the bed, encouraging me to follow. I undressed and did as he instructed, autopilot guiding me into the little spoon position. He put his arms around me and pulled me close so our bodies warmed each other.

"Is this okay?" he asked tentatively.

NO!

"Yes," I said, and I closed my eyes. Despite my best efforts, his arms felt exactly like where I belonged, even though I didn't deserve it.

We lay together in silence, his rhythmic breaths warming the back of my neck, until he began to snore in the darkness. I moved from the bed, pulling my underwear back on, and headed out of the bedroom, closing the door behind me.

The candles were still lit but had all but burned out. The food was still there, cold and unappealing, and I reached for my plate, intent on taking it to the sink.

The wine glass stopped me.

I sat in a dining chair and stared at it for a few minutes with nothing but the dull sounds of the outside world—a car, crickets, whatever—to interrupt the moment.

TAKE IT.

"No," I whispered.

TAKE IT.

I grabbed the glass.

BREAK IT.

"He'll hear."

BREAK IT!

I gripped the stem in both hands. It snapped more easily than I'd imagined. The bowl of the glass now back on the table, I stared at the sharp edge of the broken stem.

And smiled.

TEN

I JOLTED AWAKE, NOT even realising I'd drifted off. The memory was so fresh, I could still taste the alcohol on Aiden's breath. Could still feel his body against mine. My bottom lip trembled as I thought about him. I tried to move my hand to my face, forgetting that both wrists were restrained.

"You were out for a little while," Rachel said. She was next to me again, and I fought the urge to look at her. To plead with her to untie me. I knew she wouldn't. She wouldn't do anything. "You looked restless."

"I was dreaming about Aiden," I said, instantly regretting it.

"You should try to stay awake." It was like she hadn't heard me. I turned my head to face her, still fighting the urge to scream in her face. "You might be concussed from that nasty punch."

SHE'S RIGHT, CHARLIE.

Too many voices all at once. Rachel, the voice in my head, my own thoughts. All I wanted to do was cut off my ears and go back to sleep. Nobody wanted my help. Nobody wanted *me*. The ropes around my wrist were evidence enough of that.

But Aiden wouldn't quit, I thought. *And neither will I.*

"What was the dream?" Rachel asked.

"I told you. It was about Aiden."

She seemed distracted. Staring up and down the aisle, like she was searching for something. Before I could ask, she turned back to me. No hair twirl this time. No fiddling with the necklace. She was focused now.

"Tell me later," she said, and she craned her neck over the seats in front of us. "Have you seen Calista?"

My heart sank. "No," I said. "I haven't."

Craning my own neck to search the vicinity, I felt the straps tighten around my wrists, digging into the skin. It didn't matter: the pain was secondary to my immediate concern. If Calista was nowhere to be seen, that meant one thing.

The monster had jumped again.

And I hadn't tracked it.

"When did you see her last?" I asked Rachel.

She shrugged. "I don't remember."

"Weren't you watching her?" My voice rose.

"I tried," she said. "I'm sorry. I lost track of her."

"Why didn't you—" I stopped myself. Her inability to watch one person in a confined area was beside the point. "You need to go and find her."

She looked down at my wrists and bit her lip. "I can't. Charlie, I—"

A scream interrupted her.

We both shifted our attention in the direction of the scream. It came again. I couldn't see well, so I craned as much as I could, the straps digging further into my skin. The wire rope sawed through me as I struggled and winced through the pain.

"What's happening?" I asked.

Rachel shrugged and got up from her seat. Moved a few steps up the aisle to see.

"What's going on?" I pleaded.

She didn't answer me, just cupped a hand to her mouth and raced back to her seat.

"Rachel!" I called to her. She shook her head and grabbed her necklace again. Right then, I decided she was fucking useless. I wouldn't depend on her. Not again.

I leaned down as far as I could so my mouth was almost touching the restraints. I pulled my wrist up a little until there was a bit of give. My teeth met the restraints, and I gnawed at the ropes.

It was no good. They were thick and wiry. After a minute or so, with the screaming and the fuss toward the front of the plane, I gave up.

"Someone help me!" I shouted. "What's happening?"

WHat'S haPpeNinG? WHAT's happening? WHAT'S HAP-PENING?

The fucking voice was laughing at me again as I struggled harder and harder and kicked the back of the seat in front of me. My effort made the laughter more intense.

I could feel Rachel's eyes on me, and in the corner of my vision, I saw her smiling, too. Laughing to herself. Laughing at me. I swallowed hard and moved to chew on the restraints again as someone else screamed from the front of the plane.

"Jesus Christ!" I shouted. "Someone let me out!"

Nobody came for me, and the screaming stopped. Craning my neck again, I saw a crowd of passengers, but I couldn't see what they were looking at. One passenger stepped away from the crowd. Bending to her knees, she vomited in the aisle.

As the stream of regurgitated plane food splattered against the carpet and the seats, she wiped her mouth and straightened.

Stared right at me.

ELEVEN

15A

THAT GUY WAS A fucking nightmare. All April wanted to do was shut her eyes and listen to music. Then that crazy arsehole started his nonsense about what? Aliens? Demons? She tried to ignore him, tried to keep to herself, and just sleep away the drama. Except she couldn't. He was always there, screaming or pointing or harassing that poor old woman.

When the old lady had tottered off to the toilet, April had thought her movements a bit strange. Old people didn't move like the rest of us anyway, but even so, it was like she'd been unfamiliar with how to put one foot in front of the other.

Minding her own business, like her father had taught her to do, April stared out the window and then closed her eyes again. Until that *fucking* guy had started banging on the door, ordering the old woman out. She had taken her headphones off and watched him, seen the desperation on his face, the sweat pouring from him, and part of her had wanted to help him.

Mostly, though, she'd just wanted him to shut up. To go away. Getting involved was nothing but trouble.

When he'd finally settled back down, April relaxed a little. Ordered a tonic water and sipped away as Taylor Swift's new album serenaded her eardrums. Like any peace she'd ever had, it was short-lived.

"Fuck's sake," she'd mumbled, and taken her headphones off again. Crazy guy was back, storming around the place and insulting the staff. April just shook her head and watched it unfold, making sure to pause the music so she didn't miss out. "What's his problem now?"

"She isn't human!" the guy shouted.

April rolled her eyes and went back to listening to music. She didn't need to see another psychotic episode. Watching her dad dig holes in the backyard to build a bomb shelter was enough for her. She tuned in again when some dude with neck tattoos snapped him in the head. He went down like a ton of bricks, and suddenly, Taylor Swift wasn't so interesting.

"Holy shit," she giggled, unbuckling her seat belt.

Moving to the aisle seat, she watched him kick and flail as three men and a woman carried him to the back of the plane. She felt bad for the guy, who was clearly in need of a medication review. Still, it wasn't her problem.

Her dying mother in Perth was more of a concern, as was the fact that she had two years until she could call herself an adult and move away from her doomsday-obsessed father. When the plane landed, she would have to take a bus for forty minutes and then walk a little to get to her mum's place. When she got there, she was sure she'd be the caregiver, like she used to be before the divorce. If it wasn't cancer, it was her head.

Just like that guy, now restrained and calling for someone named Rachel.

Whatever.

The male flight attendant, Eric, had tried his best to appease the masses, telling everyone the old woman was merely sick, and they were going to leave her in the bathroom for a while. But then why did they have garbage bags, a dustpan, and a brush? Something was wrong, even if the guy did seem crazy.

She remembered when she was five and her mother had shouted about their cousin, Donny, jumping off a cliff. She and her dad had thought it was the last straw, the final snap in her brain. It wasn't until the next day that the police found what was left of his body at the bottom of a cliff.

Even then, people thought her mother was crazy. All except April. Somehow, the courts had decided she should live with her dad after the divorce, even though he was prepping for the end of the world and buying beans on special every second day.

Maybe the guy at the back of the plane was onto something. He could be like her mother: misunderstood, even if they were both medicated. He'd shouted something about Clonazepam, which she knew was an antipsychotic.

However, as she watched Calista—the flight attendant he'd tried to strangle—resume her work as though nothing was wrong, April grew curious. The woman's movements were much like the old lady's: the way she reached for the drinks, the way her hands grabbed at things like pincers, like she didn't know how to use her fingers. Her steps were awkward, too.

And the smile.

It sent chills down her spine.

Sipping her tonic water, April continued to watch her. Calista slowly became more fluid in her movements, but something was wrong with her face. She couldn't quite articulate it, but it seemed different from earlier.

"C'n I got youu ennyting?" Calista pushed the snack and drink cart to her aisle with a broad smile.

"Uh—" April cleared her throat. "No thanks." She stared at Calista as she shrugged one shoulder at a time.

"Swit yarselve," Calista replied.

April raised an eyebrow. "Huh?"

Clearing her throat, Calista licked her lips. The movement was slow and jerky. "Suit... yourself."

"Uh-huh," April said with a nod and watched Calista continue on her way.

As the flight attendant moved past, April saw that her elbows were red and sore. Not unusual, but the thin veins spiking from the redness gave her pause. Calista kept walking, now moving like someone who had been doing this for years.

"Actually," April called.

Calista spun around, that dopey smile spread wide. The woman's eyes were growing dark, and her skin was pale.

"Can I grab a Coke?"

Moving to the drinks drawer, Calista pulled out a can of Coke. She walked back to April. "Here," she said, and the smile faltered for a moment. Her lips trembled, and Calista grabbed April's wrist. "Help me."

The words were so fast and hushed that April wasn't sure she'd actually heard them. Except the trembling lips and the fear in Calista's eyes told her she wasn't imagining it.

"What's wrong?" April asked.

Calista returned to the fake smile, stood straight, and released April's hand. Without another word, she sauntered off down the aisle, back to the cart.

"The hell was that?" April muttered to herself. Opening the Coke can released a sharp hiss, and she took a swig of the dark liquid.

She watched Calista continue to serve people, her elbows getting redder by the second. When her eyes wandered to the crazy guy, now asleep in his seat, Calista pulled the cart back. April wouldn't want to go near him, either, not with the violence and the screaming. But something struck her about the way Calista came back. The way her head started to loll to one side, the way her right shoulder dropped a little. Calista walked past April, pushing the cart along, and the young girl noticed Calista's fingers. Pale, with a hint of blue. Like poor circulation.

Swallowing hard, April thought maybe the crazy guy really wasn't so crazy. That perhaps he knew something the rest of the passengers didn't. Her mother probably would have sprung into action right then and there, accusing Calista of something untoward. Her father would do the same, she had no doubt. She was a different breed, though, and knew she needed evidence. Or she'd end up restrained, too.

Calista was on the other side now, pushing the cart with newfound enthusiasm, and April's eyes bounced around the cabin, searching for Eric and finding him nowhere. Usually, there'd be one flight attendant on each side.

WHERE IS HE?

"This isn't what I asked for," someone said, and April's eyes rolled back to the cart. To a guy shaking a can of lemonade in Calista's ever-smiling face. "I asked for a Coke. C-O-K-E."

"I'm sorry." Calista swiped the lemonade from his hand. It landed on the carpet, drawing attention from the other passengers. "I'm so fucking sorry."

The guy looked between the fallen can and the flight attendant. "I... sorry." He withdrew a little, his voice soft and full of
regret.

April smiled at the awkwardness, at his cheeks growing more
flushed by the second. Her mouth turned downward when Calista's hand swiped again, this time, at the guy's face. The slap rang
through the cabin, and April felt tension thicken around her.

Leaning down to the man's face, Calista breathed slowly. "I am
so sorry for the inconvenience to your flight." Her words were
now perfectly formed, but her voice was robotic, like she was
reciting them without knowing the full context or meaning. Like
she was putting it together as she went.

"Listen," the guy said quietly, holding up a defensive hand, "I
just wanted a Coke."

"You'll get your fucking Coke," Calista replied, her eyes nar-
rowing. She reached into the cart and pulled out a red can. Held
it in front of the man. "What do you say?"

He stared at the Coke can and swallowed hard. "Th-thank
you." His voice cracked, and April wanted to laugh at the guy
for being an arsehole. Instead, she held her breath.

"You are so welcome, sir." Calista beamed at him as she raised
the can above his head and brought it down with a fierce *crack*.

"What the—" the guy started.

She brought it down again, harder, and raised it. The can
dripped with sweat and blood. April stood but stopped herself.

What could she do? She was sixteen and all of 45kg. Her ankles were the same size as her wrists. She wasn't helping anyone.

The guy was screaming now as Calista brought the can down again and again. He tried to fend her off, but Calista—with that everlasting smile—kept slamming that can into his face. One of the passengers tried to grab her, but she swung at him. Even as two more passengers approached, neck tattoo guy pulling her arms back, she kept pummelling the Coke into the other guy's face.

Blood splattered around her smile and all over her uniform as she pummelled the guy. "I hope you enjoy your refreshment," she said. The can had begun to dent and deform, the aluminium contorting into an odd shape, pointed edges forming. She twisted the can and slashed with a jagged edge at the man's hands and arms.

He screamed again and again as his skin tore apart, and Calista punched at him with the can, stabbing his face until his cheeks were like juicy pulled pork.

"Hey," Neck Tattoo guy shouted at her, finally gaining enough control to force her away. "The fuck you doin'?"

April watched as he thrust Calista to the side. She edged closer to the action as a small crowd started to form. To watch on like they were at a boxing match. Begging for blood and pain. Phones were raised, cameras were out, recording the moment. Not one other person stepped in, just Neck Tattoo guy.

Through the gathering of passengers, she saw the guy in his seat, slumped over. Blood drooled from his mouth down to his chest.

Slowly, he lifted his head to look at Calista, still blubbering an apology.

Neck Tattoo guy let go of Calista, and she lowered her arm and dropped the bloodied and misshapen Coke can to the carpet. Turning to the passengers, she clasped her hands together and gave a small bow of the head.

Holding her breath again, April waited for Calista to speak. Instead, she appraised the crowd with that awful fucking smile, now marred with splotches of blood. No words came, only a few nods, as though she was thanking the crowd for watching.

"What did you do?" a woman with jet-black hair asked and rushed to the bloodied man. "He needs medical attention."

"He got his Coke," Calista said and turned to walk away.

As her body twisted, the skin on her forearms a deep red, Neck Tattoo Guy grabbed her by the shoulder. "Hey," he said. "You can't just walk away. You've just beaten this fucking guy." His words got lost in the screams that followed them.

April covered her mouth and rushed to the edge of the gathering. Jumped onto a seat to get a better view. "What... "

Where Neck Tattoo Guy had grabbed Calista, there was now a vacancy. He'd swiped her shoulder away, her arm falling to the ground and exploding into dust. Calista didn't even seem to notice. She kept walking.

The passengers erupted into screams. Neck Tattoo Guy followed her, took her by the only hand she had left. It came off, like she was a mannequin. Her hand was perfectly formed in his own, but dust drained from the inside, hollowing it out.

"What is this?" he asked, dropping the limb to the floor and wiping his hands on his jeans. "Am I going to get sick?"

Calista turned around, still smiling, but her expression faltered. Pain filled her eyes, and her lips trembled. No words came, though, as she fell backwards into the aisle. One of the passengers tried to catch her, arms open wide. As their bodies collided, Calista burst into dust and ash, bits of her swirling around the cabin as the passengers screamed. The passenger who'd tried to catch her crouched, motionless, arms still outstretched as sand and dust rained down on him, powdering his clothes and face. He wheezed on miniscule fragments of Calista's body and scraped her sandy remains from his open eyeballs, crying for help as other passengers stepped back for fear they might get some Calista on them.

After a few more seconds of blinking dust from his eyes, his screams faded into terrified and confused weeping. Gagging, he wiped furiously at his tongue. "Get her—*gak*—off me!" he managed, clawing dusty remains from his mouth.

Parts of her were in thick chunks, like bits of broken charcoal, but April could see that it was decay. The shell of her body crumbled further as the passenger who'd tried to catch her fell backwards as well, crab-crawling away from what was left of the flight attendant. Dust shook loose from his hair as he went, and he wiped again at his mouth, face, and hands.

April stepped down from the seat, vomited into her hands and onto the carpet, and held her knees to steady herself. People didn't just collapse into dust. People didn't just fall away like they never existed. There wasn't any blood, no internal organs, nothing. Just... dust.

She wretched at the thought that she'd breathed some of Calista into her lungs, remembering the dust swirling through the air. And she remembered Neck Tattoo Guy's words: "Am I going to get sick?"

Standing, eyes wide, she wiped vomit from her lips and looked toward the crazy guy, who was staring right at her.

HE KNEW.

Through the screaming and the crowd dispersing with nowhere to go, she stared at that guy. He was watching it unfold, pulling at his restraints, begging to be set free. Whatever had happened, he wasn't the villain here. Despite his behaviour, despite the violence, despite everyone looking at him like he was less than, he'd been trying to warn them.

To save them.

April headed towards him, but stopped. Something else caught her attention, from the corner of her eye. Turning to face it, she saw a jelly-like blob. It was translucent, with blue lights zapping through what could be thought of as a body. It was above her now, floating on the ceiling.

Pointing up at the entity, she screamed. Nobody was watching. Nobody saw. Too concerned about Calista's remnants to pay her any mind.

Except the man.

He saw.

He was watching her, his mouth moving but no words coming.

April got down to her knees, as far away from the creature as possible, as it shuddered above her. Crawling down the aisle, praying it hadn't seen her—if it could even see—April headed towards the man. He'd know what to do. He was the only one who'd know what to do.

As she continued on her way, army crawling now, April chanced a look at the ceiling.

It was gone.

Whatever it was, it was gone.

Standing, April searched the area as another passenger pushed past her to do god knows what. Just running for the sake of it. Panicked. They had no idea what the real panic was, though. She raced down the aisle, the man still staring at her, eyes full of hope.

"Please," he said as she approached, "please let me out."

"What is that thing?" April asked.

"You saw it." It wasn't a question.

April nodded.

"I don't know what it is," the man said, "but it was inside Calista. We have to find her."

Taking a deep breath, April swallowed hard and brushed away a tear. "She's dead, man. She's a pile of fucking dust."

The man swore and pulled at his restraints. Without being asked again, April untied him, and he shot up fast to search the aisle with darting eyes.

"What?" April asked.

"I saw it above you, but then it shot away. I didn't see where it went."

"Good, maybe it's gone," April replied.

The man looked at her, his expression full of pity and fear. "It's not gone," he said.

April looked around, too, and asked, "Then where is it?"

"That's the wrong question," he whispered. "The question is, *who* is it?"

TWELVE

The girl, April, had set me free. She'd done more for me than Rachel had, and her eyes were human—for now. Though she was young, she'd handled herself well with that thing looming above her only moments earlier. Everyone else was running around screaming. She'd been present enough to be aware of the danger and act accordingly.

For the moment, I had an ally.

I flashed a look over at Rachel, who was still in her seat, melting as close to the wall as possible to stay out of sight. Something about her was wrong. The way she didn't interact with anyone. The way she refused to help me or advocate for me when she'd seen the same thing I had. It wasn't fear; I hadn't seen that in her face. It was something else.

EXCEPT SHE DID COME TO HELP YOU. SHE TOLD EVERYONE TO LEAVE YOU ALONE.

The voice was right, as always. And she'd knocked on the toilet door, to no avail. The efforts were there, just... lousy.

"What do we do?" April asked, and I turned to her and shook my head. "I thought you'd know what to do."

"We have to find it," I said, "but I don't know how to do that."

April thought, then snapped her fingers and pointed at me. "She was all red around the elbows. I noticed she had trouble speaking and moving at first, too. And that weird-arse fucking smile that just wouldn't go away."

I nodded, taking it in. "Keep going. Anything else?"

She licked her lips and breathed hard. "I think, maybe, she was like... still in there. She asked me for help, but it was only a flash of her real self, if that makes any sense. Whatever this thing is, it takes you over."

"But it doesn't last long. It dries us out," I said. "Turns us to dust."

Looking into the passengers now—all of them acting like the world had ended instead of rallying to solve their shared problem—I scanned for Eric. I imagined he'd be front and centre, trying to calm everyone and ordering them back to their seats. He was absent, though, and that terrified me. As much as we'd clashed during this flight, he was a beacon of stability, and I really needed some fucking stability right now.

"Have you seen Eric?" I asked.

April shrugged and frowned. "Not for ages. Why?"

I didn't know how to answer that, but his disappearance shook me to my core. He should have been there, within the chaos. I looked over my shoulder at Rachel, her eyes on me again. She had shrunk into her seat, trying to hide from the other passengers.

SHE ISN'T SUPPOSED TO BE HERE, CHARLIE.

"I know," I said.

"You know what?" April asked.

I waved her off as a thought started to form. The voice was right—it was always fucking right, even when it was laughing at me. Even when it told me to do things. Hard things. Things I never would have imagined. But it was always the right thing to do, and I hated the voice for it.

It was right again.

Rachel wasn't supposed to be here. It couldn't be a coincidence that she was on the plane when the creature came knocking. It couldn't be a coincidence that people started dying, and all she wanted to do was avoid being seen by anyone.

As I watched her sink further and further out of sight, it hit me. I didn't know how she did it, how she got past security or the staff. I thought back to when we'd all boarded. I hadn't seen her. She was already on the plane.

STOWAWAY. SHE'S A FUCKING STOWAWAY.

"Does that even happen anymore?" I asked.

"What are you talking about?" April patted me on the arm.

"Nothing," I said. "Thinking out loud."

She eyed me curiously. It was a look I was all too familiar with, even in the hospital. The nursing staff acted like they were judgment-free, but their eyes always betrayed them. Eyes betrayed everyone.

Even Aiden.

I didn't want to think about that now. Couldn't think about it. The problem at hand was more important. Find the monster. Kill the fucking thing.

Before we land, I thought.

That's what Rachel had said earlier, too. What would happen when we land? This thing hopped around from person to person, and we'd lost track of it in a confined space. If we landed and it got out...

"Okay," I said. "We know there are some signs. Language, movement, the... red skin. I noticed her face was pale and gaunt, too."

April nodded. "Like the life was being sucked out of her."

"We can find it. We just have to look." I paused and looked back at Rachel. "You go ahead and see what you can see. I need to talk to someone."

That look came again. The '*He really is batshit*' look. I ignored it and watched April go. If I was going to find this thing and kill it, I needed to know everything I could. And Rachel knew more than she was letting on.

I sat next to her, rubbing at my wrists. She nodded at the injury and asked me if it hurt.

"Tell me what you know about what's going on here," I said, ignoring her question.

She studied me like I should already know, but didn't say anything.

"You aren't supposed to be here, are you?" I asked.

She shook her head and chewed the inside of her cheek.

"You're a stowaway."

Rachel sighed and breathed hard through her nose. "Charlie, I want to help you, I really do."

I laughed. "No, you don't. At every turn, you have let me down. Typical psychologist, always saying you want to help and never actually doing anything."

"I'm sorry you feel that way." Rachel flashed a little smile at me and continued. "How does that make you feel?"

We both giggled a little, and the tension between us dissipated.

"Look, I don't care who you are and what you're doing here. I don't want to get you in trouble. But you need to tell me what's going on," I said.

"Charlie..." Rachel frowned and paused when my phone lit up in my pocket, vibrating and sending out a hollow version of John Barry's "The Beyondness of Things." "You should get that."

A phone call. On a plane. That wasn't supposed to happen.

I fished it out of my pocket and looked at the screen.

Aiden.

DON'T ANSWER IT!

I hit the green ANSWER button and breathed down the phone. "Aiden?"

"Oh, Charlie, thank god," he said, sighing. "Where are you?"

"I'm on a plane," I said. "Listen, something is happening here. Something is very wrong."

"What is it, Charlie? Talk to me." His voice was laced with concern. I imagined his arms wrapped around me, the way he cocooned me and kept me warm and safe. Just his words made me melt, and I felt tears start to well.

"People are dead, Aiden," I whispered. "There's some kind of... creature on here with us."

Silence.

"Aiden?"

"You can do this," he replied. "Whatever is happening, you can handle it."

I creased my brow, confusion overtaking the joy I felt at his voice. "You believe me?"

"Are you alright?" he asked, avoiding my question. "Where are you going?"

HANG UP!

"I... I need you." The tears were almost ready to flow, and I knew if he told me he loved me, that I'd fall apart. "I have to go."

The phone call ended, and I stared at the wallpaper on my phone. A picture of me and Aiden, arms around each other, faces nuzzled together, embraced in a slow dance at our wedding. The memory was too painful.

How I'd yelled at him moments later for missing a beat in our favourite song, and now the moment wasn't perfect, and everything was ruined. How he'd followed me through the wedding hall, placating our guests with, "He's just a bit overwhelmed." How he'd given me that calm, beautiful smile and made me dance out of step until we'd laughed and laughed. It was that moment I knew he'd made a mistake marrying me.

Thrusting the phone back into my pocket, I focused on Rachel again. "Tell me what you know."

"How's Aiden?" she asked instead. "I saw his name on the screen when he called."

"I didn't ask," I said, a dagger of pain shooting to my heart. I never asked.

"Hmmm," she replied.

I tried to call 000, but the reception went to SOS. Aiden always had the best timing. It wasn't like anyone on the ground could help us anyway. I put my phone into my pocket.

"Look, that doesn't matter now. We have bigger problems." I motioned around the plane. People were starting to settle now, coming to grips with the reality that Calista was dead. The old woman was dead. And they might be next.

April was moving slowly through the aisles, watching people. Taking notes on her phone as she walked. She stopped at piles of Calista's remains, her uniform tarnished with blood and dust. I saw the flash of her camera. The girl was collecting evidence.

SHE'S SMART. SMARTER THAN YOU. YOU NEED HER. SHE DOESN'T NEED YOU. NOBODY NEEDS YOU.

"Please," I said to Rachel, closing my eyes to focus my thoughts. "Will you *please* tell me what you know?"

Another flash as April collected more evidence.

Rachel looked down at her hands and clicked her nails against each other. "I don't know anything." She turned away.

I started to speak again, but April was back at my side. She gazed into her phone like it was the only thing that existed, her eyes wide. Her breath came in waves. I craned my neck to see what she was looking at, but it was a blur.

"I found something," she said, turning her screen to me.

"Fuck." I took in the image. "If this plane lands, everyone is going to die."

SESSION #6

St Vincent's Hospital, Psych. Ward
30 May 2025
Patient: Charles M. Reed
Referring Psychologist: Dr R Schwarz
Consulting Psychiatrist: Dr J Mathis

I HAD HOPED OUR previous sessions would be enough to gain some trust with Charlie. In the days since our first meeting, I've researched all I can about doppelgängers so that I might find a way to break through to him. To show him reality, rather than what he is currently seeing or what Other Charlie is showing him.

Dr Schwarz had written in his patient files that Charlie was desperate to hide from these doppelgängers and was searching for a way to keep his husband safe from being replaced. The more I read about Charlie, the more it sounds like a bad movie. *Invasion of Body Snatchers* or something. It is incredible to me that there are so many versions of reality where this seems entirely possible. To Charlie, this is his reality.

In my research, I learned doppelgängers arose from German folklore, sometimes presenting as ghostly apparitions, other times simply as doubles. It occurs to me that Other Charlie could be seen as a doppelgänger in that ghostly sense. He is a double, a lookalike, yet not actually there. Mostly there in mind, and sometimes in body when Charlie needs a reprieve. It is a risk to mention this comparison to Charlie, especially so early in our sessions, but I feel he is ready.

The following is an account of our session, based on my audio recording:

"Good morning, Charlie," I said as I entered the room.

He was in the corner again, but sitting, legs crossed, elbow on his knee. Hand under his chin. "Morning," he replied.

"Faring well today, I hope?"

He didn't reply but bit at a nail. He was pensive and nervous, his muscles tight. His mouth curved down in a frown. That was my Charlie, the original. Nevertheless, I was conscious that Other Charlie might have been listening, as alters sometimes do.

"Charlie, I want to ask you something," I said. "It's about doppelgängers. Is that okay?"

He nodded and looked up at me. There was a table in the middle of the room, with a chair on either side. I sat in one and encouraged him to the other. My silence indicated I wouldn't ask until he'd sat where I demanded, so he moved to the seat. Sprawled in it, like simply sitting there was an effort.

"Thank you, Charlie. My question will be difficult; I want you to know that." I paused so he could ready himself. He stared at me and breathed with resignation, so I continued. "How do you know *you're* not a doppelgänger?"

Charlie frowned like he had never considered the possibility. "What do you mean?"

"Well," I said, choosing my words with caution, "you are burdened with Other Charlie. He is, in a way, an apparition with your likeness. And when he takes control, he *is* your double."

"He's nothing like me." Charlie teared up, but he refused to wipe the moisture away. His cheeks went red, and he sniffed. "He's not me."

Despite the upset, I pressed on, thinking the line of inquiry could be critical for Charlie's recovery. "Isn't that what they are, though? Imitations? Evil versions of ourselves? Isn't that why you are afraid of them?"

He swallowed hard and shook his head. "I'm me. I'm not one of *them*."

"Okay, Charlie," I said. "But how do you know?"

He sat quietly for a moment, the words lingering in the room. I let the silence remain. I let him ponder the implications. Patients often lashed out when their sense of self was threatened or questioned, but Charlie didn't. Yet another aspect of his identity that fascinated me. As he sank a little in his chair, it occurred to me that he was resigned to sharing himself with Other Charlie. That he considered this other personality as a part of himself, as a way to recognise his humanity.

He confirmed as much when he said, "Me and him— we're in this together. We know we're human. That's all that matters."

We know *we're* human. I sighed, and he latched his eyes onto me, daring me to question or challenge him. I would not openly do so. That wasn't the point of today's session.

"Do you still think I'm a doppelgänger?" I asked.

He shook his head, just once. "I was wrong. Your eyes are fine. You're still one of us, for now."

I found an odd satisfaction in his response, almost as though I'd gained his trust. "Other than the eyes," I continued, "how do you recognise them?"

"They act differently than they used to," he said. "Like the nurse out there. Last time you came, she was human. Now… I don't know how, but they got her."

"How can you tell?" I pressed him. There would be no rational answer here. There couldn't be. I hoped that by getting him to examine his own thoughts and observations, really examine them, he'd come to see his delusion.

"Beyond the eyes?" he asked. "She walked with a slight hunch, which is still there. But she's more upright than she was two days ago. Her smile sags on one side. They imitate us, copy us, but it's never perfect. You have to look. You have to see."

I nodded as though it made perfect sense to me. These things could be easily explained. The hunch? Perhaps she had back problems and had gone to a chiropractor. Her smile? Maybe she wasn't as happy today as she was a few days prior. These observations were not compelling evidence, and I could tell Charlie sensed my doubt.

"Watch her," he said. "Just watch. The way she moves is different. When she checked off my chart this morning, she only clicked the pen once. Every other day, she's done it twice."

Again, easily explained.

"Charlie," I said, "these things are all circumstantial. How do you know, without a doubt, that she—or anyone—has been re-placed?"

"I… " He trailed off, but not because he doubted himself. No, it wouldn't be that easy. He trailed off because he knew I didn't believe him. I was another person who was treating him like a patient instead of a human being.

And it was that—being human—that was so important to Charlie.

"Just look at her eyes," he said. "Just look."

When I left the session that day, after almost a week of him pleading with me to see—truly *see*—the slight variations in people's eyes, I caught myself looking. I didn't know the nursing staff well and had only given them my cursory attention as I signed in and out each day or when I took a coffee break. However, in that time, I had unconsciously learned the movements and tendencies of some of the staff. A habit of my profession is to be… watchful. Detail-oriented.

So, when the nurse smiled at me upon my exit down the white, stale hallways of the facility, I stared right into her eyes. I took a moment to register what I saw, and of course, I dismissed it. Like a canvas yet to be painted, or a section of herself not yet made real.

There, in her left eye… a blank spot.

<u>Recommendation</u>: The increase in medication seems to be taking effect, though after a longer period than expected. The nursing staff has reduced his television and music allocation. The reduction in stimulation seems to be having a positive impact, though it is not sustainable. The

patient may get bored and is prone to fantasy. As such, I am further increasing medications for anxiety and deepening the therapy to target his trauma. I believe this may aid in the dissolution of the delusions concerning doppelgängers.

THIRTEEN

Eric was strewn across the galley in pieces. Bits of skin, like shredded paper, slipped down the walls. A torn-off leg, bent backwards at the knee, hung limp off one of the counters, blood seeping from where his toes used to be. As I took in the scene, the other body parts seemed to melt together, as though baked into a half-made pie. Chunks of human limbs covered in thick red blood jutted up from the floor.

"We need to alert the captain," I said as April examined her phone again. "The captain will know what to do."

"How did that even happen?" April asked. "Nobody even noticed."

I looked at the image again and shook my head. I needed to see it for myself in order to truly understand what had happened. Without turning to Rachel, I said to her, "I'll be back."

April let me pass her and trailed me as I headed to the galley.

Pulling a fabric curtain across the thin track, I stepped back. "Fuck me," I said, and held my nose.

This was why Eric had been out of play.

The carpet squelched under my feet as I stepped into the scene, April hanging back with her phone up, recording.

"What the hell are you doing?" she asked.

"I need to be sure this is Eric," I said, crouching to inspect the scene.

The stench of the rot burned in my nose, and I pulled my shirt up from the waist to cover the bottom half of my face. Even so, I gagged with the knowledge I was breathing in human remains.

"How can you even tell?" April asked through a hand clamped over her own mouth.

Sifting through a tangle of intestines, a half-eaten liver, and a discarded heart, I wiped my hands on my dirty jeans. The chaos of Eric's remains was like a puzzle. It kept me grounded somehow.

A larger piece of remains caught my eye toward the edge of the scene. Reaching for it, I took an awkward step in my crouched position and lost balance. My left foot slipped in the puddles of blood, and I fell to my side, splashing in Eric's coagulating life force. I heard April ask if I was okay, but she did not attempt to help me up. Instead, my slippery hands gripped a handle on one of the ovens, and I pulled myself up.

I regained my balance and rested on my knees. I was filthy already anyway, so more gore on my jeans wouldn't matter now. I reached again for the larger object and felt the unmistakable matting of wet hair. I turned the piece around. Eric's face stared at me. His expression unnerved me, the way his eyes remained open, his mouth hanging ajar.

April spewed again. The butter chicken she'd had swirled in the blood beneath her feet. "What the fuck did that?" she asked, gagging and puking over herself.

"I don't know," I said, somehow keeping calm. Ordinarily, I would have descended into a bumbling mess by now, but my heart was beating at a steady pace, and my thoughts were my own. "This thing is powerful."

"No shit." April spat the last of the vomit from her mouth, the phone still pointed at me, filming.

I stood, gripping the matted hair on Eric's head, and looked around. For what, I had no idea. Just looked, just took it in. To keep the mess contained like this took precision. Not an ounce of blood strayed beyond the curtain line. The monster had done this. It had been purposeful, meticulous— planned.

Dropping Eric's head back to the floor with a wet, dull thud, I raced past April and headed to the cockpit door. I didn't care that my hands, shoes, and clothes were dripping in blood and vomit.

I banged on the metal door. It was thick and hard against my fist.

"Hey!" I screamed. "Captain! We need help out here!"

There was no answer, and I wasn't sure the pilot could hear me. I banged again, harder and harder, until I wasn't sure if the blood on the door was mine or Eric's or both. April put a hand on my arm, and I turned to face her.

"What do we do?" I asked her. The calmness I'd felt only minutes earlier was vanishing. My sense of self along with it. I could feel the internal wheels spinning again, bringing forth the voice. Bringing forth my self-doubt, the need for Aiden to fix all my problems.

Except he isn't here, I thought.

"I've seen the crew chatting on these phones here." April pointed to a cream-coloured phone hanging from the wall by the cockpit door. "Maybe they use that?"

I grabbed at it, the cord bouncing up and down as I thrust it to my ear. "Hello? Captain, are you there?"

Nothing.

April took it from me, lowered her own phone, and smiled. "Let me try."

Nodding, I stepped away and raced back to the galley. Eric's head was lopsided now, the tear marks on his neck still seeping.

LOOK INSIDE, the voice nagged at me, its words like a snake, stretched out in a hiss, tickling my inner ear. *LOOOOK INSSS-SIDE.*

Lifting the severed head with both hands, I brought it up to eye level and stared into Eric's eyes. They weren't human anymore. They were just nothing. His jaw became slack and hung wide, the tongue sliding out a little.

I gulped hard as the voice ordered me to look inside again.

Flipping the head a little, I peered into the neck hole. The dark blood glistened under the halogen ceiling lights, and inside, I saw it. The hole was a tight squeeze, but I managed to get my hand all the way in, keeping my fingers layered and squished together like a pincer. There was something in there, and the deeper I went, my fingertips scraping at brain matter, I felt it.

"Jesus fucking Christ," someone said from behind me.

I turned around and stood, my hand still deep inside the neck hole. "It's not what you think."

It was Hoodie Guy.

"You're a *fucking psycho!*" he shouted, pointing at me and jumping backwards against the wall. "Keep away!"

"There's something in here," I said to him. I knew what it looked like and couldn't blame him for thinking the worst. "I didn't do this."

"He killed the flight attendant!" Hoodie Guy screamed. "He's fucking ripped off his head!"

"No, no, I—"

He leaped on top of me, rage and fear and tears all over his face. I was on the floor again, flapping in the blood and guts, begging him to listen to me. His fists were in my face. I felt the bones in my nose crack again and again as he beat into me.

All I could do was swipe hard with my arm, Eric's head slamming into Hoodie Guy's shoulder. He was knocked off balance but quickly recovered. I hit him again; my wrists burned with the force. I made it to a sitting position, but his fist came at me again, and I was face-first in Eric's messy remains.

"Stay the fuck down, psycho!" Hoodie Guy was on my back, pressing my face into the carpet until I could taste blood. Something squelched against my cheek, and as he pushed my face down harder, I felt a knuckle jutting into my cheekbone.

"Hey!" Another voice—older, female. "Get off him!"

Hoodie Guy didn't listen and kept pushing me against the carpet, his knee pressing into my spine.

"Please," April said. "I've told the captain what's going on. We need to figure this out."

"Get the captain, then," Hoodie Guy said through clenched teeth.

"I'm here," the gruff voice said, clearing her throat. "Now get off him."

"Who's flying the fucking plane, then?" Hoodie Guy asked.

The captain flashed an angry look and said, "The co-pilot. Obviously. Now get off him."

Hoodie Guy complied but dug his knee into me one more time before getting up. I stayed where I was, looking up at the captain, Hoodie Guy, and April. April was still filming, capturing my hand inside Eric's neck.

"Sir," the captain said, her hands raised in a *Calm the hell down* way. "Put the... head... down." Her gaze betrayed her. She was struggling, taking it all in, unsure what to do. It was written in her pupils, the lines around her eyes. She was sucking in bile and vomit, her chest heaving. She was weak, like the others.

She couldn't save us.

"We're going to get you some help," she said.

And that's when I saw what was really in her eyes. She wasn't taking the scene in. She was taking *me* in—the guy covered in blood, swimming in a stew of Eric's remains with my fist inside his decapitated head.

All I had left was what was hanging off Eric's brain matter. And I didn't even know what it was.

I raised a hand to indicate I wasn't a threat and slowly brought my hand from Eric's head, clutching the object I'd felt in there. Everyone stepped back, Hoodie Guy ready to jump at me when needed. As my hand slipped free from the slack neck muscles, slick with the goo from Eric's brain, veins, and tendons, I presented the object to the crowd.

"What is that?" April asked.

"It's his fucking brains, that's what!" Hoodie Guy pointed.

I looked at it, shook my head. "No." I wiped it against my jeans, a spot on the leg that hadn't been tarnished yet. "Look."

Holding it up, now cleared of most of the gunk, it was what I'd hoped it was.

What the voice somehow knew it was.

A translucent, stringy mass with tiny veins branching off inside it, like discarded skin. It was evidence. I wasn't crazy. I hadn't imagined it. I spread my bloodied lips wide.

"This is part of the... the *thing*."

"Holy shit," April said. "He's right. It looks like the thing I saw earlier."

VALIDATION VALIDATION.

I breathed through the voice's celebration that I wasn't crazy and nodded. I moved closer to the captain and Hoodie Guy, getting to my feet. I showed them the portion of whatever that creature was.

The captain stepped back, looked between me and the stringy mass, uncertain. April looked at me and smiled, though her lips were laced with fear. Mine were too, as I smiled back, and the voice called to me from the depths of my own mind.

YOU DID IT, CHARLIE. THEY BELIEVE US.

"You believe me," I said. "Right?"

A moment of silence, and the captain looked away, catching April's gaze. April nodded to her, and she sighed. "I don't know what I believe. But I do know what I see. You... covered in blood, holding a... holding that."

"But... " I trailed off, holding up the piece of the monster again.

The captain snapped her eyes to mine. "We need to detain you. Again. Until we can sort out... all this." She motioned around the galley.

Don'T LET THeM TAKE Us, CHArlIE. YOU KnOw WHaT HAPPENS TheN!

"I know how this looks. I'm not stupid." I dropped the translucent mass to the floor. Held my hands out, wrists together. "Restrain me. I won't resist. But please, you have to find the creature. It's in one of the other passengers now, and they don't have long. It killed the old woman and Calista in minutes. And... it did this."

The captain moved toward me. She held plastic handcuffs before me and gulped as she slipped them over my wrists.

"How long until we land?" I asked her.

"Just under three hours." She tightened the cuffs around me. They reminded me of zip ties but were thicker.

"We have that long to find that thing. If it's alive when we land... " I didn't need to finish the sentence and let the implications hang in the air. The weight of what I *didn't* say hit them harder.

The captain nodded towards Hoodie Guy and said, "What's your name?"

"Derek," he replied.

"Okay, Derek, can you take him to the back of the plane, please? Away from all the other passengers. Stay with him; make sure he doesn't do anything." Her voice wavered with each word, and her eyes darted left and right as she thought on her feet. Surely, nobody had ever exploded on her plane before, and she was way out of her depth.

We all were.

I shuffled towards Derek and let him lead me to the back rows. The other passengers, fretting over Calista's remains, formed a path to let us through. I ignored the whispers and hushed words, keeping my head high as we went. Again, phones went into the air to record, and, not for the first time in my life, I felt like a circus freak on display. However, despite being restrained again, despite my bloodied and broken nose, despite being led through a crowd like a man on death row, I knew I was the hero this time.

YOU ARE, CHARLIE. YOU ARE THE HERO. WE BOTH ARE.

"Thank you," I said.

"What for?" Derek asked.

I smiled as he headed to the back of the plane. "Nothing."

We moved past Rachel, who gave me a sad nod, and I took my seat in the back corner. Rested my head against the chair and closed my eyes. Three hours to go before we landed. I needed to rest, to process.

If the entity could tear someone apart without anybody even noticing, it was stronger than I'd realised. It could also lose parts of itself and function, which meant... what?

Three hours, the voice said. *We're running out of time.*

"I know," I whispered.

"Dude," Derek said, scowling at me, "why are you always talking to yourself?"

I sighed. "I always have. But it's like... It's another person in there, you know?"

He shook his head. "No idea, mate. I'm not crazy."

NEitHeR ARe wE, CHARLIE.

"Neither am I," I replied, and when Derek raised his eyebrows and looked away, I repeated it, more to myself than to him. "Neither am I."

"You need an extra set of hands?"

It was Neck Tattoo Guy, coming to offer Derek some help to watch the psycho in the back row. I smiled at him, not realising my expression was clouded by the blood caked across my face and teeth.

Derek nodded, and the two shook hands.

"Brett," Neck Tattoo Guy said, and sat across the aisle from us. He folded his arms and stared at me, and I realised I was still smiling, the same way Calista had been. I shut my mouth and cleared my throat.

"I'm Charlie," I told them.

"We don't give a shit, mate," Derek replied. "You're a fucking killer."

I didn't bother replying. The voice was yelling at me to defend myself, to show them the truth, to tell them to go look at the weird glob of discarded stringy mass in the galley. I just stared at the back of the seat, watching the flight path on the monitor and counting down the minutes until the monster would be let loose on humanity.

Until then, we needed to figure out who it was in.

WRONG QUESTION.

"What's the right question?" I asked, ignoring Brett and Derek's angry stares.

WHY IS IT DOING THIS?

"What does *that* matter?"

WHAT DoeS It WaNT, CHARLIE?

"I don't know."

WHY DID YOU SEE IT WHEN NOBODY ELSE DID?

"Rachel saw it. April saw it. Everyone's seen it now."

HAVE THEY? WHERE IS IT? WHO IS IT? WHAT DOES IT WANT, CHARLIE? CHARLIE! CHARLIE, WHAT DOES IT WANT?

"Hey... uh... Derek... " I whispered. "Could you please take one of my pills from my pocket and put it in my mouth?"

NO NO NO! I WON'T BE SILENCED AGAIN!

"SHUT UP!" I screamed and then apologised to Derek and Brett. "I just... um... I need my pills."

Derek gave me one and then studied the bottle. "What's this for, anyway?"

I shrugged and asked for another one. He slipped a second pill into my mouth. I knew it wouldn't silence the voice, but it would dull my senses enough to stop it from screaming at me.

CHARLIE, I'M SORRY. I WILL STOP YELLING. BUT YOU NEED TO ASK THE RIGHT QUESTIONS. YOU—

"What does this thing want?" I asked, feeling my chest grow heavier and my breaths unsteady. It was hard to draw in oxygen, no matter how hard I forced myself.

The guys stared at me. Over Brett's shoulder, I saw Rachel perk up.

"Huh?" Brett asked.

"Just go with me. If this thing is real, this creature," I said, "then what does it want? Why inhabit people only to turn them to dust? Why tear Eric apart?"

They both shook their heads, and Derek sniffed. "I don't know what happened to Calista or the old woman. But you can't blame what you did to Eric on whatever happened to them. You did that."

"With my bare hands? You took me down in a second; do you think I could really tear a man's fucking head off?" I let the question settle for a moment. "Pretend I'm not lying. What then?"

Brett scratched at his chin, the cogs turning in his mind. "It was pretty weird," he said. "Ain't no way he coulda done that. Turned 'em to dust, I mean. As for Eric—"

"How could I tear someone's head off? What with? I mean, look at me!" I tried to stay calm, but Brett's face was making me anxious. The possibility that I might be believed.

"Okay," Derek conceded, "let's say—just for a second—that you're not completely psycho and that there is something on board with us. What is it? Where did it come from?"

WRONG QUESTION, WRONG QUESTION.

"No," I said, "the question is, what does it want? People fly all the time. Have you ever heard of this happening before?"

They both thought about that for a second.

"Exactly. It *hasn't* happened before. So why now? It's absurd to think this thing just popped into existence a few hours ago. So, what does it want?" I asked.

Nobody had an answer, but I could tell my words had made an impact on them. Rachel was still watching over Brett's shoulders, contemplating what I'd said. I still needed to get her to talk to me, to tell me what she knew. She wasn't supposed to be on the plane, and neither was this monster. It couldn't be chance.

YOU ArEN't SUppOSeD TO Be HErE, EItHEr, CHARLIE.

I told the voice it was wrong. I needed to be on this plane. I needed to get to Perth.

YOU SHOULDN'T BE HERE.

FOURTEEN

1 DAY BEFORE TAKE-OFF

"I don't know why I thought about doing it," I said, fidgeting with my hands in my lap. I didn't want to look at her, to see the disappointment in her face. After the confession, I was worried she'd call the police or have me taken away.

"Do you think it was a *real* thought?" Dr. Schwarz asked.

"A real thought?"

Her mouth twitched downward. "You know what I mean, Charlie."

I shrugged.

"It was your first night back," she continued, stifling a sigh. "You are bound to be having trouble readjusting. It sounds to me like you were anxious and feeling guilty. Those sorts of bad thoughts can sneak in."

Nodding, I looked up. "I know. But to fantasise about stabbing my husband in the neck with a broken wine stem?"

Dr. Schwarz put her pen down, rested it against the yellow notepad in her lap, and sighed. "Was it a fantasy? Or just a passing thought?"

I thought back to the night before, how I'd sat with the wine glass for hours after Aiden had gone to sleep. How I'd held it to my chest and whispered at the voice to go away. How I'd refilled the glass, holding the broken stem, and emptied the wine bottle, then held it upside down to get the last drops of merlot.

WE CAN'T GO BACK TO THAT HOSPITAL, CHARLIE.

"I guess it was a passing thought," I lied.

"See," she said, motioning toward me with a pen in her hand. "We all have thoughts like that."

A psychologist saying everyone thought about killing their spouses didn't sit right with me, and I felt the voice settle in the depths of my mind. Curling up with a blanket, getting comfortable. I swallowed hard and thought about what she'd said.

"You think about murdering your wife?" I asked.

Dr. Schwarz nodded. "I have thought about strangling her a few times," she said, "especially when she's snoring. It's not a serious thought. It's just something that happens when people get frustrated. And, Charlie, it's okay to be frustrated."

The truth was that I felt frustrated all the time. Deciphering who was one of *them* and who was human—it was exhausting. The psychiatrist at the hospital had told me *they* weren't real, that it was my imagination. I'd said what I'd needed to say, taken the drugs I'd needed to take, and done whatever they'd required to get out of there.

Now I was home, and I wasn't ready.

YOU ARE READY, CHARLIE. WE. ARE. READY.

"Charlie?" Dr. Schwarz guided me back to her with a calm voice. "Where did you go just now?"

DON'T SAY TOO MUCH.

"I just... I'm a bit tired, is all." I yawned to sell the lie.

Her eyes were inside me, the way they always were when she stared. Her pen started to flow on the notepad, but her eyes stayed right on me. The ink was messy, but it formed words, and as my brain twisted the spiral handwriting into words like *"unfit"* and *"too early,"* my heart pounded in my ears. The voice was yelling at me—*DON'T YOU FUCKING SAY A WORD, CHARLIE!*—and her eyes were so narrow I couldn't see if she was still human, and I never looked at my own eyes anymore because I didn't know if I was human, and Aiden just wanted to love me, but I—

"I still see them everywhere," I blurted.

Schwarz looked up, and the scratch of her pen stopped. "Them?"

I nodded.

FUcKInG PatHEtIC, CHARLIE. YOU PieCe oF SHIT.

"I know I shouldn't," I said. "But they're real."

"We've talked about this, Charlie. *They* aren't real."

I nodded again. "I know. But then... why are the eyes so hollow? It's not everyone, but the numbers are growing."

"You are a highly empathic individual, Charlie. You are seeing emotion, or a lack thereof. That's all."

NO NO NO!

"If I argue with you about this, you will send me back to that awful place," I said. "So I can't even justify myself."

GOOD, CHARLIE. GOOD.

I smiled.

"This is a safe space," Schwarz said. "You can say whatever you need to say."

DO NOT TRUST HER.

Breathing as calmly as I could, I said, "I can trust you, right?"

Her eyes flashed with something I hadn't seen in her before. Just a hint, but it was there. The deception she was about to give me. "Of course."

LIAR. I thought that. The voice echoed me a moment later.

SHE PUT YOU IN THAT HOSPITAL TO BEGIN WITH, CHARLIE. AND NOW YOU WANT TO TRUST HER?

"Did I ever tell you what *they* are?" I asked.

Schwarz shook her head. "You never said."

"They look like us; they aren't us." The voice was screaming at me again, but I kept on. "I think they're doppelgängers. They're replacing people, and I don't know why."

"Doppelgängers?" Schwarz asked, her pen scribbling again. "Why are they here?"

I shrugged and leaned forward in my chair. "Does it matter? They *are* here, and nobody is doing a goddamn thing about it. But you can tell because of the eyes. The eyes don't look right. It's like they can't fully take our form; there's a little part missing."

"Well, what do they want?" Her pen was poised again, and I knew she was documenting my perceived insanity.

"They want us. They want to *be* us."

YOU'VE DONE IT NOW, CHARLIE. The voice sounded sad, which was unusual. I leaned back in my chair and looked inward for a moment as Schwarz kept scribbling. It was like she'd hit the jackpot, scrawling down the page with a speed I hadn't seen from her before.

"I've said too much, haven't I?" It wasn't a question. My eyes jumped to the door, half of me wanting to bolt, the other half expecting men to come and take me away.

"I told you," Schwarz said, "this is a safe space."

Except she didn't look at me. She faced her notepad. Her notes about the crazy guy talking about doppelgängers. Why wouldn't she look at me? Right after I told her, I knew the eyes were different.

SHE'S AVOIDING YOU, CHARLIE.

"She's not," I whispered.

"Not what?" Schwarz asked, still not looking at me.

THE NurSeS, ThE PSYCHIATRISTS—TheY WeRe AlL THEM in ThE HOSPITAL, anD YoU THINK SHE'S INNOCENT? SHE'S WITH THEM, CHARLIE! SHE WORKS FOR THEM!

My leg bounced up and down, and Schwarz looked at it. Considered it before she looked at me again—finally looked at me. I studied her eyes. Human, not human, human, not—

"I wonder if you might benefit from taking a trip back home." She paused. "To your childhood home. Where this all began." Her mouth twitched again, just a slight tug to the right, and I jumped from my seat. "What's wrong, Charlie?"

"You're going to fucking put me away again," I said through heaves. My chest was full, but I couldn't breathe.

Schwarz put her pen down and set the notepad on a small table next to her chair. "No, Charlie. We're having a chat."

A flash of something was in her expression again. Another lie. She could deny it, but I saw it. I fucking saw it. Her face was full of lies, and her eyes were changing. She was changing right in front of me. Is that how it worked? I hadn't seen it before, but it didn't mean it wasn't real.

"I think you would benefit from revisiting the site of your trauma. I know it sounds awful, and it will be confronting, but I can go with you. It was beyond words, what happened to you, Charlie. What happened to—"

"Stay away from me," I said, stepping back until I hit the office wall.

The door to my right felt a million kilometres away. My struggle for breath became harder, panting for air because there wasn't any. I wiped at sweat falling into my eyes, and as Schwarz walked toward me, I pressed harder against the wall.

"Stay away!" I screamed.

She did. She stopped mid-step and reversed, moving away from me. "Everything is okay, Charlie," she said. "You're having a panic attack."

JUST A PANIC ATTACK. JUST JUST JUST!

"I won't go back," I said, sliding down the wall as tears started to pour from my eyes. "Please leave me alone."

I saw her step towards me. Through my tears, I couldn't see her eyes. Blurry, all of it. I wiped at my face, but it made no difference. She came closer, kneeling before me but out of reach. She rested on her laurels, hands on her knees.

"Charlie," she whispered. "You're okay." A pause to let the words sink in. "Come back and sit down. Have a glass of water."

DON'T DRINK IT. DON'T DRINK IT.

I shook my head.

"You don't want to take me home; you want to put me back in that place. You're going to call them."

"There's nothing you can say to me that's going to make me call anyone. It's just you and me here, Charlie."

She was right. It was just the two of us.

My body broke into goosebumps at the realisation she could take me right then and there. She could do whatever she wanted, whatever doppelgängers did. She could make me one of *them*.

I wiped at my eyes again, the tears paused by my fear. I wasn't ready. I didn't want to be like her.

"Just come sit down," she said. "We can do some breathing exercises."

THIS IS HOW IT STARTS, CHARLIE. GET THE FUCK OUT OF HERE!

"Okay," I said, trying to keep her calm.

NO. RUN!

"Good." She reached out to me, encouraged me to take her hand. I did, and we stood together. She turned her back to me and walked to her seat. To turn her back on me was cocky. She thought she was in charge. She thought I didn't know.

BUT WE DO KNOW, CHARLIE.

I swallowed hard. I could run and go home and tell Aiden what I'd seen. He'd know what to do. Or I could stay here. And fight.

As she sat down, inviting me to do the same, I saw the coy smile. The way she believed, I still thought of her as human. The way she still acted like the real Dr. Schwarz. I moved toward her, stood above her.

She looked up at me. "Charlie? Take a seat, and we can do those breathing exercises. Are you sure you don't want some water?"

There was nothing to say. No response would be meaningful.

"Charlie?" she asked.

"You're one of them," I whispered, "and there's only one thing for that."

Before she could reply, I grabbed her by the neck.

FIFTEEN

9B

THE FLIGHT ATTENDANT COLLAPSING into dust in his arms was the least of Jim's problems. Let alone that he'd gotten some of her in his mouth and swallowed it. The bigger issue was that Eric was fucking torn to shreds, and a psycho killer was on the plane.

He should have stayed quiet in his seat instead of playing the hero and getting involved. Chivalry wasn't dead, but maybe it should have been. Then he wouldn't be spitting out bits of Calista-dust and having people talk to him, asking if he was okay.

How can I be okay? I just had a woman turn into dust in front of me.

After the initial freak-out of people running around like they had somewhere to go, the reality of the situation began to sink in. He didn't know who'd finally checked on the old woman in the toilet, but someone had discovered she was dust, too.

And Eric had lied to everyone about it.

The only person who hadn't lied, seemingly, was the crazy killer guy. The young girl, April, had tried to convince everyone he hadn't done it, that he was innocent. She stood up on a chair and showed everyone the photo she'd taken *before* he was released from his restraints. The first round of restraints.

"I don't know," someone said. A woman with jet black hair. "There's something off about him."

Others agreed, and Jim was inclined to favour that view.

"Guys," April said, her voice urgent and pleading. "He didn't do it. He's innocent."

"He's dangerous!" someone else said. Jim tried to find the voice and couldn't.

"Keep him locked up!" another cried.

April sighed and showed them the time stamp of the photo again. "I found the body and I rushed to tell him."

"He's babbling about a fucking monster on board!"

Nobody knew where that voice came from, and nobody cared. The captain, standing by April, didn't silence anyone. The situation reminded Jim of a town meeting, the kind that always descended into a modern-day witch hunt.

"He was right about that, too," April said. "I've seen it!"

The crowd went quiet.

"He found some of it," she continued, and held up a piece of something. A blob of jelly, as far as Jim could tell, but something was odd about it. Little veins stretched and convulsed inside the globby shell.

"He's been trying to help us," April said. "And we've treated *him* like a monster. You think he's responsible for... that?" She pointed right at Jim, remnants of Calista all over his clothes.

Jim looked around the cabin at the eyes staring at him. One pair caught his attention. It wasn't just the eyes, though. It was the smile.

The same one Calista had before she tried to bash a guy's head in with a Coke can. The guy was still holding his bloodied face. At least he had a jumper and an ice pack, courtesy of the captain. Everyone knew he needed more, but the flight crew just weren't equipped for that kind of thing. His skin was falling off his face; the ice pack was less than bare minimum.

Following the smiling passenger with his eyes, Jim saw him head away from the crowd and back to his seat. He was walking with a strange gait, planting each foot firmly on the floor before taking the next step. Almost like his feet were too heavy for him.

April was still shouting about the guy—Charlie—and his innocence, telling people we had a serious problem and needed to work together to solve it. The captain was nodding, though Jim wasn't sure why. Maybe the monster, if there was one, was inside her. Otherwise, why would she be so quick to accept all this as fact?

As Jim continued thinking about that, still following the smiling guy with his eyes, he saw him slump down next to a woman. She fawned over him, hands on his chest and cheeks, her lips moving to his mouth. Jim watched as she kissed him, and he sat unresponsive. After a few moments, she pulled away. He couldn't hear what she said, but she looked upset.

"What are we going to do about it?" April asked the crowd.

"Go sit down, you stupid girl," someone replied.

"You're just causing trouble," another said.

Jim wasn't so sure. He didn't think those outspoken few were sure, either. When something you didn't understand happened right in front of your eyes, you could do two things. Deny, or believe. Denial usually won out.

Not for Jim.

Seeing was believing.

Tasting was irrefutable.

Scraping his tongue once more to try and rid himself of the taste of Calista's dust, Jim took his eyes away from the young man and put them on April and the captain. The captain was nodding again, gazing up at April like she was in charge. That wasn't a captainly thing to do.

"What do you think, Captain?" Jim asked, his voice louder than the dissenters.

The captain cleared her throat and took the stage from April. "I'm joining right in the middle of this thing. But there's no denying *something* is happening here. Whether there's something on board with us or not is actually beside the point. We need to trust each other. We need to work together to find out what happened to Calista and Eric. And the old woman."

People nodded, trusting the captain's authority. Except her words didn't make sense. Trust each other? How could they trust each other when someone was making people turn into dust? When Jim posed this question to the captain, he folded his arms.

"We don't know if someone is responsible for this or not. We just know it's happening," she replied. "To be safe, I have ordered Charlie to be restrained. I have two passengers watching him; he won't cause any more trouble. The areas where... the bodies are... have been quarantined. That's all we can do until we land. I will be placing calls to emergency services on the ground, so they'll meet us, and I dare say each and every one of you will be questioned."

"No emergency landing?" April asked.

"No point. This is a pretty short flight as it is. Like I said, I'll have emergency services on the ground."

"So, what are we supposed to do until then?" Jim asked.

"What if it's a virus?" someone called.

Thinking for a moment, the captain nodded. "We treat this like an outbreak. Anyone who was in the vicinity of the old woman or Calista will need to be quarantined. That means you, sir." The captain's long, slender finger pointed at Jim.

He'd half-expected that. Wasn't that always the way? Trouble-makers get quarantined or sent off to some island somewhere... *Like Charlie.*

"If we can get anyone within two seats in each direction of the incidents with the old woman and Calista to move to the back of the plane, we might be able to start figuring out if this is a virus and if anyone else is going to get sick." The captain looked happy with herself as people started willingly moving to the back of the plane.

Jim followed along with them, though he wasn't sure why. "What about Eric?" he asked over his shoulder.

The captain considered for a moment. "It's a crime scene," she said. "We need to stay away from the area. I will secure the scene. Everyone who hasn't been in close contact with either Calista or the old lady, move to the front of the plane. Use the other aisle to maintain distance." The captain disappeared back towards the cockpit a moment later with a final announcement: "I'm going to speak to my co-pilot to inform him of what's happening and to arrange emergency services. Everything will be okay."

Jim walked past the young guy and his girlfriend as they headed back to the front of the plane. The guy was still moving awkwardly, his arms swaying but not bent at the elbows. He was stiff and struggled to bend his knees. His girlfriend took him by the hand and led him down the aisle, not noticing that he seemed to be on autopilot.

Smiling.

Who in their right mind would be smiling now, with all that was going on? Still, he continued on his way to the back of the plane and lost sight of the couple. Instead, he focused on what was in front of him and the fact that he'd just been quarantined in the same area as the supposedly crazy killer.

Looking at him now, Jim didn't see a killer. He saw a guy who, while covered in blood, looked desperate and scared. Just like him. Their eyes met for a moment, and Charlie frowned at him.

What's that about? Jim wondered as he took a seat in the very back row. From now on, he was staying as far away from the plane's drama as possible. They had only two hours to go, and the plane would once again be on solid ground. All he had to do was sit in the corner and act like nothing was wrong.

Wiping at the dust on his sleeves, he knew it wasn't that simple. The Coke can guy sat next to him with a heavy sigh, still weeping at the pain and the embarrassment. Jim turned to him with a sad smile. "Did you notice anything about Calista that seemed odd?" he asked.

Coke-can guy stifled a laugh. "You mean between thumps in the face?"

"Sorry." Jim looked toward the front of the plane to see if he could spot the captain or the young guy. The captain's orders didn't make sense, nor did her willingness to go along with April without much evidence. And the young guy, moving like that. That weird smile.

If something was on board, it was in one of them.

SIXTEEN

The dusty guy and I exchanged a glance. I couldn't help but frown at him. What he'd been through, having Calista erupt on him like that. I felt bad for him, not understanding what had happened or why.

My heart ached at the thought because none of us knew, and time was counting down. I wanted to take another pill—several, to be honest—but the voice told me not to touch them. I only listened because I was starting to appreciate the insights it provided. It had known to check inside Eric's decapitated head, and it had told me to watch the lightning. That was the only reason I even knew this thing was on board.

The creature.

A blob of goo, jumping from passenger to passenger. The questions Derek, Brett, and I had asked were circling in my mind: What is it? What does it want? Why now? I didn't even know if we had time to answer those questions before the plane met the earth again. There was only one question that mattered anyway: who was it inside now?

I knew one thing for certain. It wasn't in me. I may have had a voice in my head telling me to do things—which I often obeyed—but I didn't have a strange being possessing me, drying me out into dust. Looking over at Rachel, I knew it wasn't in her, either. She was hiding, but she was vigilant. She was smart—smart enough to stay out of trouble and let me do the dirty work. Smart enough to betray me, and yet I kept going back to her. Her role as a psychologist gave me both hope and filled me with fear. I couldn't trust the doctors at the hospital or my psychologist back home, Dr. Schwarz.

Doctor Schwarz...

My phone beeped in my pocket and vibrated three times. Neither Derek nor Brett seemed to notice, deep in their own conversation. They would each look at me now and then, to make sure I was still there, behaving. Not killing anyone.

Me, a killer. What a joke.

Reaching into my pocket, I scooped my phone out into my cuffed hands and sighed at the screen. The text asked where I was and where I was going. Aiden wasn't normally that possessive, which told me something was wrong. I texted back that I was on my way to Perth, as we'd agreed. I needed to go home, to face what had happened there. He was free to meet me there if he wanted, but I had to do this either way.

With or without him.

I wasn't expecting his reply.

HE BELIEVES US!

I rushed to reply, unsure if he was trying to trap me. Aiden didn't trap, though. He just loved. That's all he ever did.

I waited for his reply, staring at my phone screen without breathing. Without blinking. Derek and Brett exchanged words between themselves, satisfied somehow that they were doing their due diligence in watching over me without paying attention to me. As long as I was seated and quiet, they felt they were doing a good job.

That's all I got. No more bouncing ellipses. No more assistance. Somehow, it was all I needed. April had talked about the signs earlier. She was out there now, scouring the plane for someone with the symptoms. As far as I knew, though, she and I were the only ones who knew there *were* signs. I hadn't had a chance to tell Rachel about them and probably wouldn't. She'd betrayed me. I wasn't going back to her.

EXCEPT SHE KNOWS. The voice was fierce about that point. *SHE KNOWS SOMETHING.*

My fingers were unsteady as I waited for a reply that I wasn't sure was coming. I'd lost time before, had gaps in my own life that Aiden was always filling in. People describe autopilot, but that's not what it was for me. It wasn't like I was distantly aware that something was happening and could recall vague memories to laugh about over dinner. For me, it was pitch black.

Like the time I slammed my fist so hard into a wooden table that it left a dent.

The time I held a blade to my throat and promised to die, to fucking end it all, if Aiden left me.

The time—

It didn't matter. Reliving my own history, or some version of it that I'd only been told about but never experienced, wasn't going to help me. Not now. Not here. Breathing hard, I started to put my phone back into my pocket when it vibrated and beeped again.

AIDEN

Look for the signs.

He'd already said that. Was there signal interference? Except there wasn't, because I scanned upward to see he had texted that to me twice. He'd ignored my question and simply repeated himself.

Something was wrong. Aiden wasn't like that. He was patient, explained things, and always let me know when I was overstepping. He tried to keep me focused, and he—

That was it. He was trying to keep me focused. Wondering how he knew about the signs, wondering if I'd lost time—and what I might have done during that period—could only fracture my ability to focus on the matter at hand.

SEE THE SIGNS, CHARLIE. THE SIGNS.

They were right, Aiden and the voice. There were signs.

Of what, though? The veins on the elbow, the redness—I knew about those. The gaunt face, sure. I still had no idea what this thing was, though. What it wanted and why it was here at all. Rachel knew. I just had to get across to her. Putting my phone back into my jeans pocket, I tuned into what Derek and Brett were talking about.

"... if something really is on the plane, that is," Brett said.

"What?" I asked. "You believe me?"

His eyes were still human, thankfully, as he turned to me and shook his head. "April showed us the picture. She took it before you were untied earlier. Timestamp says so. But just 'cause you didn't kill Eric don't mean you aren't a crazy."

The phrase grated on me. "A crazy". Like I was some kind of different species. I was medicated, and I heard a voice in my head, but I wasn't crazy. I saw things others didn't; that's how I noticed the monster to begin with. They should have been thanking me.

"Even so," I said, "you admit there might be something on board with us."

"The woman collapsing into dust is... "—Derek searched for a word—"bizarre. Not something we've ever heard of."

"Right!" I jumped in my seat, held back by the seatbelt. "We need to kill it before we land."

"How do we find it?" Brett asked.

RACHEL KNOWS! TELL THEM ABOUT RACHEL. TELL THEM TO LOOK FOR THE SIGNS.

"There are signs," I said. Rachel and her involvement were for my knowledge only. At least until I figured her out. "April saw them, too. We're looking for someone who has redness around the joints and a gaunt, pale face. Maybe some weird, splotchy veins on their body."

They stared at me in silence, taking in my words. I couldn't believe it. I couldn't believe they were listening to me, believing me, *trusting* me. Even after the way I'd been found with Eric's remains. What I'd done to his head. They didn't care that I had conversations with myself, just that I had seen something.

Except Brett smirked.

FUCK YOU! FUCK YOU!

"What's funny?" I asked.

He and Derek began to laugh, breaking into fits and holding their stomachs. Brett snorted as he laughed, and Derek wiped an involuntary tear from his eye.

"You're... making fun of me?" I asked.

Derek repeated my words in a high-pitched sing-song voice. "Of course we are, dickhead. Fucking psycho."

EveRYbODy hATes you. EVERYbody HATES YOU!

"People are dead," I whispered, "and you're laughing at me."

Despite the situation and the rage bubbling inside me, my heart beat like normal. I didn't break into sweats or start with a trembling bottom lip. I just stared at them, wishing they would be next... Wishing them to dust.

The voice cooed in my head, and I was convinced it would clap if it could. It would dance and dance, grabbing me into a tango.

The laughter was immense, both outside and inside of me. Yet I just stared.

YOU CAN'T DO THIS, the voice said, calmer now. *LET ME TAKE CONTROL.*

Part of me suspected the voice was in charge during my blackouts. I wasn't aware of exactly when they had diagnosed me with dissociative identity disorder, yet it was on my chart. Other Charlie had had that conversation. Now, as the voice goaded me to let it take over, I shook my head.

"People are dead, you fucking arseholes!" I screamed. "And that thing is going to kill all of us!"

They laughed again, shaking their heads at me like I was pathetic, and I struggled in my chair, fighting at my handcuffs even though I knew it was impossible to get them off. I could dislocate a thumb like they did in the movies, but I was sure everyone on board knew I wouldn't do that.

COWARDCOWARDCOWARD.

The voice cooed again, insulting me again and again until I was repeating the word of my own accord. Yet I still stared at Derek and Brett, letting the anxiety and fear and anger wash through me as the voice kept screaming about my cowardice.

My ears almost burst with the sounds, and I turned to look around at the group of quarantined passengers. Each face was laced with anxiety and fear, and I noticed nobody had sat with Rachel.

She was still melted into the fabric of her chair, almost entirely hidden from view, but I saw her. I needed to get to her, to ask her what she knew. The more I thought about it, the more I questioned whether she knew anything at all. The coincidence was too much, though.

She was a stowaway.

The creature was a stowaway.

They were connected.

DO IT.

"No."

Brett and Derek stared at me, squinting like they could see into my brain.

DO IT.

"NO!" I screamed.

"No... what?" Brett asked.

TELL THEMMMM.

The words spilled out before I could stop myself. "Rachel knows. She saw it too."

They exchanged glances, eyebrows raised. "You called that name before. Who's Rachel?"

"She... She's a stowaway," I whispered, ashamed of how easily I gave up the knowledge.

"Does that even happen anymore?" Derek asked. "How does someone sneak onto a plane?"

"She saw that thing come on board," I continued. "She's over—"

Rachel was gone, her seat empty. I scanned the plane, my gaze roaming up and down the aisles. Nothing. Everyone was seated, and her curly red hair was missing. I'd only looked away for a moment. It wasn't possible.

A lot of things on this plane aren't possible, I thought.

Scanning again, desperate to catch a glimpse of her, I knew it was too late. She was a stowaway, so she must have had hiding spots. Didn't the crew have sleeping spaces or something, or was that just on international flights?

"Where is she, huh?" Brett asked, staring at me with wide, expectant eyes. When I didn't reply, he chuckled. "That's what I thought."

I looked once more and saw the guy, still covered in dust, looking at me. The would-be Calista saviour. He eyed me with something like curiosity and motioned toward the front of the plane with his chin.

A MESSAGE. The voice laughed, but it wasn't directed at me for a change. It was joy. *THE GUY WANTS TO TALK TO US, CHARLIE.*

He motioned again, and I slowly twisted my neck to follow his gaze.

My eyes landed on the aggressive guy and his girlfriend making out at the front of the plane amid the passengers deemed uninfected or whatever. I shot my glance back to the dusty guy, who raised his eyebrows and motioned once more.

Look again, he was telling me.

I obeyed.

The pair were all over each other, as though nothing was amiss at all, and they weren't in public. Her hands were around his face, her lips tight to his, and I could see the bulge of cheeks as their tongues explored each other's mouths.

I was about to look away, to shrug at the dusty guy, when I saw it.

Subtle, but it was there.

The guy, his movements. He was slow and sharp, like he didn't know what to do. In another context, one might think he was a virgin or maybe just shy, but here? On this plane? It was all wrong. I'd seen them before, when we boarded. He was fine, groping at his girlfriend and giving me the stink eye.

Now he was a shell of himself, kissing because that's all he had the sense to do. I craned my neck, unable to stand because of my seatbelt, and tried to get a better look. Among the front-end passengers, April was still filming. Collecting evidence, I guessed. Her back was to me, and I swore.

She had to look at me. She had to. I couldn't get a better look at the guy, so checking him would be on her shoulders. I was aware she was only sixteen and had already witnessed so much today. If I could have spared her, I would have.

SHE'S OUR ONLY HOPE, CHARLIE.

I sighed and leaned into my chair. Stared at April's back, willing her to turn around. I didn't know what she'd found or what she was filming, or why she was even still doing that. She was walking backward down the aisle as the captain did something with tape. Sealing the crime scene, like she'd promised she would.

A few more steps, and April slowly began to turn.

Yes!

A little more.

YES!

She wasn't quite facing me, but she was near enough. I raised my arms as far as I could and swayed, only for a moment, before Brett noticed what I was doing. He nodded to Derek, who pulled my arms down and sneered at me, "Just sit there and don't fuckin' move, will ya?"

It didn't matter. She'd seen and was studying me with caution. She raised her hands and shoulders in a *'What is it?'* gesture and waited.

I gave a quick, sharp nod across to the couple making out, and she sucked in her bottom lip. Winked at me and turned back around. Headed towards the guy and his girlfriend with her phone outstretched, ready to record whatever was about to happen.

SEVENTEEN

APRIL

THE CAPTAIN HAD ASKED April if she was near the "infected," and she'd shaken her head with such sincerity that the captain had believed her. For good measure, April pointed to the other side of the plane and said, "I was in my seat, over there."

"Well, get back there and stay seated," the captain replied. "Something strange is going on here, and I don't want a teenager involved."

Strange. That was one word for it.

April headed to her seat but stopped after a few steps. The captain had just joined them; she didn't know what was going on. April knew better than most—she'd seen it, she'd cowered from it. She'd discovered Eric's body for Christ's sake.

"Fuck that." She turned back to the captain. "I'm collecting evidence. I'm going to find this thing."

"I really think—"

"No," April said, grimacing. "I don't give an ounce of a shit if you're the captain. Go be a captain and fly the fucking plane. I've been tracking this thing already. I know what to look for."

"I'm ordering you to take your seat." The captain's voice grew deep and firm.

"What are you going to do, tie me up next to Charlie?" April sneered.

The captain blinked at her, and a smile slipped onto her lips. "I'm not going to win this, am I?"

April shook her head again. "This might be the most important thing we ever do," she said. "That *thing* made quick work of Eric... "—she paused as the memory made her gag—"just let me do this. Teenager or not, I've seen it. I'm the only one who can help."

Nodding, the captain stepped aside and motioned for April to do her thing. Whatever that might be. And she did, taking her phone out and hitting record on the camera app. If she didn't see something straight away, it would no doubt be captured there.

And if I don't make it home...

She didn't finish the thought and tried to keep her focus. Tried to focus on what she knew, what she was looking for. Charlie had pulled a piece of the monster from Eric's head, which meant two things.

One: it had been inside Eric and tore him apart from the inside.

Two: it somehow damaged itself.

Which meant the inevitable third thing.

We can kill this motherfucker.

As she scoured the seats, searching around and underneath each one, her mind ticked over. Whatever it was, it was translucent and could move through walls and other solid objects. So how did a piece of it get stuck inside Eric's head?

Maybe it's weak. Injured.

She got down on her hands and knees, crooked an elbow, and held the phone up to get a look at the carpet where Calista had fallen to pieces. Still lying on the carpet were her earrings, necklace, and her uniform. She sifted through the remains with her bare hands, ignoring the sense of the captain's eyes on her.

Yes, she thought. *It's weak. It's using us, taking our energy to heal itself.*

In the dusty remains of the flight attendant were no clues. At least, nothing April considered a clue. She'd hoped for some sign of the monster—another separated glob or some kind of markings left behind where it had entered the plane.

Nothing.

Standing up, she faced the captain with a sigh.

"Done?" she asked April.

"I don't know." April shrugged. "I know what I saw. I know it's real. Charlie didn't do that to Eric, and he sure as shit didn't turn people to dust."

The captain folded her arms as April raised the phone to record her image. She checked the screen and panned left and right. At the front of the plane, eight passengers, her, and the captain. Ten people total.

That left thirteen people at the back of the plane.

Too many suspects.

She bit her lip and thought about how she might narrow it down. The captain might have been on to something with her quarantine of the passengers. She and Charlie didn't know how far this thing could jump. Assuming the old lady was right by the creature's entry point, it wasn't far. And when she crumbled, it jumped into Calista, who was in proximity.

If that was true, and her assumption of the monster being weak was also true, then it stood to reason that it had jumped into someone close by. Like the guy who'd tried to catch Calista. Or the Neck Tattoo Guy who'd grabbed her.

Or anyone else in the fucking crowd.

She sighed again and turned around to capture the images of the thirteen quarantined passengers. They were all just sitting there, frightened and concerned, but not actually quarantined, not locked up and secluded. Just sitting there like sheep waiting to be given orders. They could get up at any moment and mix with the rest of them.

And the entity could still be anywhere.

*Any*one, she thought. "Fuck."

In the corner of her eye, she saw flailing hands, and instinct drew her gaze to the movement. It was Charlie, staring over at her with wide eyes and a look that said, '*Pay attention.*' He was nodding, motioning with his chin across to somewhere else on the plane.

Over to some of the passengers.

April didn't like looking at people making out. On screen, in images, but particularly in real life. So, when she'd noticed the couple sucking the air out of each other's lungs like horny teens, she'd looked away. Now, Charlie was motioning to them. She was sure of it.

She shrugged at him—*What?*—and he motioned again.

It struck her in an instant.

The creature.

She headed for the couple, swallowing hard, and passed the captain, who was leaning against the wall with her arms still folded. The captain seemed pretty useless, but it was clear she was thinking things through. She was the type who was slow to action until all the possible outcomes were known. In this plane, here and now, the captain was way out of her depth.

The plane must have been on autopilot, April thought. Otherwise, they'd be in a nosedive, screaming for their mothers.

"You found something?" the captain asked.

"Maybe," April replied. The captain followed her to the couple's seats.

The couple fondled each other, oblivious to the eyes on them as the other passengers awkwardly tried to avoid looking at and hearing them. April cleared her throat, unsure of what she was about to do or how the monster might react.

She didn't even know which one it was in—both of their movements were odd, and with their cheeks so immersed in each other's faces, they both looked gaunt.

She cleared her throat again, louder this time. "All this death making you horny, huh?"

The woman broke free of the passionate embrace and wiped a thumb over her lips. "Sorry," she said, her cheeks reddening. "Sometimes we forget we're in public. Right, babe?" She leaned into her boyfriend, who hadn't moved.

He only smiled.

April breathed hard and stepped away. The same smile as Calista. It was him. It was fucking inside him. The woman frowned and sized April up. "It wasn't *that* bad, was it?"

"Ma'am, we need to speak your boyfriend," the captain said softly.

"He's possessed," April whispered, holding her phone up to him.

His image looked normal, like any other, and her eyes darted between the screen and reality. Just to see. Just to know that what she was seeing was real.

The woman turned to her boyfriend and noticed the smile. Noticed his cheeks. "Babe? Are you okay?" She put a hand to his forehead. "Babe, you're burning up."

"That's not your boyfriend anymore," April muttered, her chest heaving, and the captain tugged at her arm.

"Get back," the captain said. "Get away from him."

She stayed put, some part of her wanting to run, but another part knowing there was nowhere to run to. From the corner of her vision, she saw the other passengers moving away, ducking, and cowering. She heard the scared murmurs and terrified pleas to God that they wouldn't be next, and the "No more, no more, please God, no more" and the whimpers.

The woman stood up, still asking her everlastingly smiling boyfriend if he was okay, when his head cocked, and his gaze landed on April.

"Oh fuck," she whispered.

"Howwww"—he paused, his mouth turning dark and grey, almost bruised—"d'youuu kno'?"

"Your face... " April replied, letting the words hang. "It's all fucked up."

The guy felt around his face, the lips stretched way too far, and poked a finger into his cheek. The skin tore apart, and the guy wiggled his finger through the hole, pulling at the skin until it met the split of his lips. His mouth began to hang, teeth exposed and crumbling away, as his girlfriend screamed.

"Babe, what the fuck?" She sat next to him again and tried to hold his cheek together, but he tore at it again, pulling flesh from his face until he reduced the right side to exposed nerves and teeth.

April was aware phones were up again, people filming and talking to their screens, narrating the fucked-up shit they were seeing. Yet not one person put their phone away to try and help. Not one.

The guy's cheek splatted to the carpet next to April's feet, and she wanted to move, to run away and scream, but she held firm. Her phone was up too, capturing the moment. *I'm no better than the others.*

The boyfriend kept his eyes on April as he began to stand, his fingers scratching at his eyeballs. Even as the captain tried to intervene, tried to push the guy back down into his seat and pulled at April to force her back.

The guy moved away from his girlfriend, who watched on as one eyeball hung from its socket. He pulled hard on the thread of the extraocular muscles, and April winced at the wet snapping sound as it came loose. A small stream of blood puked out of the hole, followed by a line of dust. He was hollowing out.

"You... sssseeeeee me?" he asked, holding the eye out to her.

Nodding, April lowered her phone and looked at the eyeball. Her guts churned and she held the vomit inside, finally letting the captain move her aside with a "Please, get back!"

"I ssseee... you." Despite half his face lying on the floor, the man smiled. "W-w-wannnt you."

She met his eye again, pushing into the wall as much as she could as he approached her. The captain came to help, but it was useless. The boyfriend slapped her hard and punched her in the solar plexus. With a deep "Oof", the captain hunched over, unable to do much of anything.

Nobody else even tried to help. The passengers fled, crying and screaming as they begged for their own lives while April stood trembling before the entity.

"What's happening?" she heard Charlie roaring from the other end of the plane. "Let me out!"

"W-w-wannnt *out*."

"What?"

It dropped the eyeball to the floor and stepped on it, delighting in the squish as the discarded organ popped. His girlfriend screamed again and raced away into the captain's arms.

"Babe! Stop!" the girlfriend begged from the sidelines.

"He's sick!" someone said from over April's shoulder.

"Maybe there is an alien on board," someone else said. "Fuck, fuck, shit!"

"It's the virus; he's going to explode!" a third voice added.

"Help her, for fuck's sake!" Charlie roared again. She knew he was restrained. He couldn't help. "Rachel! Rachel! For Christ's sake, Rachel, fucking do something!"

She didn't know who Rachel was, but whoever she might have been, she was like the rest of them. A coward. Content to let April die.

Worse, she thought. *To let me turn to fucking dust.*

"Let me out," Charlie cried as April realised her fate. "Why is nobody helping her?"

There was nothing she could do. The creature was right in front of her. She clutched at her phone and held it up, the last thing she could do with the monster blocking her from escaping. "What do you want?" April asked, shrinking down the wall.

And in a clear, strong voice, the thing replied, "Everything."

The word sank in as the being pulled April to her feet by the neck and seethed its rancid breath into her. The one remaining eye seemed to stare right into her soul, sizing up its weight and mass, ready to devour it.

"Everything," it repeated.

April widened her eyes, ready for whatever was coming, prepared to die, and thinking about her mother and father and all the shit they did to her that she'd never get to yell at them for. How she wanted to give them hugs and tell them she loved them, hold them and cry and cry and cry. Defiantly, she stared into the thing's eye, daring it to do its worst.

"April!" Charlie yelled. "Jesus fuck, April!"

Nobody cared. That's all she could think about in that moment. Among the twenty-three passengers left on the plane and the captain standing a metre away, she was truly and utterly alone. Charlie's cries echoed through the plane, his pleading and begging going unnoticed.

She'd end up on some viral video on TikTok and be forgotten a few moments later. That's all her life would amount to.

She saw the man's face grow gaunt and pale, but splotches of those veins appeared down his arms and on his hands around her neck. The smile widened, but hung loose at the jaw he'd torn at earlier.

Whether it was the fact that she'd been abandoned or the fact that her fate was knocking ever closer, she didn't know. But she wasn't going to die screaming, and she sure as shit wasn't going to die crying.

"Do it," she spat, and she waited.

The hands tightened around her neck, but in the next instant, they went slack. Confused, April waited for the grip to come again, but it didn't. Instead, she pushed against the guy's chest with as much force as she could and sent him reeling backwards into a seat.

"Babe!" the girlfriend shouted and raced back to him. "The fuck are you doing?"

He tried to stand, but April saw what was happening. The missing piece in the remaining eye told her that time was up. It was moving to a new home. A new body. She crawled away, grabbed the woman by the ankle, and begged her to come too. She kicked April off and returned her attention to her boyfriend.

"Babe?" she asked. "Oh, babe, your face... "

The creature looked at her. The smile dropped.

April stood and ran to the captain's side, aiming her phone at the scene.

"He... loved... you... " the thing mumbled and started to laugh. The sound was more of a bloodied gaggle than a laugh, but April recognised it for what it was. She heard the cruelty behind it.

In the next instant, the man broke into dark veins across his body, and he caved in. His face was first, the nose pressing backward into his skull until it was just a concavity of dust and shattered teeth. April breathed a sigh of relief as his chest went next, his clothes deflating like a balloon, his girlfriend grabbing at them as though she could save him.

April's neck was red and raw from where he'd grabbed her, but her breathing was okay. Still, her hands trembled as she caught the scene on her phone's camera. The girlfriend screamed again, tears flowing as she pulled the now-empty shirt to her face and cried into it.

April ignored it and kept filming. Unlike the others, she wasn't doing it for social media. She was doing it because what happened next was the important part.

The next host.

As the guy's body continued to fall away to the carpet, April stared. She wasn't going to miss it this time. And when she found the next host, they could kill the fucking thing.

From the ashes of the guy, it began to rise.

A translucent glob, though it wasn't as bulbous and fleshy as it had been before. It wasn't as loose and freely formed. April watched on as it rose into the air and seemed to turn around, searching. It had said it wanted her, but it had also said it wanted *everything*. Stepping back a little, she held her phone out as far as she could, ignoring the gasps and whimpers and pleas to God to please let this not be real.

The blob was darker now. Still translucent, but in the centre of it—like a nucleus—was growing dark matter. It looked more solid, and April wondered if that was what had broken off from it earlier. Maybe it was a shell, some kind of skin it had shed.

As she stepped back again, the monster twisted in the air, its surface rippling. She heard the captain gasp, and the other passengers, too. But nobody moved, too intoxicated by the vision before them. They'd all seen it now. It had been unmasked, revealed. Now they could track it. Stop it.

It spun again, and April braved a step forward.

The being shot down the aisle, and April raced after it, intent on finding the next host while the monster adapted to their body. She jumped over people cowering on the floor, slipped on someone's shirt sleeve, and banged her head on an armrest, but she got up fast and kept her eyes on the enemy.

Zooming through the plane, it hovered above quarantined passengers who stared at it with awe. It zoomed again, the other way, and April ran after it, yelling at people to get the fuck out of its way. The captain ducked as it approached her, and the creature kept going.

Searching.

It's not weak anymore. Is it looking for a permanent home?

Finally, it stopped.

Heart racing, sweat forming at the edges of her hairline, April breathed hard and watched. "Get away from it," she said, and the passengers did. She reminded herself to laugh about it later, that she was giving orders as a sixteen-year-old. The adults were supposed to take charge, but instead, they hid. She thought they might as well have been in the doomsday bunker with her father.

It was in the middle of the plane now and could go anywhere. April didn't know why it hadn't chosen its next victim yet. What was it searching for?

It wants everything.

She scrambled to think of how it might achieve that. Take the strongest host it could and then walk out of the plane? Nobody would believe what had happened, even with the bodies of dust and with Eric's shredded remains exploding all over the place. Even with all the footage, it would be deemed a hoax.

The monster hovered across to Charlie, levitating above him for a moment, and then shot into the guy sitting next to him. April raced to the seat and watched on as the guy writhed, coughing and retching and spasming.

"Oh fuck," Charlie whispered, "get me out of here!"

The other guy, Neck Tattoo, bolted from the scene like a child, tears flying from his face.

April rushed to the seat in front of him, leaning over it. She jumped over, her head scraping the overhead baggage compartment, and untied his belt. His bodyguards had tied it up in a knot, so unbuckling wouldn't be enough.

Cunts, she thought, even as one of them was being possessed.

With Charlie freed, they both climbed over the seat and stumbled into the aisle once more, twisting around to see.

They looked at the former bodyguard just in time to see his body explode.

EIGHTEEN

I DIDN'T HAVE TIME to blink before bits of Derek erupted into my eyes. Flecks of skin and chunks of brain and bone and muscle slapped against my face. I raised my arms to shield against most of the viscera, but somehow a bit of him—an earlobe—straddled my tongue.

The plane filled with screams. I was vaguely aware of the cries to God and Allah and whoever else, the sign of the cross doing nothing to abate the fear in the passengers. Someone simply wailed and moaned, the sound an ear-shattering, heartbreaking one, from the darkest depths of their soul. People were running, fleeing to the front of the plane—pushing each other over, sacrificing their peers for the belief that their own lives were worth more.

Dusty Guy, April, and I stayed put. I noticed Rachel had fled her seat, too, the fucking coward. When I caught up with her, I thought I might kill her myself, and the voice cackled at that in glee.

Spitting Derek's earlobe to the floor and retching, I rubbed my eyes to see the entity hovering again. It was larger now, the shape changing and shifting. The surface still rippled, indicating movement, but it was changing. Instead of a glob of translucence, it was now a shade darker, the black orb in the centre slightly hidden.

It's more solid. We can get this fucking thing. I smiled at the thought.

WE DON'T WANT TO, THOUGH, CHARLIE. DO WE? The voice echoed a few times, snickering at me.

"Of course we do," I muttered.

April stared at the rippling thing while she pulled a strand of exploded stomach lining from her hair and wiped blood off her arms. She hadn't heard me, or at least hadn't acknowledged me, talking to myself.

"What do you want from us?" I asked the shape-shifting orb.

"It wants everything," April answered on its behalf. "Whatever that means."

I stepped toward the entity, legs shaking, hands trembling in front of me as I raised them. "Please, just go." I motioned to the side of the plane. "You came in with such ease. You can just go."

It hovered towards me, and I stayed put, too afraid to run. Too afraid to breathe. As it stopped an inch from my face, studying me, I resisted the urge to close my eyes. A few tears slipped out, streaming down my cheeks, but I kept them open.

SEEEEEEE. The voice was intrigued, curious... Excited. *IT'S BEAUTIFUL, CHARLIE.*

I felt it watching me, despite its lack of eyes. Felt it search inside me for something. It turned away and shot to the left.

April and I followed it with our eyes as it leaped into Dusty Guy, and he exploded, too. It was so fast, he didn't even have time to writhe or spasm. His eyes widened slightly at the realisation that his life was over.

And it was.

The crack of his skull, the tearing of his muscles—it was all so fast, but I heard each noise as if played at half speed. I managed to duck in time, missing the spray of organs, but I saw April put her hands to her face as she was drenched in Dusty Guy's insides. She gasped a long and painful "Fuuuuuck," and I pulled her down to my side.

"I didn't sign up for this shit," she said, too shocked to cry. "I just wanted to see my mum."

I looked at her, a tangle of veins and shards of kidneys in her hair and strewn across her face and chest. I wanted to tell her everything would be okay, and even though it was the most ridiculous sentiment in the world, I mumbled it to her.

The voice in my head laughed at me again.

"Why is it laughing?" April asked, covering her ears.

"You hear it too?" I crossed my eyebrows. "How?"

It wasn't the voice she heard. It was the creature. Somehow, as a disembodied glob, it was laughing. I poked my head up to see what it was doing and gagged at the sight of it swimming in the stew of Dusty Guy's bloodied remains.

IT'S TAKING SHAPE, CHARLIE. LOOK.

The voice was right. With each kill, the entity was gaining strength, changing shape, becoming something else. I almost wanted it to take more passengers, just so it was more tangible, and I could stab it in the fucking heart.

IT DOESN'T HAVE A HEART, CHARLIE.

"It will," I said. "Once it's more human."

The realisation struck me without warning. As I took in its form, that's what it reminded me of—a human foetus. I could see the beginnings of arms and legs, little mounds where the ears would eventually be, and the curvature of a still-forming spine.

WE'RE HAVING A BABY, CHARLIE! A BABY!! The voice was excited.

I was terrified.

I couldn't kill a kid, let alone a baby. I wondered if this thing was one of *them* in its primal form. If I'd stumbled upon the origins of the doppelgängers.

April nudged me out of my thoughts. "We can't stay here."

Despite myself, I giggled. "Where do you want to go?" I asked. "A café down the street? We're locked in a fucking plane."

"I know that," she snapped back. "But we can't stay *here*."

Looking around the seats, the creature was still swimming and laughing, an innocent, gleeful sound. Splashing in the pools of blood, tiny malformed fingers slapping Dusty Guy's shredded, floppy penis up and down against the wet carpet. I nodded for April to move down the aisle, toward the remaining passengers.

When we'd crawled as far up as we could go, huffing and panting, the captain called us over with a hurried wave. "What's it doing?" she hissed.

"Uh,"—I didn't quite know how to say it, so I fumbled with the truth—"having a... bath."

She looked past me to try to see for herself, but gave up fast. Fear, panic, whatever the reason, she rested back on her calves and held a hand to her chest.

"How long until we land?" I asked.

Checking her wristwatch, she said, "Just under two hours."

I took a long, deep breath, ignoring the voice in my ear whispering that I should go join the entity. *TAKE A BATH. CLEAN UP, OLD BUDDY.* Now it was the voice laughing inside my head.

"It's getting stronger," I told the captain. "But it's also more solid. We can hurt this thing. Do you have a gun or... anything?"

The captain shook her head. "Not a thing."

"Then we make do," April said. "We make a fucking weapon. All of us."

Glancing at the other passengers, I frowned. "You think they're going to help us?"

"We have to try!" April replied. "Right?"

The captain and I exchanged worried expressions.

"I can take charge on this," I said. "I can do this."

YEAH, CHARLIE. TAKE ANOTHER PILL; YOU'LL BE GOLDEN. The voice laughed. *OR LET ME TAKE OVER FOR A BIT. HAVE A NAP, FRIEND. I'LL GET IT SORTED.*

Breathing through the words, I repeated myself, firmer this time. Neither of them believed me. I could see it in their eyes. It didn't matter. I wasn't losing more time. I wasn't letting the voice take me over and do who knew what.

No, I thought, and it was *my* thought. *I am doing this. I have to do this.*

"How many people can fit in the cockpit?" I asked.

The captain looked at me, thinking. "Not all of them, but some."

"We need to find a way to block it off from this part of the plane. Quarantine it; lock it away somehow. Now that it's becoming more tangible, it might not be able to leave the plane on its own. It might not be able to levitate or go through walls or whatever."

"Is that why it's exploding people instead of inhabiting them?" April asked.

I shrugged. The only way we'd know for sure would be if it told us. We needed to focus on what we knew or what we could find out.

Rachel. I looked around but couldn't see her.

"Where can someone hide on this plane?" I asked the captain. "I think there's a stowaway on board."

The captain shook her head. "Impossible. It can't happen these days; there's too much security."

"Well," I said. "I think she slipped past your security. I've seen her, I've spoken to her. She's on board. And I think she knows something about the monster."

NINETEEN

The captain—Jessica Thorpe, as she'd finally introduced herself—told me there was only one place to hide on the plane—the cargo hold, where the checked luggage was kept.

"It's not easily accessible, though," Thorpe said. "There's no way this woman—Rachel—could sneak in and out at will. And it doesn't make sense for her to come inside the cabin and just sit there to be caught."

"I didn't say it made sense," I said. "But it has happened. I know what I saw." Thorpe opened her mouth to speak, but I silenced her, as shitty as that was. "Nobody believed me about that thing, jumping from passenger to passenger. Yet here we are."

She nodded, accepting her role in his restraint earlier. I took it as a sort of apology, but didn't care. I had to stay focused.

Find Rachel.

Find out what she knew.

Kill the creature.

BUT IT'S BEAUTIFUL, CHARLIE. HAVE YOU EVER SEEN SO MUCH BLOOD?

"How do I get down there?" I asked Thorpe. "To the cargo hold."

She sighed, knowing we had limited time before the entity had finished bathing or playing or whatever it was really doing. Limited time before the wheels hit the earth and the monster was set free in a new playground.

"Follow me," she said, and we crawled towards the start of the right-side aisle. "There's a door back there, in the floor. A small set of stairs, like a ladder, takes you down."

JUST LIKE THE MOVIES, CHARLIE. YOU'RE A REGULAR SCHWARZENEGGER!

Thorpe took a key chain from her hip and slipped a key from the coil. "You'll need this to access it. It's locked, though. There's no way someone could come and go as they pleased."

IF IT'S LOCKED, HOW IS SHE GETTING IN AND OUT?

The voice raised a good question, but my immediate concern was getting past the entity, whose laughter was still echoing throughout the plane.

"Okay," I said. "Can I have the key, please?"

"I told you," Thorpe continued, clutching the key in a closed fist, "it *cannot* be down there. You're wasting your time."

GRAB IT! GET THE KEY!

"Listen," I snapped at the captain and snatched at the key. "I have to try, okay? I know it doesn't make sense, I know that! But what else are we supposed to do?"

"It's not down there!" Thorpe fought me, but I had her hand in both of mine now, and was already loosening her fingers. The key was mine and as the captain began to argue once more, I turned my attention to April. "Can you try to get some of these passengers to take their luggage down from the overhead compartments? They might have something we can use."

April was visibly shaken, as we all were. Nevertheless, she nodded. Just once, up and down. She was braver than I'd ever be.

Gripping the key in one hand, I started for the door. It was at the other end of the aisle, no big deal. In ordinary circumstances, I would be there in a minute, maybe less, with decent strides. Now, on my hands and knees, as close to my belly as I could get, the journey would take considerably longer.

As I approached the monster's laughter, I stole a glance under the seats. It was bathing in the blood, but its shape had changed again. The beginnings of a face were visible now, the moulds of the ears more defined, and arms and legs shot out from what was fast becoming the body.

Still no eyes.

No way for me to tell if the creature was one of *them* in its primal form.

I saw no reason it should be, but something in the back of my mind—something separate from the voice whispering in my ear—wouldn't let me shake the thought. Doppelgängers were everywhere on the ground. I saw them all the time. But never when they were made.

Halfway down the aisle, I risked a look over my shoulder to see April talking to the other passengers, drawing them out of the corners one by one.

That April, I thought. *She's a force.*

If we could all work together, find some weapons—*make* some weapons—there was hope. A chance. And if I could get to the end of the aisle and locate Rachel, I was sure I could find a way to end this.

Crawling to the end, pulling myself along with grinding teeth and worn-out, carpet-burned fingers, I saw the door in the floor. I'd noticed doors like it on other planes, but never gave them a thought. Now, it was all I could think about.

I didn't have any checked luggage on this flight—nor any handheld—but I was sure it would be full. I twisted the key, lifted the door, and slid down into the hold, grabbing onto the ladder.

The light was dim, and I fumbled for a switch or a button or a string—anything to turn a light on. A panel on the wall by the ladder emitted a faded blue light, and I stumbled towards it, squinting to see the options.

A small lightbulb on the panel indicated the light switch, so I tapped it, and the cargo hold lit up. Spinning around, I saw the hold was full of suitcases, pets, and other belongings. It wasn't a large space, with the plane intended for domestic travel only, and the luggage stuffed into the area made it seem even smaller.

Cramped.

OH, the voice said with a solemn sigh. *THAT'S RIGHT. YOU HATE TIGHT SPACES.*

I breathed slowly and fought the urge to take a pill. It would dull my senses, make me weak. And I needed to be strong, now more than ever.

LET ME TAKE OVER, CHARLIE. LEEET MEEEE.

"Shut the fuck up," I snapped. I took another steady breath as I eyed the cargo hold.

The hum of the plane's engines was louder in the hold, and the temperature was slightly above freezing. Wrapping my arms around myself, I walked a few steps, grimacing as the cold air slapped against my blood-stained body. I had to duck a little; the hold was a narrower space than I'd realised. My head brushed against the ceiling as I scanned the area.

A flash of red in the corner of my eye made me turn fast.

"Rachel!" I said.

Nothing.

"I saw you," I continued.

Slowly, as I stepped towards where I'd seen the red flash, her head poked out from behind a pile of strapped-in suitcases.

"Why are you hiding from me?" I asked.

She stayed half-hidden behind the suitcases. "I'm scared, Charlie. I'm not supposed to be here."

"None of us are," I replied, my voice soft and low. "But we are here, and I need your help."

She shook her head.

"For once, don't chicken out on me." I stepped closer. "You let me down up there,"—I pointed to the ceiling—"a few times. I needed you, and you let them all think I was crazy."

Rachel frowned, her eyes showing how desperately sorry she was. "I know, Charlie."

"Why have you been hiding when you could have helped me?" I asked, my fists shaking at her.

"I'm not ready for people to see me."

The words sank in, silencing me for a moment, and chills ran down my spine. Even the voice was quiet, subdued. Whatever she meant by that was a question for another time. I refocused, wrapping my arms around me again, and said, "You know something."

She nodded.

"You need to tell me." I shivered, the sound of the engines drowning the chattering of my teeth.

"You're not ready to hear it, Charlie." Her voice was almost inaudible. She hugged her suit jacket to her body, and I saw her breath puff out of her. Mine too.

"We need to know," I said, urging her. "People are fucking dead up there."

She nodded again. "I know they are. But you're not ready to know what I know."

I stepped forward again until we were face to face. Grabbing at her collar by the shoulder, my cold fingers almost numb, I spat, "Tell me!"

"Charlie, I don't know anything about the... the monster!" She struggled out of my grip. "I know something about *you*."

"Me?" I stopped. "What the hell are you talking about?"

Rachel straightened up and smoothed out her clothes. "I'm a psychologist, Charlie. A very good one."

"I don't need a psychologist right now," I said. "Whatever you think you know about me, whatever the reason you're a fucking stowaway, nobody cares right now. We have bigger problems than whatever you're hiding. We need to kill that fucking thing upstairs before it's too late."

I could see she wanted to say something, but the words weren't coming.

"We land in less than two hours." I hoped that knowing time was running out for all of us might give her a change of heart. She stayed silent.

SHE AIN'T HELPING, CHARLIE. WHAT CAN SHE DO ANYWAY? TALK IT TO DEATH? PSYCHOANALYSE THE MONSTER? The voice chortled and snorted. The joy it felt at the hopelessness of our situation nauseated me.

"Please," I begged.

Shaking in the cold and avoiding my eyes, she put a hand on my shoulder, traced it down my arm, and sighed. "I don't know anything about this... whatever it is, I promise. But I will help you."

Taking her by the hand, I rushed back to the stairs and climbed the ladder—four steps in total. Rachel was right behind me, her freezing, clammy fingers intertwined with my own. I flipped the door open and moved up the ladder again, letting go of Rachel's hand to pull myself back into the plane.

Halfway out, I paused.

The plane was silent.

"What is it?" Rachel asked.

I looked back at her, the terrified expression on my face matching hers. "I don't know," I whispered. "It's quiet."

Scanning down the aisle, I didn't see anyone. No Thorpe, no April.

Just a path of coagulating blood leading to the front of the plane, with bits of flesh and bone scattered across the carpet and the seats. I moved back down the ladder and closed the door as quietly as I could.

"What's happened?" Rachel asked, pushing against my shoulder to turn me around.

I swallowed hard and thought about April. Thought about how brave she was and how fucking stupid I'd been to let her be involved in any of this.

"I think... " I said through a fresh stream of tears, "Everyone's dead."

SESSION #10

St Vincent's Hospital, Psych. Ward
4 April 2025
Patient: Charles M. Reed
Referring Psychologist: Dr R Schwarz
Consulting Psychiatrist: Dr J Mathis

CHARLIE'S DELUSIONS ARE NOT improving. It can take months, sometimes years, for patients to see progress. However, even in those instances, there would be flashes of hope where the treating psychiatrist could see a glimmer of critical thinking, something to demonstrate that the patient shows signs of knowing that their understanding of reality is inhibited by their condition.

This is not the case with Charlie. Despite my encounter with the nurse four days prior and the fact that I have since noticed this same thing in several people around me, I am convinced Charlie has gotten into my head. This can happen on occasion, and I am aware of the impact this has on my ability to treat him effectively.

A colleague/mentor of mine from my university teaching days recommended I take a step back from the case to re-evaluate the notes and my learning so far. Taking his advice, I reviewed Dr. Schwarz's extensive files on Charlie. He'd been treated by Schwarz for several years, and while Charlie sometimes demonstrated violent tendencies, these were almost always attributed to Other Charlie. The real Charlie, the original, is sensitive and caring but burdened by a traumatic history that causes him to retreat inside his own mind. Schwarz had difficulty pinpointing when the doppelgänger fascination had begun, and so, upon my review of the files, I've determined this might be a useful point of analysis.

The session today, then, is directed at establishing the origin of his delusion.

The following is an account of the session, based on my audio recording:

"Good morning, Charlie," I said.

By now, he was comfortable seeing me. Expected me. He greeted me with a smile. "Morning." His voice was happy and energetic. It gave me pause, but I acted as though this were normal for him.

"How are you?" I asked.

"Really well, how are you?"

I smiled at him as I sat at the table. Charlie was already there, arms folded on the surface like a schoolboy awaiting the start of class. "I'm well, thank you, Charlie."

"What are we talking about today?" he asked. When I looked at him with curiosity, he added, "I look forward to our sessions."

"You do?"

"Oh yes," he said. "You're starting to believe me."

"Do you still think the nurse is a doppelgänger?" I asked.

Charlie nodded.

"Why is that?"

He considered the question, looking over my shoulder into the distance. I suspected he was conjuring the words he needed, so I would set him free. Allow him to go back home to Aiden.

"Charlie?" I prompted.

"You saw her eyes, didn't you?" he asked.

This was dangerous territory, and I was wary of playing another of his games. I asserted my authority as the one who asks questions, and Charlie relented. I could tell, though, that he knew the damage had been done. He'd asked the question, and not answering it out loud didn't mean I wasn't thinking about it.

"I'd like to ask you about doppelgängers," I said. "Can you tell me, Charlie, when you first started seeing them?"

He shifted in his chair now and sniffed. He rolled his folded arms up to his body and tightened them around himself. "Why?"

"Was it the same time as when Other Charlie appeared?" I asked.

"He didn't *appear*. He's always been there."

I found this interesting because a lot of D.I.D. patients were aware of what some of them called their "splits." The moments or the events surrounding the creation of their alters. The terminology wasn't consistent, and patients often referred to their alters in many ways. Even as friends. Saviours. Rarely was it the case that patients believed their alters were always already there.

"You can't remember?" I asked.

"It's not a case of not remembering," Charlie said, retreating into himself. "He's just always been there."

Could it be that their personalities, their identities, were formed at the same time? A twin inside the one body? The thought was preposterous, and I dismissed it immediately. No, there was something else going on, and I had to push a little more to find out what.

"When did you first discover him?" I asked.

He shrugged. "I didn't."

"Because he's always been there."

"Exactly."

It felt like he was trying to tell me something. No, that wasn't right. Something he couldn't answer, because he didn't know, outside of the fact that his trauma had been perfectly recorded by Dr. Schwarz during their sessions. As is often the case, the trauma occurred early in life, and the mind fragmented as a coping strategy. The violent persona emerged to help Charlie, the real Charlie, manage the trauma at the hands of both his mother and father.

His lack of knowing told me that perhaps the memories were locked. Bound with Other Charlie.

"May I speak to Other Charlie?" I asked.

Charlie flashed a smile. It was awkward and shy.

"I'd like to ask him about this," I said.

Giving in without pause, Charlie nodded and closed his eyes. I saw his tension dissipate. His whole body relaxed. The transitions were often like this with him, like his mind stepped out of his body and another walked into the empty shell.

"Hiya, Jamie boy," Other Charlie said.

"Morning," I replied. "I suppose you heard what I said to Charlie?"

He nodded. The difference in such a minute gesture between this Charlie and the original was astounding. Where the real Charlie would lift his head first and then let his chin quickly fall to his chest, Other Charlie gave only a slight, slow-motion, almost imperceptible nod.

"Can you tell me when the fascination with doppelgängers began?" I asked.

Other Charlie took a deep breath and loosened his arms so they sat in his lap. He pushed the chair back with his feet and drew one foot over his knee. I'd never seen the real Charlie sit like that, so casual, so carefree.

"1994."

"What happened in 1994?" I asked. This year was significant for Charlie's trauma, of course, but I needed to hear it from him.

"My mum and dad tried to kill me." He stared at me, daring me to look away. "But you know that already, right, James?"

I nodded. "I'd like to hear it from you."

Blowing out a sigh, he ran his fingers through his hair. "They hated me since birth; I don't know why. Don't much care. When I was ten, in 1994, they tried some ritual on me. You know from my file that they worshipped an ancient spirit, a demon. Not just any old, run-of-the-mill demon worshippers. Nah, they went for the heavy shit." He took a deep breath, uncomfortable but reciting Charlie's history without missing a beat. "So, apparently, I was conceived to be a sacrifice on my tenth birthday, which coincided with a blood moon or some shit. Out to the woods we went, dressed up in our fucking goat head masks and white gowns, all ready for the big night."

"What happened then?"

"Well, I'm still here, so you know it didn't go down how they wanted. My mum had a book, reading passages, and speaking in tongues, her tits all out, rubbing herself. Dear old Dad had the knife, and he's stroking himself while I'm strapped to a fucking tree. A bunch of people were surrounding us in a circle, stripping and making animal sounds. You know how this goes, Doc; fucking cultist rituals are all the same more or less."

I didn't know. I had no idea. I nodded anyway so he'd continue.

"I was sure I was gonna die, and I won't lie. At ten years old, part of me hoped I would. The shit they did in that basement, I'm surprised poor old Charlie hasn't slit his wrists already. Anyway, the AFP came crawling out of the trees, guns blazing, screaming at my folks to drop the knife or they'd shoot. I never saw my mum or dad again." He spat on the ground next to him. "Good fuckin' riddance."

"And that's when you first appeared?" I asked.

"Like I'm a magician or something? Just appearing and disappearing?"

"You know what I mean," I said.

"No," he replied. "I've always been around. Charlie told you that."

"You know what I find interesting?" I asked. Without waiting for a response, I continued. "You call them *your* mum and dad," I said. "But you know they aren't. You don't have parents."

"What makes you say that?" Other Charlie wondered.

"You're not real," I said flatly. "Those things you described didn't happen to you. They happened to Charlie. You exist only in the mind."

He pinched at his arm and winced. "This feels pretty fuckin' real to me, Jamie boy."

"I mean, you're not the original Charlie."

"Who says?"

I understood that remark for what it was—another game. A poor attempt to make me question which Charlie was the original. It wouldn't work, and I believed he knew that. Still, Other Charlie did like games, as sordid as they might be.

"And after that, when you went to stay with foster families, you began to see your parents everywhere; is that right?" I asked.

He nodded. "Sure. Wouldn't you?"

"So, it's safe to assume the event in the woods and the subsequent PTSD—in Charlie's case, visions of his parents stalking him—led to a belief in doppel-gängers."

It wasn't a question, and he didn't offer an answer.

"What I struggle with, though, is how that's broadened from a specific fear of his parents to a generalised fear of the public."

"I'm not afraid of the general public. I'm afraid of *them*. The doubles, the fuckin' body thieves."

"Don't you find that ironic?" I asked.

He narrowed his eyes and rubbed at his nose. Looked away. "What do you mean?"

"You're a body thief," I told him. "You are, as we speak, inhabiting the body of a person who is not you. The real Charlie is in there now,"—I pointed at his forehead—"a passenger in his own body."

Other Charlie laughed.

"What's funny?" I asked.

"You still think he's the original."

Recommendation: I am concerned about the session today. The patient has regressed, as noted with the persistence of Other Charlie. I will review the medication and take a more direct approach in future sessions. Charlie must confront his trauma, as well as his secondary identity, in order to overcome his delusions.

At this stage, **release is not recommended.**

TWENTY

APRIL

She watched Charlie half-crawl, half-drag himself down the aisle and turned back to the other passengers. She couldn't believe she was the one in charge, a fucking teenager with abandonment issues. Even the captain, who'd almost let her get choked to death, was looking at her like she was humanity's saviour.

Swallowing the fear that maybe she was, April opened her mouth. "You all heard him, right?" she asked.

A few nods here and there, and April fought the urge to roll her eyes and shake them all by the shoulders.

"Well, what the fuck are we waiting for? While it's busy, get to your hand luggage and find something we can use against it." She got up to leave, to return to her own luggage, when she noticed nobody was moving. "Are you pricks fucking serious?" Her face turned into a scowl. "You want to sit there like little fucking cunts and die?"

The severity of her words knocked a few of them back, their eyes shooting up to meet her.

"It's busy back there,"—she thumbed over her shoulder—"so what the fuck are you waiting for?"

A couple of people stood, shaking and wide-eyed, and April nodded. Encouraged more to stand with a reassuring smile. She counted eight who sat there like mannequins, too afraid to blink or breathe. It wasn't up to her to inject them with courage, so she left them to stick their heads in the sand.

Her own hand luggage was mostly just stupid shit, and she rifled through her bag, tossing clothing, shoes, and make-up to the floor. There was nothing she could use as a weapon, unless she wanted to throw a shoe at the fucking thing.

Abandoning her own luggage, she raced to another passenger. A woman with jet-black hair, digging through her possessions without taking one item from the bag.

"Anything?" she asked.

The woman ignored her, digging, digging, until April put a hand over her own.

"Hey," she said, and the woman met her eyes. "Is there anything in there we can use?"

"I-I... I don—... I don't know... " The woman breathed in short bursts, stuttering and confused.

April wanted to slap her, to knock some fucking sense into her. Instead, she said, "I need you. I can't do this without you."

The woman's expression changed, and she gave a short, slow nod. Went back to sorting through her bag, items falling to the floor and the surrounding chairs.

Better, April thought.

She moved on to someone else who'd found a pair of drumsticks in his bag. "We can maybe use this... " the youngish guy, maybe twenty-five, said.

"How'd they get on here?" April asked.

"They were wrapped up in a jumper. Whoever owned them snuck them through. Who knows why," the guy said with a shrug.

"Sharpen those," April said, nodding, "and you've got something to stab it with. Get to it."

April glanced down the aisle, saw the entity lapping at the pool of Dusty Guy's bloodied remains with a half-formed tongue. Knowing they were running out of time, she urged people to hurry. All they had so far were some blunt drumsticks.

"Fuck," she muttered. She went to the captain.

"I've got the flare gun," Thorpe said, holding it out to April, "and we've got the fire extinguishers. They're heavy, but maybe—"

"It's better than nothing. Look, you know this plane better than anyone," April said. "Is there anything we can use?"

Thorpe shrugged. "Maybe in the cargo hold. Maybe Charlie will bring something back for us."

The monster was starting to move, so April ignored Thorpe's defeatist attitude. Waiting for someone to save them wasn't an option. It had never been an option for April. She watched as the thing began to form longer arms and longer legs, jutting from the solidifying body more with each passing second.

"What about in the galley?" April asked.

Thorpe's eyes dropped for a moment, thinking back to Eric sealed up in there. "Yes. There will be some knives in there. Only small ones for chopping up lemon and that sort of thing, but it's better than nothing, right?"

"I'd rather have a knife than nothing at all," April conceded, and rushed to the galley. She hadn't even considered crawling or staying out of sight. There wasn't time. Whatever the creature was doing, it was happening then and there.

She reached the galley, stepped into the river of blood, and grimaced at the squelch of her shoes on the soaked carpet. Her stomach flipped and churned, but there wasn't time for that, either. The guy with the drumsticks ran from the galley, having sharpened them into a weapon. April saw a flash of metal in his hands, too, and figured he'd taken a knife.

Eric's body parts were still lying around, an arm here, a leg there, and a trail mark where a kidney had splattered on the cabinetry and slowly slid down to the floor. Slipping in his entrails, April pulled at drawers and flung canisters out of their tightly sealed locations. Food trays, fridge units, and spare cutlery. She picked up some cutlery and tested it. It would barely cut through the airplane food. Tossing it, she searched again.

"Oh fuck!" someone yelled.

Poking her head into the aisle, she saw the entity hovering again, blood and skin dripping to the carpet as it headed to the front of the plane. It was laughing again, despite not having a fully formed mouth. As it went, April saw the translucence fading. The surface, its skin, still rippled, but it had taken on a fleshy, tan colour.

Little legs dangled and grew as it glided up the aisle, zigzagging in odd patterns.

Hunting.

April resumed her own hunt to find a fucking knife. Even a tiny blade was better than nothing, and she tipped out cupboards and kicked at long-life milk cartons and juice bottles in frustration. Muttering to herself, berating herself, she continued the search, throwing out shitty fucking sandwiches and packets of biscuits.

A cabinet at the other end was untouched, though covered in shredded... something. April couldn't even begin to guess and didn't want to. She tugged at the handle, but it was locked. She pulled harder, as hard as she could with both hands, but it didn't budge.

"Fuck you!" she screamed at the door. She could see the lock and guessed that the key was held by the staff at all times.

"Please, leave us alone!" someone cried from beyond the galley.

She looked around the corner again. The creature had entered someone else, their remains spraying across the seats like rain. The laughter that followed was the cruellest thing she'd ever heard. Half of her wanted to stay put, to hide away in the shell of Eric's torso. The other half, the half that won, wanted to join the fight.

The guy with the drumsticks stabbed at the monster as it entered him next. Realisation hadn't even set in when he exploded. A drumstick protruded from the entity, seemingly unnoticed. The other had fallen to the floor. April raced to it as the thing went from passenger to passenger, exploding them one by one with that hollow laugh.

She gripped the drumstick, thanking the guy for at least sharpening them, and stabbed the monster hard.

It didn't even notice.

She pulled it free and stabbed again. The drumstick entered its body, but it absorbed the wood. She thought back to Eric's head, how a piece of it had been stuck there, detached.

How? she wondered.

As the entity paused, deciding between two passengers, she tried something different. Instead of stabbing, she grabbed at it. Thrust her fingers into its body and clawed, taking a chunk back with her.

That's how.

She held it in her hand and dropped it as the monster spun to face her with coalescing eyes. The chunk of globby flesh rolled back to its master, absorbed into its foot. April stepped back and turned to run, sensing that was it for her. She readied herself to be entered, but Thorpe appeared from somewhere behind her. She sprayed the fire extinguisher, a steady flow of white cloud filling the space.

Coughing through it, April ran. The creature spun back to Thorpe, giving April a chance to escape.

Escape, she thought. *There* is *no escape.*

She didn't look back, didn't see what happened to Thorpe, but hoped she got away, if only to land the plane. April made it back to the galley, grateful to be alive, and knew the best thing she could do was find those knives. To do that, she needed the key to that cupboard. More screams came and went as the monster attacked.

April didn't want to know what was happening out there; she only needed to find the key. Dropping to her knees, she sucked her lips in and pulled them tight, knowing what she was about to do betrayed any sense of reality she thought she had.

On her hands and knees, she moved her fingers through Eric's sticky remains, picking at things that felt solid. His clothes were torn to shreds, too, and she hadn't seen a belt or anything that a keychain might attach to.

Another scream from beyond the galley, and April searched faster, convinced the knives were locked away in that cupboard.

More screams.

"Come on!" she yelled at herself.

A small glint just out of reach.

She crawled to it, grabbed at the item, and held it up.

The key.

"Yes!" she hissed and raced back to the cupboard as the passengers screamed. She heard the unmistakable sounds of flesh tearing apart and bodies exploding and fumbled with the key in the lock. Twisting it, she yanked the door open, ready to grab the knives.

Bottles.

Alcohol.

"You've got to be kidding." She elbowed the door hard, and it swung on its hinges. She grabbed the first bottle she could find and raced from the galley, holding onto the wall to stabilise herself as she slipped on Eric once more.

She wished she'd stayed in the galley.

Upon entering the aisle, she saw the entity flying into passenger after passenger, each one exploding as their bodies connected with the thing's still-gelatinous form. She didn't know how many were left, or if she was alone

The woman with jet-black hair ran towards April, their hands outstretched to each other so April could pull her to safety, but the creature entered her, expanded, and the limits of the woman's body shattered.

April fell backwards, shards of the woman's ribs stabbing at her face.

The entity only *looked* more solid. She'd seen it before, but it hadn't clicked. They'd assumed because it was becoming more tangible that it couldn't go through walls anymore, but they were wrong. It *could* still travel into people. That meant it *could* still travel through walls. Which meant a knife, a pitiful fucking knife she couldn't even find, wasn't going to be of any use.

All she could do was take a chunk from it, and it hadn't even noticed. Hadn't cared.

Which meant they had no way to fight it.

The monster moved through the spray of the exploded woman and hovered above April. Beyond it, she saw Thorpe racing down the aisle, the flare gun in one hand, the fire extinguisher in the other.

It's useless, she thought. *Even if I get away now, it's all useless.*

"Yessss," the thing replied, the words dribbling from a malformed mouth. "Uuuuselesss."

Defiant, April swung the bottle at the monster, screaming and spitting at it to leave her the fuck alone. It hovered above her, watching.

Laughing.

Playing with her.

It jerked to the left, and April swung. Jerked to the right, and she swung again.

"Please!" April begged. "Don't fucking kill me."

And the being entered her, rummaging around in her body. April screamed and screamed, begging for help, though she knew none would come. None *could* come. The monster told her it was useless again as it filled her insides, drowning her in its globby, fleshy existence.

You feel good, it hissed inside her.

She waited for the pain of her body being torn apart.

She waited for her organs to burst from her body and for the entity to fly away, discarding her as garbage.

She waited.

Her fingers lost their grip on the bottle of alcohol, and it rolled on the carpet, thunking against a wall somewhere.

And she stood, though it was with legs that she didn't control.

Useless, the entity said. *It's all useless.*

TWENTY-ONE

CPT. THORPE

Flare guns were designed for open spaces—like the woods or the middle of the ocean—not for an airplane cabin. It was all she had, though, and as the being approached April's body, Thorpe fired it. The flare shot from the pistol, igniting fast and penetrating the monster.

I've done it! She smiled, but her expression faded as she saw the flare jutting from its back.

Smoke started to fill the entity, and Thorpe continued toward it, tossing the empty flare gun. Lifting the fire extinguisher, she began to cough as she sucked in lungfuls of the thick black smoke.

The monster hadn't even noticed, too consumed with April to care. The flare was pushed from the creature's body and fell to the floor, Thorpe's grand plan amounting to nothing. It fizzled and smoked on the carpet like a dying cigarette butt. She hadn't known what would happen; she hadn't really thought much about the end result. But as she stared down at the dead flare, the situation's direness sank into her. Even with the exploding passengers, she'd assumed they'd find a way out. A way to fight back, to beat the fucking thing.

Drawing her eyes back to the enemy, then back to April, she knew it was useless. Still, the girl was in trouble, and she wasn't about to stand there and let it take her. Thorpe raised the extinguisher to what she supposed was the monster's head, but stopped as it entered April. It was almost like the entity had blanketed her, cocooned her, until it enveloped her in a translucent, gooey sheen. Their eyes met, and April was begging for help, and all Thorpe could do was drop the extinguisher and pull at the layer of globby flesh.

"I'll get you out of there," Thorpe said, digging at the monster's gelatinous flesh, even as it sank into April's skin and spilled down her throat. "Just hold on!"

April's eyes began to change. Easy calm, a quiet confidence, replaced her terror. Pulling back from the teenager, Thorpe sized her up. A missing piece in her eyes told Thorpe April was no longer alone.

She was no longer herself.

"What are you?" she asked.

April sighed. "You're about to die, and all you want to know is what I am? Does it matter?"

"I-I'm... about to—"

April smiled and gave a small laugh. "About to die, yes."

Thorpe turned and ran, sensing April right behind her. She imagined April would stretch out with new, strange limbs or jump on her back and tear at her throat, but the monster was just a teenage girl now. Riding along in that body.

Not riding, she thought. *Driving.*

April had to be in there somewhere. The entity surely couldn't push her consciousness from her body in an instant.

"April," Thorpe called over her shoulder. "April!"

Nothing but footsteps, matching the rhythm of her own as she continued to the front of the plane. She reached the cockpit door and pulled the handle.

Locked.

It automatically locked itself, a safety feature embedded into every plane since 9/11. In her panic, she'd forgotten one of the basic tenets of airplane safety. Scrambling for a keypad at the side of the door, Thorpe punched in the code. Her finger moved to the OK button.

April tugged at Thorpe's neck, the fingers soft but the grip exceptional. She stumbled backwards, April leading her away from the door by her gullet. Thorpe wheezed and gasped through the ever-declining passageway of her throat. She felt the cartilage crush and snap under the force of April's fingers.

"P-pl-pl—" she stammered.

"Shut the fuck up," April spat, annoyed.

She tugged again and threw Thorpe to the ground. Hands up defensively, she tried to plead, but her throat was sealed. Crushed. Struggling to breathe, she instead crawled away, with April towering above her, following her.

"What to do, what to do," April teased. "You thought you were safe because you're the pilot, didn't you?"

Thorpe grabbed at the corner of the wall and pulled herself towards the aisle, towards Calista's remains. She hadn't even had a chance to mourn her or Eric, to even let it sink in that they weren't even dead. They were nothing. Eradicated into spots of trampled dust and pools of blood.

And she was next.

Desperate, she got to her knees, ignoring April's mocking applause, and stumbled down the aisle. She clutched at her neck, wheezing and trying to breathe through her nose. She tasted the tiniest amount of oxygen, but the stench of death tainted it, and she coughed it back up.

Behind her, April sucked in the air and expelled it with a satisfied "Ahhhhh." Thorpe entered the aisle, cut through the seats in the middle row, and headed back to the fire extinguisher. It was all she had, even though she was convinced it wouldn't work.

Nothing worked on it.

She reached the extinguisher, with April still stalking behind. Picking it up, she aimed the hose at the girl, still coughing and wheezing, desperate for air.

It's about to get much, much worse, she thought.

"What are you going to do with that?" April asked, a dirty smile splitting her lips.

Thorpe waited for April to step a little closer.

"Bang me on the head?" April continued.

Another step.

One more. That was all she needed.

April took that last step, and Thorpe pressed the trigger on the extinguisher. A puff of white gas sprayed in April's face, and Thorpe rushed her. She knocked the girl down, climbed on top of her, and smashed the extinguisher down into her face.

The girl laughed at first, but as the metal came down again with a dull thud, the glee turned to anger. Thorpe's knees were on April's arms, the weight of her body keeping the girl pinned to the carpet.

The extinguisher came down again, and even though Thorpe was glad to see the blood pouring from April's nose, she was also horrified at what she was doing. April was still in there somewhere. Suffering.

"I'm sorry," Thorpe managed through the smoke and the crushed windpipe before bringing it down once more into the girl's face.

Her eyes were closed now, her body unresponsive. Thorpe knew April was merely the vessel, though, and if she had in fact killed her, the entity itself was still alive. Abandoning the fire extinguisher to a nearby seat, Thorpe stood and headed for the cockpit.

Punching the code in again, she hit OK and pulled at the door. With one final look at April's body on the floor, Thorpe entered the cockpit and slammed the door behind her.

"What the hell is going on out there?" her co-pilot, Kevin, asked. "Are more people dead?"

Thorpe took her seat and rubbed at her throat. Her breathing was returning—only a little, but enough to spit the word "Mayday" into her radio.

"Mayday?" Kevin looked at her, his eyes wide. "Oh Jesus, what's happening now?"

Thorpe shook her head at him, and he took in the blood on her uniform. "It's all real. He wasn't crazy."

"Captain?" he asked.

"Mayday," Thorpe repeated. "Several... dead. Landing... not... not viable."

Kevin didn't say anything. He knew enough to stay quiet when the word "mayday" was even whispered on a plane. She'd already informed him about Eric and the other dead passengers, but he had no idea about the... whatever that thing was out there. There was no time to explain now. Thorpe shot Kevin a glance, wishing she could explain further, but instead reached for her phone.

Swiping to Favourites in her contacts list, she pressed SHERRY and let it ring.

And ring.

"Answer, please," she whispered.

"Hi—"

"Sherry, baby, listen—"

"—I'm not available to take your call right now. Please leave a message and I'll call you back."

Thorpe shed a tear and waited for the beep. "Sherry, it's me. I... " She paused, knowing these were the last words her ex-wife would hear. Her windpipe ached and pulsed as she forced the words out. "I'm sorry for everything. Please forgive me and know that... I love you." She hung up and turned to Kevin. "There's something on board with us," Thorpe said. "That guy we thought was crazy; he was right. If it gets to civilisation, everyone's going to die."

"Captain, with all due respect, what the fuck are you talking about?" Kevin asked, his voice a few octaves higher than usual.

"It's not human. Charlie was right all along. He was right. He was fucking right about all of it."

"I don't know what—"

"Kevin!" Thorpe screamed at him as much as her throat would allow. "Shut up and listen to me. We need to crash this plane."

TWENTY-TWO

12 HRS BEFORE TAKE-OFF

It wasn't me who had done those things. The voice— it was the voice. The voice had told me to do it, and I wasn't strong enough to ignore it.

And it was right.

The voice was always right.

I couldn't go back to that hospital, to be surrounded by *them*. Dr. Schwarz knew how I felt, and I couldn't take the chance. It was my fault; I'd been honest. Too honest. And I knew I wasn't ready to come home, but I needed to be home. Not my childhood home, like Schwarz had suggested. No, I needed to be at my home with Aiden.

Sitting in the car, I looked at the front windows of our house. The wide front door he'd wanted when we built the place a decade earlier. The voice had whispered to me then, too. Told me it hated that door.

I did hate that door.

Gripping the car door handle, I paused. My other hand was on the steering wheel, sliding down to the PRESS TO START button. Dr. Schwarz had intended to call the hospital.

But here I was, an hour later, and nobody was coming for me. I thought back to what had happened, hating myself and the voice for what we'd done.

Her neck was feeble in my hands, the veins pulsing and popping, her face fragile and pleading. She punched at me, clawed at my forearms, and pried at my fingers, but in my rage and fear, I didn't let go.

"P-pl-pleeease," Schwarz sputtered. "Ch-Char-Charlie!"

KILL HER!

The voice echoed through my mind, and I tried, I really tried to shut it up. My hands wouldn't move, though, as Schwarz's face turned blue, and she gasped again and again for the air I was stealing from her.

YES CHARLIE!

"No," I said.

It was like my fingers were not my own, as though I was a passenger in my own body, fighting for control. My fingers loosened a little, and Schwarz pushed me away, coughing and spluttering.

She moved to her desk and scrambled for the phone. I beat her to it, swiping it from the desk. A landline, of all things. The handset careened through the office, bounced on the coiled cord like a bungee, and we both heard the dial tone.

"Charlie," her voice came as a hoarse whisper, "stop this."

"I won't go back," I said. "I won't."

Holding up a defensive hand, her eyes begged me to stay where I was and listen. A look could carry many meanings, and hers was clear. She thought I was going to kill her.

"I don't want to hurt you."

"Prove it," she replied.

I moved to the phone, picked it up, and placed it back on the desk. "Here. See? I'm cleaning up."

Schwarz stared at me, then at the phone. I could see she wanted to grab for it, to call the police or the hospital, but she stayed still, one hand attending to her sore neck. It was red and bruised, and I apologised for my role in that.

"It's okay, Charlie. But you need to leave."

NO, CHARLIE BOY, YOU CAN'T LEAVE. YOU GO, SHE PICKS UP THAT PHONE. AND THEN WHAT? The voice paused for a moment to let me think. *AIDEN WILL BE SO UPSET IF YOU GO BACK TO THAT AWFUL PLACE. HE WON'T LOVE YOU ANYMORE.*

"He will," I whispered.

Schwarz studied me, not saying a word. She knew better than to interrupt me during these moments.

NO, CHARLIE. THIS'LL BE ONCE TOO MANY. HOW LONG WOULD YOU STICK AROUND IF YOUR HUSBAND WERE IN AND OUT OF A PSYCH WARD?

"I can't leave."

Trying not to frown, Schwarz lowered her eyebrows as her hand crept closer to the phone.

"I'm so sorry, Doctor Schwarz," I said, and I meant it. "But if I leave, you're going to have me put away again."

"Then let's talk."

I shook my head. "We've done that. It doesn't work."

She gulped hard, and I wasn't sure if she couldn't swallow properly or if I'd destroyed something in her neck when I'd squeezed. "Then... what?"

The voice didn't even need to instruct me on what to do next. I took care of it all by myself, quickly grabbing the phone as Schwarz reached for it. I snatched it up, and she must have seen something in my eyes or on my face, because she turned to run.

My hand was on her before I realised it.

She lunged away from me, running for the office door, calling for help. I grabbed at her hair and pulled it back. Her head jerked backward, but she kept running. Her fingers clutched at the door handle, and I leaped at her. I was on her back. She scrambled to open the door, and I forced her away. Knocked her to the wall.

Schwarz was down, crawling away from me on her hands and knees, calling for help. Someone would hear. Someone would come.

She headed back to her desk, back to the phone. I towered above her, my heart hammering, my thoughts blank. As she reached for the phone once more, I bent down to grab it.

"I won't go back." My words were cold and empty.

The phone cord was around her neck. Her poor neck, already so bruised and battered. I pulled the cord so tight I thought it might snap, but I stayed there, letting her body sag against mine. She struggled and fought, but as the cord wrapped tighter, her energy sapped fast.

YES, CHARLIE. YOU'VE DONE IT!

The voice was eager to keep at it, but I dropped the cord and let her unconscious body fall into mine. Lying her down on the office floor, her eyes pried open and hollow, I studied the emptiness there.

"Is she—"

OH YES, CHARLIE. YOU KILLED HER.

I'd fled to my car and come home, and now I couldn't get out. Aiden opened the front door, the one he'd chosen even though it was supposed to be *our* decision, and waved at me. I waved back and got out of the car, wiping my sweaty palms on my jeans.

Aiden came towards me with a smile, arms out wide, and embraced me. "There you are," he said as he drew me into his chest. He gave a small moan as his arms tightened, and I melted in his warmth.

"Sorry I'm late," I said, my voice muffled by his shirt.

"How was your session?" He kissed my forehead.

Pausing, I searched his demeanour. Did he know? Had he heard? Who was inside? Why was he meeting me out here, almost on the fucking street? "It was good," I said.

Aiden let go and took me by the hand, leading me inside the house. My heart raced. My eyes were wide. I had to get out of there. Someone would come for me, and I could only hope they'd be human.

"Hungry?" Aiden asked.

"No," I said, and I realised I was too short. Too sharp.

BE COOL. The voice was frustrated. I was giving too much away.

"I mean, no thanks. Maybe a coffee?" I smiled and tried to make sure my face didn't betray me. That it didn't tell him I was a killer.

He nodded and moved through the house to the kitchen. I heard the click of the kettle as he switched it on. He always made instant coffee, even though we had a coffee machine sitting right there. He knew I liked the coffee machine and knew I hated—*hated*—instant.

Shutting the front door, I followed him to the kitchen. He was already looking at me with a sad smile.

"What?" I asked, my eyes returning to the front door.

He sighed. "I'm sorry, it has to be instant today. The machine is broken."

"Broken?" He was lying. It wasn't broken.

"Yeah, I have to take it back to the store. It broke while you were away." He folded his arms, putting a distance between us—a coldness.

HE KNOWS, CHARLIE. HE KNOWS.

"No worries," I replied, though I was aware my face said I didn't want the coffee anymore.

"How about some wine?" he asked.

"I can't. You know that."

Aiden smiled, a big, wide grin. "Ah, but guess who went shopping today?" He went to the fridge, opened it, and pulled out a bottle of white wine. "All the taste, zero alcohol. I hunted for it, but there are actually quite a few options."

"For medicated psychos, you mean?" I took a deep breath and muttered an apology, thinking about how much I hated the front door.

Aiden unscrewed the cap and put the bottle down. "Hard session? You want to talk about it?" When my lips twitched, he continued, "No pressure. We can just have a nice drink and cuddle on the lounge."

He doesn't know, I thought. *He only wants to spend time with me.*

I wanted nothing more than to take a glass of wine, even if it was some alcohol-free imitation, and sip it while my beautiful bear of a husband cuddled me.

"Got any cheese and crackers?" I asked with a coy smile.

Aiden nodded and busied himself with preparations.

GOOD PLAN, CHARLIE BOY. KILL THE PSYCHOLO-GIST, GO STRAIGHT HOME, AND EAT CHEESE.

"What do you want me to do?" I asked.

"Nothing," Aiden replied, thinking I was talking to him. "Just go relax."

If he only knew I was incapable of relaxing. The front door thing was still pissing me off. Sometimes it did, sometimes it didn't, and I was aware that right now, I was channelling my rage and upset into that stupid door.

The house was open plan, so the kitchen wasn't far from the lounge room. I took a seat on the chaise lounge and stretched out to give the illusion of a carefree attitude. Show him I was relaxing, even if my chest was heaving, my heart was hammering, and I couldn't swallow the fact that I was a killer.

I sipped the wine, surprised that it tasted like the real thing.

"How is it?" Aiden asked.

I told him I liked it and sipped again. Not too fast, a casual, calm sip. I tried so hard not to shake my hand.. I saw it trembling, but Aiden didn't say anything. "How was your day?" I asked, watching Aiden rip open a packet of Jatz with his teeth.

He spat a small bit of foil onto the kitchen counter and poured the biscuits onto a plate. "Interesting," he said. "I heard something alarming that I wanted to ask you about."

FUCK. FUCK, FUCK, FUCK.

"Oh?" I rested my hands on my stomach, fingers interlaced.

GoOD, CHARLIE, GOOd. BE INNocENT, be calm. FUCK. Be CALM!

"Yeah," Aiden said, and paused as he unwrapped the triple-creamed brie.

"I think I should go home," I blurted out.

"You mean… " He knew what I meant and let the question drift into nothingness. "Are you sure that's a good idea? I mean, after what happened there?"

"Doctor Schwarz thinks I might benefit from revisiting the site of the initial trauma. She thinks it will cure me or something."

CURE You? CHARLIE, We AreN'T SICK.

"Initially, I thought there was no way, but maybe if we go together?"

Aiden gave a slight, slow nod. "We can talk about it, I guess."

"Anyway," I smiled at Aiden, "are you going to ask me?"

He looked at me with those beautiful eyes and smiled again. "It's nothing," he said. "We can talk later. Just relax."

RELax, CHARLIE. Relax. FUCKING RELAX!

I made a conscious effort to relax my shoulders and take a deep breath. My hands were clammy, and I tightened the grip of my interlaced fingers to disguise the trembling. "I *am* relaxed," I said, hoping Aiden didn't see my knuckles turning white. "Ask me."

It was almost a dare.

Aiden walked over, carrying the plate of cheese and crackers in one hand and a glass of alcohol-free wine in the other. Setting the plate and his glass on the coffee table, he sat next to me and leaned close. I felt his breath on my neck and hated myself for having a neck that wasn't broken and shattered like poor Dr. Schwarz.

"Some building firm wants to build a new development up the street," Aiden said, kissing my cheek.

I sipped the wine.

"They think it'll increase the housing prices around here," he continued, "but I think the area is becoming a little overcrowded now."

That's all, I thought. *Housing bullshit. He doesn't know. He doesn't know shit.*

I settled into the lounge a little more and asked for a biscuit and some cheese. Aiden handed it to me, sat up, and ate some himself.

WE'VE GOTTEN AWAY WITH IT, CHARLIE.

Except I knew I hadn't. It had been an hour, and her body was still there. It hadn't even started decomposing yet. When the smell set in, someone would notice. They might have noticed already. Another client, another "crazy," poking at her with curious fingers.

No. I hadn't gotten away with it. Not with anything.

I looked at Aiden as he talked about Sydney property prices, the cost of living, and whether we should move to a small town somewhere. He sipped the wine, the stem lifting to his nose, and I watched his Adam's apple bob up and down as he swallowed.

So easy to snap, those stems. I smiled and took another slice of cheese.

TWENTY-THREE

"Stay quiet," I whispered, resisting the urge to put a hand over Rachel's mouth. "Something has happened up there."

Rachel waited for me to continue while I stared up at the door, listening. Thinking. If only she'd helped me earlier, we could have come up with a plan. If only she'd been willing to step outside her own situation and look at the bigger picture.

Look who's talking, I thought, and swallowed my guilt. *Murderer.*

I had killed Dr. Schwarz, strangled her to death with a phone cord, and now I was playing the hero. I wasn't a hero, not by any stretch of the imagination. Yet, here in this cargo hold, Rachel and I were the only hope the passengers had.

If there were any left.

"What did you see?" Rachel whispered, her teeth chattering again. She wrapped her clothes and arms as tight as she could around her, but the cold was getting to both of us, seeping into our bones.

Cupping my hands, I breathed warm air into them and flexed my fingers to stop them from going numb. I tucked my hands into my armpits to maintain some of the heat.

"Charlie," Rachel said, "what did you see?"

I tuned into her words and hissed back, "Blood. Lots of blood."

She muttered a curse word and stood silently.

Through the door, a sound.

"What is that?" I asked, and Rachel shook her head.

It sounded like knocking. A deep *tap-tap-tap* from right above us.

"Someone's alive up there," I said, my eyes widening. I reached for the door handle, ready to lift it open, when Rachel put a hand on my arm and pulled me back. "What is it?"

"What if it's the... thing?" she asked. "We're safe down here. Out of sight."

I stifled a laugh and motioned around the cargo hold. "Look around. We're going to die in here. If not from the creature, then from the cold. We can't stay here."

Nodding, Rachel added, "I guess if the pilot's dead, it's all for naught anyway."

MAYBE IT'S FOR THE BEST, CHARLIE. YOU DON'T DE-SERVE TO LIVE.

"No, there's a co-pilot," I said.

Rachel smiled. "Of course!"

"Then there's still hope."

I tried to mean it, but the idea of hope felt far beyond my reach. The aisles of blood, the strewn body parts, the complete absence of human sounds. The thought that, amid all the carnage and death, the co-pilot was in the cockpit, oblivious to what was happening, was almost comedic. I imagined them sipping Red Bull and staring into the night sky, navigating the clouds without a fucking care in the world.

Tap-tap-tap. It was louder this time and definitely right above us.

"We have to go back up there," I whispered, a shiver travelling through my entire body. "Creature or not, we can't stay here."

Rachel looked away, drew some hair behind her ear, and then met my gaze. "I won't go back," she said.

Those words echoed through me.

Spinning to face her, my eyes drawn, I said, "What did you say?"

SHE KNOWS, SHE KNOWS! HOW DOES SHE KNOW? WHO IS SHE? The voice wasn't laughing now. The voice was scared.

"I said I won't go back. I'm not supposed to be on this plane. If it lands, if we somehow get out of this alive... I won't go back home. You have to promise me you won't let them take me."

"I don't know your story," I replied. "And I don't know you. As far as anyone else knows, we never met." I gave a small smile, the best I could muster in that moment. "If we land—*when* we land—you get back here and hide. I won't say a thing."

Rachel smiled back, though we both knew the odds of landing safe and sound were becoming slimmer by the moment. The monster was up there, killing everyone one by one, and we were about to join it.

Tap-tap-tap.

I lifted the door and slowly climbed the ladder, peering once more down the aisle towards the front of the plane.

"There you are," April said, her kind eyes filled with terror.

"April?" I asked, re-entering the cabin. She helped me up, her hands slick with blood. I could tell she'd tried to clean it off, with streaks up and down her arms and smears around her eyes where she'd wiped at it. Her nose was a mess and looked broken.

"What happened out here?" I asked. "What happened to you?"

"I got... attacked. My nose really hurts." She held her face, and I went to her.

"Let me see," I said.

She put her hands down and let me look at the mess. A first aid kit had to be around somewhere. I searched for it, April and Rachel in tow.

"The other passengers?" I asked April, hopeful but knowing in my heart what she'd say.

"I think it's just us left, maybe the pilot, too," she said, looking around. "You should have seen it, Charlie. The monster... It flew into every passenger, and they just... exploded."

"No more dust?" I asked.

She shook her head, and I noticed Rachel standing in the cabin by the cargo hold door. She looked at April.

"This is Rachel," I said, "the stowaway I mentioned. See, she is real."

April's eyes shot to Rachel and back to me, and she gave a slight nod. "Uh, hi." Rachel nodded, and April said, "Come on. I have a plan."

She dragged me up the aisle, stepping over flayed skin and discarded body parts like they weren't even there. Was that shock setting in? Survival instinct? Or something else?

"Where are we going?" I asked, shrugging at Rachel, who followed along.

April didn't answer, and as she dragged me, I glimpsed the bluish-black outside. It was an eerie twilight, and I guessed we had slightly more than an hour before we were due to land. Whatever April had planned, it had to work fast.

I almost slipped in a puddle of someone's blood when April steadied me, unusually strong for a teenager. She mumbled something like "Keep moving," and I yanked my hand free from hers.

"April," I said, "tell us what's going on."

She turned to face us and smiled.

The eyes were changing and I held back the urge to scream. The voice in my head did that for me, the ringing in my ears deafening.

"It hurts, doesn't it?" April asked. "The voice's screams."

"What?" I wanted to put my hands over my ears, and I wanted to take another pill, to swallow happiness and serenity, to make this all go away.

But the voice. The voice was screaming, *IT'S HER, IT'S HER, IT'S HER!*

"I can hear it, Charlie. It knows about me. *You* know about me." April was calm, just standing there, leaning against one of the seats. She didn't care that her elbow was sinking into the blood-stained fabric of the chair or that Rachel and I were slowly moving backwards.

She moved forward, confident, her stare unwavering.

"Just like I know about you," she said.

"What do you mean?" I asked.

April smiled. "You don't even know it yourself, do you?" Tilting her head, she looked into me, searching my eyes for something. "You really don't. I wonder... Does Other Charlie know what I mean?"

I turned to run, Rachel now in front of me, but April cleared her throat and said, "Where will you run to, Charlie? We're on a plane in the middle of the sky."

"She's right," Rachel said. "There's nowhere to go."

"Why are you doing this?" I asked as we ran.

April was slow to follow us, though her movements were perfectly human. Fluid. It was different than it had been with the old woman and Calista. Like there'd been learning curves—as if the entity had to figure out how to use our bodies.

INCREDIBLE. The voice, even now, saw beauty in that thing when all I wanted to do was vomit and cower and pretend it wasn't real.

"It is real, Charlie," April said.

I didn't care how she knew what I was thinking. It didn't matter. I needed to get away from her. The voice was laughing again, poking fun at me, telling me it was useless, useless, useless. But Rachel and I ran back to the cargo hold door. I flipped it open, knowing what lay beneath was my coffin. I wouldn't last ten minutes in there before the cold got me.

It's that or the creature, I reminded myself.

"Charlie," April said. The way she called my name gave me pause. Something in her tone, the cadence. I looked back at her and saw the fear in her eyes.

"April?" I asked. "It's you; you're still in there?"

She nodded and fell to her knees. "It wants... everything." She tried to stand, but her arms trembled and shook. "I don't... have much time."

"What can I do?" I wanted to run to her, but my feet didn't move. Rachel was halfway down into the cargo hold, pulling at me, urging me to abandon the girl. After another breath, so deep and filled with detritus that it burned my lungs, I took a step back to her.

"Charlie, no!" Rachel called after me.

I went to April, her eyes somehow back to human and her expression of a person who knew they were about to die. "What can I do?" I asked softly.

"I never got to... tell my parents... I love them," she whispered. A tear crept from her eye as she struggled to keep control of her own body. "Tell them for me."

I held her, clutched her in my arms, and brought her body into mine in a hug. "I'm sorry," I said. "I'm so sorry for all of this."

"Charlie," she muttered, and met my gaze.

Her mouth moved, but no more sound came. Her jaw started to sag, her tongue lolled, and I could do nothing but tighten my embrace as her skin fell away like sand, crumbling to the carpet one piece at a time. I hugged her tight, begging for this not to be true, for it all to be a dream, as her shoulders collapsed onto me, breaking into clumps.

"No, April, please no," I whimpered.

The rest of her body fell away, and I stared down at her remains, at the broken promise of all her potential. A moment later, before I could even contemplate what to do next, her remains began to stir.

I fell backward, shooting my hands behind me, and moved away, shaking some of April's dust off as I went. From within the pile of dust, stirring beneath the vacant clothing, the glob. It was gelatinous and small but started to grow, expanding and replicating, and forming into a shapeless figure. Through my tears, I watched as the monster grew to the height of an adult, with the build of a man: arms and legs and facial features slowly melting into the translucent, globby flesh.

"What the fuck are you?" I screamed at it and stood, pointing down to the remains. "Why did you kill April and everyone else?"

As the mouth formed, what I took to be lips parted. A long tongue slithered from its mouth and licked the bottom lip. "I was done with them." Its voice was hollow and empty, hoarse.

I tried to ask what that meant, but nothing came out.

"And now," the entity said as it continued to form into something new, its flesh rippling as it changed colour, "I need you."

YES. The voice was gleeful, encouraging me to step forward. *YES, CHARLIE. IT NEEDS US!*

"No," I whispered. "I don't care."

YOU DO CARE!

"I don't!" I cried.

"We all know you do," the entity said, its face beginning to emerge but still featureless. It was like a mannequin, unable to hold a perfect human shape but trying, nonetheless.

"How are you—"

"I want everything," it said, "and I am going to take it."

INCLUDING OUR THOUGHTS, CHARLIE BOY.

The monster stepped towards me, the gooeyness of its feet leaving wet tracks in the blood-stained carpet. I recognised the shape of a smile as it raised its hands to me. It wasn't threatening. It was the way Aiden reached out when he wanted a hug.

"I need you," it said to me. "When this plane lands, I am going to need a host."

"And then what?" I asked. "You fucking blow me up like the others or turn me to dust?"

The creature shrugged.

Rachel grabbed my arm and pulled me towards her. I leaned into her and went wherever she led, my eyes still on the monster.

"You can't run, Charlie," it called after us. "There's nowhere to go."

As we headed back to the cargo hold, the plane dipped fast. Rachel and I tumbled backward; the entity toppled forward. My head crashed against the floor, with Rachel on top of me, a tangle of limbs. She tried to stand, but I held her, sensing the plane was still in a dive.

"More turbulence?" she asked.

I shook my head. I didn't know how I knew. I felt it in every inch of my body. Down to the core, I felt it. And I said, "The captain is crashing the plane."

Rachel's eyes widened, and she scrambled to stand. "I have to get off this fucking thing. How do I get off?"

The panic in her voice was clear. The illogical thought that she could somehow step off the plane mid-flight was somehow all too rational, and I wanted to show her the exit. I wanted a life jacket or a parachute or a fucking lifeboat, but we both knew we were stuck. The captain had made an executive decision, and it was the right one.

"Rachel," I said, oddly calm. "It's the best thing."

The monster was getting up, pulling at the chairs to steady itself as the plane continued to dive. We had minutes, maybe less, before the plane was on the ground in pieces. Minutes to live. I smiled.

HOW WILL YOU SPEND IT, CHARLIE?

The voice was sombre, and I smiled again. I would finally be at peace. No more voice telling me to hurt people. No more looks from strangers as they heard me talking to myself. No more medical appointments, drugs, or psych wards. No more fantasies about killing my husband.

No more Aiden.

As the creature walked towards us, intent on its final kills, my mind went back to Aiden. I saw it smile, its features now more human by the moment. It didn't matter. We were all about to die, that thing included.

EXCEPT IT CAN GO THROUGH WALLS, CHARLIE BOY.

"Then why isn't it?" I asked.

"Why isn't it what?" Rachel said, brushing away tears.

"The plane is in a nosedive, yet it's walking towards us. It's not leaving the plane." I pointed to it. "Maybe it can't anymore. Maybe it's too solid."

"Then maybe... maybe we can kill it now!" Rachel cried.

"There might still be time. Go tell the captain. We need more time."

I saw Rachel run off to the other aisle and slip past the monster. Letting out a relieved sigh, I thought back to Aiden and what he'd want from me in that moment. If this abomination was going to kill me, the least I could do was show Aiden the respect he deserved and fight back.

I remembered how April had ordered people to search their luggage, but I'd been down in the cargo hold. Did they ever get the chance? I looked around for a weapon but saw nothing. So, it was either run away again or use my fists.

I didn't have much confidence in either option, but I had to try.

For Aiden, I thought.

FOR AIDEN, the voice echoed.

And I ran at it.

SESSION #14

St Vincent's Hospital, Psych. Ward
8 April 2025
Patient: Charles M. Reed
Referring Psychologist: Dr R Schwarz
Consulting Psychiatrist: Dr J Mathis

OTHER CHARLIE REMAINS CONVINCED that he is the original, while my Charlie believes the same of himself. In a strange way, this is progress. My Charlie has asserted himself as the true identity, which is a means of silencing the alter. Erasing or removing alters has not been proven to work; however, silencing them, or sending them to sleep, for lack of a better term, is entirely possible. We are on the path to doing just that. I believe the change in medication has led to this stunning and significant improvement, and I am hopeful of future progress.

If Charlie continues in this vein, I am confident Other Charlie can be permanently silenced and that the real Charlie can soon be released, so long as he maintains constant psychology sessions with Dr. Schwarz.

The following is an account of the session, according to both my audio recordings and my personal reflections:

I had a strange encounter in today's session, which is giving me pause. Other Charlie has demonstrated the ability to disguise himself as the real Charlie: his actions, his word choice, and his demeanour. I thought I was talking to my Charlie today until Other Charlie nodded to a comment I made. It was that same slow, minuscule nod, and I knew what he was doing.

It was a test. A game. He liked to play games, but this was different. If he could fool me, he could fool others. And what then? Who would Charlie be then if he were to be sent home?

"I don't like him," Charlie said, after his alter had retreated.

"You don't?"

He shook his head and sighed. It was heavy, like he didn't have the strength to breathe. "He tells me to do things. I used to listen but… I don't want to listen anymore."

"Why not?" I asked.

"I want to go home," he said. "I just want to be normal. I miss Aiden. I miss my bed. I miss my life."

I nodded. This was progress, though I couldn't be sure I was talking to the real Charlie.

"I know I'm not right in the head, but I can't stay here." He bit his bottom lip, then chewed a nail. Classic Charlie behaviour, easy for a cunning alter to mimic.

"Have you seen any more doppelgängers?" I asked.

Charlie closed his eyes, his eyebrows drawn downward. The misery his face could convey was unlike anything I'd ever seen.

"You have to believe me," he said. "There are more here now than there used to be."

His progress had been unquestionable, and despite his persistence in this delusion, I believed that with the right cocktail of drugs, he would be alright to go home. Keeping him in the hospital would not necessarily do him any good. Being at home with his husband might help, though.

I wasn't quite ready to sign the paperwork. I believed another week was necessary to monitor his progress.

"You've seen them, too," he said.

I scratched at my chin. He was right. I had noticed the empty spot in the nurse's eye. A genetic deformity, nothing more. Imperceptible unless one was looking for it. And yet, I had to admit, I noticed it on a few other nurses and treating psychiatrists.

It meant nothing, of course, but the fact that Charlie could see it in my expression told me I wasn't helping.

"Where do they come from?" he asked me. "I've been trying to figure it out, but I'm stuck here, in these walls. You can find out for me."

"Why does it matter where they come from?" I asked. "They aren't real. They're mythological creatures."

"Myths start somewhere."

"So do rumours. They aren't real, either." I didn't know why I was so defensive, but I had to shut down the line of questioning. Feeding into his delusion was unhealthy—for both of us.

Something in his words, though, had me intrigued. I wouldn't let on, but it was true that I had noticed these flaws in the eye. Some cursory research had yielded no results worth mentioning. As much as I wanted to tell myself it was a genetic defect, the fact that no medical research existed on this phenomenon did have me perplexed.

"Doctor Mathis," Charlie said. "I know I'm crazy. Just not about this."

<u>Recommendation</u>: Patient demonstrating progress regarding alternate identity. Therapy seems to repress Other Charlie, and the real Charlie is showing signs of strength. Medication seems to be lessening his anxiety and psychosis. He is more assertive and far less timid. However, his delusion remains as powerful as it was two weeks ago.

At this stage, **I do not recommend release.** But I believe this may change soon.

TWENTY-FOUR

THE MONSTER CAME AT me, and I ducked, feeling its wet hand clutch at my shoulder. It brushed me, but didn't slow me down. I hurled myself up, jumped onto a chair, dove over a few rows of seats, and crashed into the wall. As I slid to the floor, I saw it—a weapon—a feeble thing made of wood, rolling around as the plane nose-dived to the earth.

Moving towards it, the entity pursued me like a shadow, and I searched under the seats for the wood. It looked like a sharpened drumstick. It was pathetic, a stick of wood, and I hated that it was my only hope. Just out of reach, it was rolling around with the motion of the plane. I sensed we were still diving, heading for a crash and an instant, fiery death, but I couldn't depend on that outcome.

I dragged myself to the drumstick and felt the creature's hands on my back, pulling me away. My fingers clasped it, and I drew it into a steady grip. Turning to face the thing, I stabbed it in the face as hard as I could.

The stick penetrated its fleshy skin, and it reeled in pain.

Pain. The voice laughed. *We caused it pain.*

It was more solid. With each kill, it was becoming... human. Grabbing at the drumstick, I yanked it free, and a stream of red—human blood—spurted from the wound. I stabbed again, in the chest, and the monster stumbled backwards.

"Rachel!" I called. "It's working!"

Whatever this thing was, it was taking a human shape now, and with it, human mortality. I stabbed again and watched the creature back away.

"Fuck you!" I yelled. "Fuck you for what you did here!"

"Charlie... " The voice was April's. "Please... "

I stopped for a second, the drumstick shaking and dripping red in my hand. I wondered who this entity might become. It had killed all those passengers; it had turned April to dust. But her voice spoke to me now, and I wondered if it had chosen her form.

"You aren't her," I said.

"I could be," the monster replied, getting to its feet. "I took her. All of her."

Raising the drumstick again, ready to slash and stab, I said, "What does that mean?"

"She's *inside* me, Charlie. They all are. I've collected them." The wounds healed as though they were never there.

Yes, the voice said. *They're alive in there, Charlie. Like me, they exist inside.*

"No," I said. "They're all dead."

The entity recovered further, wiping at the spots where I'd stabbed it. "Dead," it echoed. "I don't understand." Its eyes reflected confusion, bewilderment. "I know the word; the people inside me recognise its meaning. Yet... " It trailed off with a shrug.

I held the drumstick up again, and the creature spread thin lips into a wide smile. I knew the glorified twig wasn't going to help me, that this being was beyond the mortality of flesh wounds.

IT ONLY APPEARS HUMAN, CHARLIE BOY, the voice whispered in awe. *IT'S MORE THAN WE COULD EVER BE.*

"Shut up." I meant to think it, but the words came out with a seething rage.

"Poor Charlie," the monster said, its smile curling into an exaggerated frown. "Still hearing voices."

"How... How do you know about the voice?" I asked.

The monster shrugged again. "I know a lot of things, Charlie."

It stepped toward me, raising a hand—fingers like April's shifting and rippling as the abomination moved forward. Its form was unstable, and I wondered if, somehow, I could use that to my advantage.

HA! ADVANTAGE? CHARLIE BOY, WHEN HAVE YOU EVER HAD THE ADVANTAGE? The voice giggled at me, and it slapped against my eardrums.

The entity stepped forward again, its hand bent inward, towards its own body. I moved away, calling to Rachel to stay back, though

I couldn't see her. She must have been inside the cockpit with the captain.

I felt the plane diving further and took solace in the knowledge that we would all be dead soon. Even if it didn't kill this thing, it wouldn't have us. We would go on our own terms.

The creature pulled at April's form, shuddering in glee as her skin fell apart, strips of skin squelching to the carpet under its feet. "Mmmm," it moaned, "it feels good to shake free sometimes."

All I could do was stare, wide-eyed, as the entity shed April's skin like a coat, pulling on the tips of each finger like a glove to loosen the shell. It gripped the loosened flesh and tugged until the skin came off in one meaty, gooey mess. It dropped her form to the carpet and kicked the discarded flesh to the side.

"What do you want?" I asked as it continued to strip, revealing the translucent form I was sure was its true body.

"I want everything," it said. "I want the world, Charlie. And I will have it."

I ran to the exit and bashed at the door, not caring that the plane was crashing, not wanting to wait for the end to come. I needed to get off that fucking plane. My fists banged again and again on the metal door, and I saw through the scratched and bloodied window that the night sky was fading into day. We were close to Perth now, the place of my childhood home. We had to be.

And I didn't want to be there when the monster got to the ground. One way or another, I was going to kill myself. I grabbed at the wheel lock on the door, intent on breaking the seal. It was the fastest way I could think of to get off the plane, to get away from the entity.

NO, CHARLIE. The voice was gentle in my ear now. *WE DON'T WANT TO GET AWAY. THIS IS WHAT WE'VE BEEN WAITING FOR.*

"NO!" I screamed. "NO! I can't become part of that thing!"

It was behind me now as I wrestled with the seal. It was heavier and harder than I'd imagined, but the wheel was slowly turning. I felt its hand on my shoulder, the force of it pulling me back to the floor.

Teeth beamed at me as the monster smiled, a thick black tongue rolling from its mouth as it licked its lips. I crawled from its grip, knowing it was playing with me but not understanding why. Why kill everyone else and leave me? Me, of all people?

"Just kill me," I screamed as the entity skipped down the aisle.

A dreadful sound filled the cabin as the plane continued its dive. The creature was whistling.

Here we go down, now

Here we go down

I was crawling to the back of the plane, which felt like the steepest hill I'd ever encountered, ignoring the whistled tune by The Rolling Stones behind me. I was almost at a 180º angle, clawing at the carpet with my fingernails, scooping at dead bodies and tangled entrails to pull myself away from the monster.

Well, the good Lord is gonna ring your front doorbell

The thing skipped towards me as though it were the easiest thing in the world.

"I don't want to kill you, Charlie," it said. "You're the only one who saw me when I was just a baby. We're connected, Charlie boy."

Charlie boy... But that's...

THAT'S WHAT I CALL YOU! The voice was enraged, screaming at me to ask it how it knew that name, how it dared to steal his name for me.

But I knew.

"You can't kill me..." My voice was a low whimper. The pills, the anxiety, the voice in my head thrumming in my ear and giving me orders. I swallowed hard at the question I felt rising in my throat. I turned to face the abomination, my whole body trembling, and asked, "Are you real?"

It looked at me and tilted its head, which seemed to merge with its shoulder in a fluid-like state.

"*I'm* killing everyone, aren't I?" I asked. "It's me. You're just... another fracture in my mind."

The entity laughed. If it'd had a belly, it would have been a full belly laugh. If it had tear ducts, they would have leaked. Even so, it wiped at its eyes as if to rid them of laughter tears.

"No, Charlie," it said. "You are crazy, but you're not *that* crazy. I'm very much real, and I very much, as you say, *killed* everyone. I need them. It's like fuel. When I came on board, I was weak. I hid."

Hiding inside the old woman.

"I gathered strength to grow. Sucked out their soul energy. Well, from those who still had the soul energy I require. The others, well... sorry about all the mess."

The people turning to dust, the people exploding. It was about their souls, about the creature's hunger.

"And I watched you, Charlie," he continued. "I watched you watching me." There was affection there. It came toward me again, lifted me from the carpet, and held me by the neck at an odd angle so I could see straight into its eyes.

"Why didn't you leave when you got stronger?" I asked.

"Why should I leave? You still haven't figured it out." The creature's stare seemed to see beyond me, somewhere in the distance, in an imagined future it was moving towards. "You haven't figured out what *we* can have."

"Wh—"

"Join me, Charlie."

JOIN HIM, CHARLIE!

"Nobody will ever look at you like you're less than—ever again."

NOBODY WILL DARE!

The monster's grip on my neck loosened. It was sure I was going to say yes. As a part of me struggled to shout my agreement with all that made me human, Rachel appeared in the distance, clutching a seat and pulling herself forward.

"Charlie!" she cried. "Charlie!"

She had something around her torso. A life jacket. She was getting ready to take her chances, just like I had. Except that if I joined with the entity, I wouldn't need to. I'd live forever as one with this disgusting—*beautiful*—thing.

"Charlie, don't!" Rachel screamed, pulling herself towards me.

The monster didn't notice her, didn't flinch or try to tell her to stop talking. It stared at me, daring me to answer.

"I..."

"Yes?" It smirked.

"Don't, Charlie!" Rachel begged. "Please!"

"I... can't." I looked away, and the abomination shrieked. There was less anger and more disappointment. Its lips moved as if to ask me why. As if to negotiate or plead. It threw me across the aisle, and my body splintered as I crashed into the seats.

Rachel came to me, her hands cold and gentle and trembling as she helped me up. We looked over at the monster, who stared at me curiously.

"We have to go," Rachel said. "If we jump from the rear exit, behind the wings and the engine, we have a chance."

I stared at her, shaking my head. "There is no chance," I replied. "We're dead. Even if we survive this, that *thing*"—I pointed—"will take everyone."

She grabbed my shoulder and spun me to face her. "We're over water, Charlie. The captain thinks we have a chance. But we have to go now!"

I saw movement over her shoulder—someone in a pilot's uniform. The co-pilot, who'd been safe and sound in the cockpit this whole time. He was young and looked like he was about to crumble into pieces, but he moved towards us.

"Thank god," he said, "you're alive! Look, we have a chance if we—" He saw the monster. His knees buckled.

"I know," I said. "Rachel told me."

His eyes didn't move from the abomination, who still watched me. The voice was yelling at me to join it, that I was making a mistake, that *we* deserved this. Wanted this. Needed this. After everything, it was our chance. It was our only hope.

Daring to look away from the monster, the co-pilot said, "We need to go now."

I nodded, and we made our way to the rear exit. For whatever reason, the entity was neutral, just watching us like it was a game. I looked back a few times, but it hadn't moved. The curious expression hadn't shifted, either.

As the plane tilted into a deeper nosedive, we reached the rear exit. The co-pilot released the seal and began turning the wheel to open the door.

"Hold on," he shouted at me. "When this opens, it could suck us out."

"Don't we want that?" I asked.

He shook his head hard for emphasis. "No! We need the initial burst of wind to equalise the pressure, then we can control our jump better."

Control the jump... This was crazy. It was all crazy. Crazier than I'd ever been.

I held onto the nearest thing bolted down and wrapped my arms around it. Rachel did the same. She closed her eyes, muttering some kind of prayer, and I hoped like hell it would work. I hoped she made it out of here and back to her ex-wife so they could repair their damaged marriage.

Aiden.

I wanted to see him again, but I didn't deserve that. I had to die; there was no two ways about that. He'd be better off. The world would be better off.

A gust of wind, intense and loud, filled my ears, sucked at my lungs, and I felt my grip loosen. The co-pilot had strapped himself to a railing somehow, and I realised he'd cut a seatbelt from a nearby chair and tethered himself. I hadn't seen him carrying a knife, but it didn't matter. The three of us were safe.

"Go," he said, waving me over. "You first."

"No." I thumbed over to Rachel. "Her first."

The co-pilot looked over my shoulder and frowned. "Who?"

I turned around. Rachel was stumbling over to me. I grabbed her hand and pushed her forward. "She goes first."

Swallowing, the co-pilot glanced away and then back to me. "Sir... there's nobody there."

SESSION #22

St Vincent's Hospital, Psych. Ward
16 April 2025
Patient: Charles M. Reed
Referring Psychologist: Dr R Schwarz
Consulting Psychiatrist: Dr J Mathis

THE MORE I TAKE notice, the more I see the empty spot in people's eyes. Like they're incomplete. I'm sure it's Charlie's influence, Charlie in my head. Nevertheless, a small part of me does wonder. Where *do* myths come from, anyway? Are they really mere stories, or are there parts of this world only a few of us see? Certainly, Charlie might fit that profile. His delusions are the only consistent thing about him. Other Charlie, too, seems to believe in the existence of doppelgängers.

While alters share a mind, that often doesn't mean they share a belief system. It is curious. Even more curious is that I have now seen multiple people with this gap. No genetic defect can explain it. I searched. When I visited Charlie today, I noticed seven staff members with that spot in their eyes. The void, I have started calling it. Something else was different, too. The way they moved was… off. Like they were getting used to themselves, the way crash victims do when they learn to walk again.

It isn't appropriate for me to divulge what I've seen to Charlie—either of them—and so in our session, when he asked, I changed the subject.

The following is an account of the session, based on my audio recording and personal reflections:

"You've made a lot of progress this last week," I said. "Let's focus on that."

Charlie nodded, though I could tell he was distracted. His eyes darted left and right, as though he expected someone else to be in the room. I reminded myself that his treatment here was not to "cure" him but only to ensure he was not a danger to himself or others. It was becoming increasingly more likely that the real Charlie was the dominant personality and that Other Charlie was receding into the background.

In fact, it was day 5 without him emerging. I believed this was perhaps the most significant progress we'd made, and Charlie seemed generally happier, which was why his behaviour caught my attention.

"What's wrong, Charlie?" I asked.

He held his breath before letting out a deep sigh. "Doctor Mathis, I know you don't believe me. But none of the staff are real anymore. I'm… I'm scared."

"Not real?"

Nodding, he bit at his fingernails. "They've all been replaced. I don't know how many people are left." He searched my eyes and gave a relieved smile.

"The void in their eyes?" I asked.

"Void? That's what you call it?" Charlie looked hopeful. "You've seen it too?"

I cleared my throat. "What would you do if you saw one of these doppelgängers on the street?"

Charlie reflected for a moment. "I think I'd run away. They want to take the planet; they want everyone. I'd hide."

The way he spoke, the way he looked at me, the way his shoulders retreated a little. I believed him. I believed he was scared, too. Scared, but not dangerous.

"Is Other Charlie still there?" I asked.

As Charlie spoke, I made notes in my pad, the scrawl of ink against paper scratching at my nerves. No, Other Charlie hadn't made any appearances. No, Other Charlie wasn't whispering anymore. No, Other Charlie was asleep.

"Well, I think if we continue to monitor your medication, and with frequent therapy, we can keep it that way," I told him.

Charlie's eyes lit up. "I'm going home?"

Nodding, I shuffled some papers, closed my notepad, and leaned in to Charlie. "You're a nice person, Charlie. This version of you. Remember that, okay?" He drew his lips in to stave off tears. "Aiden loves you. Remember that, too."

It was a short session, but I believe it was all that was needed.

<u>Recommendation</u>: Patient, Charlie M. Reed, is to be released effective immediately. His treatment shall continue with Doctor Rachel Schwarz, with a medication review undertaken by me every 6 months.

TWENTY-FIVE

Doctor Rachel Schwarz.

I stared into her eyes, and she stared back, sadness filling me. The co-pilot was right: she wasn't there. She had never been there, not on the plane.

"I don't—"

"You *do* understand," she said, her imaginary hair flicking in the wind.

While I stared at the person only I could see, the co-pilot muttered a curse word and jumped out of the plane.

"But you've been on the plane the whole time," I said. "People saw you, talked to you."

She gave a sad smile. "No, Charlie, they didn't. Think about it."

The way she seemed to melt into the chair, the way people had moved straight past her. When I'd introduced Rachel to April and April hadn't responded. The weird look she'd given me. The way people had treated me when I called to Rachel for help. It all made sense now.

"Why?" I asked. "Why are you here? Why didn't I recognise you?"

As the wind gushed around me, thrashing at my ears, the voice laughing at me again, Rachel touched a soft hand to my cheek. "I'm here because you needed me. Your mind, Charlie, is a complex thing. You see what you want to see, and you recognise what you want to. You needed me, but if you recognised me, it would have been too painful. If you consciously remembered what you'd done, it would have destroyed you. So Other Charlie blocked that out and behaved like I was someone new—a friend."

"A friend? But I... I killed you."

"I'm just your version of her," Rachel said. "To help you when you needed it. To believe you when nobody else would."

The tears came without warning, flinging off my face into the wind. My hair flicked across my eyes as I cried, and I turned away from Rachel. It was a pointless act. She wasn't there to begin with. The physical turning away from the figment still felt necessary.

"I'm sorry." I heaved the words like they were the last I would ever speak. My vocal cords caught in my throat, my chest ached, but I repeated the words until I couldn't talk anymore. She'd tried to help me—the real her—and I'd attacked her in her office. I knew somewhere deep inside that I'd done it, but the voice had protected me and made it disappear. It had sheltered me from the truth, like it always did.

Looking down at my hands, I begged for it not to be true. I couldn't have; I wouldn't have taken a life. She was human, not one of *them*. The voice was quiet now, with no laughing or taunting or teasing. I was all alone in there, with the wind rushing through me, into my bones.

"I'm... a... monster," I whispered through my tears. I turned to face the creature. Ready for it to take me, to rid the world of all that I was and the evil inside me.

Except it was gone. I scanned the plane for it.

"You know where it's gone," Rachel said, and motioned with her chin out the door.

Moving closer to the edge of the door, the tips of my shoes hanging over the edge, I gripped the railing the co-pilot had been strapped to and looked out. In mid-air, the monster hovered, and I could see its form loosened and tangled around the co-pilot. His legs were fighting to get free, but the entity was too strong. It had turned some to dust and had exploded others, but this? This was new.

"What's it doing?" I asked.

Rachel didn't respond.

I kept watching and grimaced as the monster constricted its body around the co-pilot, like a boa, squeezing until the skin split apart, his insides spilling to the ocean below. Fish food.

"There really is no way to stop it," I said, "is there?"

Glancing at the spot where Rachel had been, I saw the space empty. She was gone. Just like all the other times when I really needed her. She'd told me she was here because I needed her, but that wasn't true. I needed her now, and she'd abandoned me.

I haven't, the voice said. *I never will.*

The abomination lingered over the scene, and I realised the only one left, apart from me, was the pilot. If she was going to make it off alive, I had to distract the monster. It wanted me, so perhaps I could give myself to it and take its attention for long enough that the pilot could get out alive.

Returning to the plane, my enemy burped. I knew it didn't need to, that it was practicing being human. It gazed over me with a knowing expression. I couldn't escape. It knew that. What it didn't realise was that I no longer wanted to. The moment the truth of Rachel's death was revealed to me was the final straw. I was a killer. I was a fucking murderer. Not Other Charlie. Me. I was no hero; I had to stop pretending to be. No, there would be no getting off the plane for me. I was going to die right here, and that was perfectly fine with me.

I just had two things left to do before I killed myself: distract the monster so the pilot might live and do something good in my final moments, and phone Aiden. Say goodbye. Make sure he knew he deserved better than shitty little me.

"You want me to join you?" I called over the wind. "Come get me!"

The sharpened drumstick wouldn't kill it. But it would inflict pain now that the monster was more solid. It could help me buy time for the pilot. She hadn't come out with the co-pilot, which meant she was still in the cockpit. I had to stay at this end of the plane and ensure that there was a clear route for the pilot to take. If she even wanted one.

I was guessing she'd do whatever it took to survive, to be the only one who made it, and not abide by the stupid rule of going down with the proverbial ship. In any case, there was nobody left to save, and I dared to assume she knew that.

Dropping to my back, I slid down the plane, now at a full nose-dive, toward the creature. I had a plan, but it was perhaps the shittiest plan I'd ever had. Get near the monster. Rush to the next aisle. Beeline back to the rear. Repeat. Use the limbs and luggage and whatever I could to impede it.

IT CAN FUCKING LEVITATE, YOU IDIOT. The voice came back to life inside me. *YOUR PLAN IS FOR SHIT.*

"What would you do?" I asked as I grabbed hold of one of the chairs. Pulling myself up, using the back of the chairs as footing, I raced to the far aisle, the abomination on my back, laughing.

I KNOW GAMES, the voice told me. *I'M GOOD AT THIS.*

The voice was right. I wasn't a game player, but the voice had impersonated me; it had pulled my strings like a puppet master. I needed it now more than I needed anything else in my life. Except

Aiden. My heart skipped a beat as I thought about all I was throwing away. I could have a life with him. I needed to get off the plane.

No, I thought. *I don't deserve it. I'm a killer.*

The voice begged me to let it take over. The last time it took over... I couldn't think about that. I needed to stay focused.

Lunging over a chair, I hit the aisle with a thump and slid through the debris of bodies, blood, and internal organs. The wetness of livers, hearts, and lungs propelled me like a slippery slide into Hell.

The enemy laughed at me, called my name in a slow drawl, and asked me where I was going. Yelled at me that I was going to die if I didn't trust myself to it; didn't give my mind and body—and soul?—to it.

My legs hit the captain's cabin, and my ankles bounced, sending spikes of pain through my Achilles tendons. Clenching my jaw, I focused on the task at hand. Get the captain out alive. Do one good thing before I die.

Just one good thing.

"Captain!" I cried, but the wind and the sound of the engines collapsing on themselves drowned my voice. "Captain, we have to get out of here!"

How? The voice, calm and cool, asked in my ear. *How, Charlie?*

"I don't know, I don't know!" I screamed. "Captain!"

The creature placed a hand on my shoulder, and I spun to see it floating again. I was going to die without doing one good thing for another person. The monster smiled with those yellowed, twisted teeth, and even as I plunged the drumstick into its chest, I knew it was no good.

"I'll give you one last chance, Charlie," it said. "Join me. We can be so much better... together."

"Why?" I asked.

WHO CARES! the voice answered.

"Why do you want me? Why am I so important?"

Again, the monster smiled, and the calm I felt sent a chill down my spine. "Because we're the same, Charlie. We're—"

The plane rocked again, a high-pitched sound drowning out the last of the monster's words. I fell backwards, and with the plane in a nosedive, my back smacked hard against the aisle, and my head collided with the corner of a chair.

Blood ran through my hair, and I blinked through the surprise of the pain. I took a moment to realise what had happened; what was going to happen. My eyes started to blur as I saw the captain open the door to the cabin and peer out.

Through the haze, I saw the enemy's face light up at the prospect of another body to devour. The captain slammed the door shut, but the thing travelled straight through it. My head felt heavy; my eyes lost focus. I heard the scream, cut short as the entity weaved its way through the captain's body.

"No," I whispered. "Please... "

YOU CAN'T SAVE ANYONE, CHARLIE.

As my eyes grew heavier and the monster returned, I saw pieces of the captain dangling from the controls, blood painted across the windscreen. There was no blue sky. No nothing. Just red.

My phone buzzed in my pocket.

In the few seconds I had left before I was to die, I looked at my phone.

AIDEN

I forgive you, Charlie.

For everything.

But he signed the paperwork… I read the messages again, each time another came through.

AIDEN

I'm not filing the divorce papers. I love you.

The blood pooling out of my head shrouded my vision further, and I wiped it from my eyes to reread the messages. The last three words felt like a lie, but I wanted so much to believe them. I wanted to believe he could love someone like me.

After fantasising about stabbing him with a wine glass.

After refusing to make love to him.

After…

After everything.

I love you... I tried to type back, my unsteady fingers pressing the wrong keys. I couldn't get the message to him. My eyes fought to stay open. The creature watched me, its eyebrows furrowed in an expression of sadness.

"How will you spend your last moments, Charlie?" it asked.

Ignoring the monster, I raised the phone to my face. "Call... Aiden," I muttered.

Through the gushing wind and the faltering engines chugging and whirring, the phone still heard me. The screen changed, Aiden's face filling my blurred vision as the phone tried to connect a call.

"Poor Charlie," the thing said.

"Charlie?" Aiden's voice came through, and I put the phone to my ear.

I shed a tear at the concern and fear in the way he said my name. "Aiden, I'm sorry."

"Charlie," he said, "whatever you've done, we can fix it."

"No," I wheezed through tears. "You know what I did. I killed her."

"You didn't mean to," Aiden said. "Look, when you land, we can sort this all out. I promise."

"We can't."

"We can. We will. Charlie..." Aiden paused, and I heard a heavy sigh. "Charlie, don't do this."

I couldn't be sure what he meant. My brain was slowing down, and the entity was prodding at my face like it wanted to taste me. Our eyes met and it wiped at my tears. Licked the salty water off its fingertip.

"Don't do what?" I asked.

"Don't do it. Just come home. For me. Whatever happens, I will be with you."

"Aiden, don't do—"

The monster slapped the phone away from me and crawled up onto my belly. I felt its gelatinous body perched on my chest, the heaviness of the blobby flesh on me as it thinned out to envelop me.

"Aiden..." I stretched for my phone, but it was well out of reach. "I'm sorry."

"Yes," the abomination said, nodding its head as its figure began to change again, "you are *always* sorry. But you don't have to be."

I gazed into its eyes, searching for the meaning. If the monster truly did see me, truly did care for me, it would let me die. It would explode into me, the way it had done all the others. It didn't need to torture me with the pain of living on. Not after what I'd done.

"We can be so much more," it said. It had told me that earlier, and I hadn't known what it meant then, either. But the way it said those words felt profound. Like the creature knew something I didn't.

"What..."

"We can be *everything*."

My eyes went back to the phone, hoping Aiden had heard the exchange, but the screen was dark. I tried to activate another call. I needed to tell Aiden I loved him before the plane collided with the earth.

The line was dead, and I'd never get to say those words again.

As my eyes closed, I saw the thing shifting its appearance once more. The curves of its head rearranged themselves. The lengths of its fingers and the shapes of its torso all changed.

Into me.

Behind the new me, something else. I blinked to make sure it was actually there, and I laughed when what I saw waved at me.

The little girl from the airport.

TWENTY-SIX

Staring into my own face, I saw the pain I wore. I saw what Aiden saw every time he looked into my eyes: the emptiness, the apathy, the darkness behind every expression.

The diagnoses I walked around with.

The paranoia that the barista or the shop attendant or the bus driver would recognise that there's something inherently wrong with me. That I can never be like everyone else.

YOU DON'T WANT TO BE!

"I do want to be," I whispered.

"I know you do, Charlie," the abomination replied.

For the first time since I'd awoken, I looked around. We were in the cockpit, the windscreen having been wiped from the inside, just enough for the enemy—the other me—to see into the blue sky beyond.

"Why didn't we crash?" I asked, feeling the back of my head. The bleeding had stopped, though I couldn't fathom why.

"I absorb the knowledge of everyone I consume," it said. "I know how to fly a plane."

"You saved me?" I asked.

It nodded. "It's not altruism," he said in my voice. "I still need you."

I stared at him again. It was hard not to think of this thing as a "him" when we shared a face. The voice was laughing at me, telling me there were three Charlies now.

HE CAN TAKE THE BLAME FOR YOUR CRIMES!

I thought about that as I looked at the monster before me. It was true enough. When we landed, I could send the police to him, and he'd take my place in prison. The thought made me smile, and the thing mimicked it.

"It won't work, Charlie," he said.

I'd forgotten he could read my thoughts.

"I can just change into someone else," he continued.

"But you want to be me," I said.

He nodded. "I need a permanent form." He turned away from the blue sky and looked at me.

His eyes were like mine.

Except—

"Tell me one thing," I said, my breaths heavy and long. "Are you a doppelgänger?"

He held my gaze for a few seconds, the empty spot in his eye taking my attention, and sighed. "Poor Charlie," he said. "You really have no idea." He paused for a moment to see how I'd react. "You were right all along. Something is happening on the ground. People are being replaced."

I opened my mouth to ask what he meant, to get the answers I'd killed for, when he picked up the radio—slick with the captain's remains—and cleared his throat.

"Cleared to land," he said, and winked at me. "We're almost home free, Charlie."

Nodding, I sat back in the chair, wondering when he would take me. Having my body wasn't enough. He needed me, in my entirety. My knowledge, my brain. My memories.

Aiden was the most prominent memory I had, but something about his messages and phone calls wasn't right. He knew about the thing on the plane. He knew what it wanted. When I'd left him at home, he'd been human. He wasn't one of *them*.

I looked toward the sky, only seeing a smattering of blue among the still-dripping blood. It reminded me of all that had happened on the plane and how it could all have been avoided if people had listened to me. If they'd heeded my warnings instead of chaining me to the chairs.

And the little girl.

She wasn't here, on this plane. Yet, she was here, in my eyes. She'd waved at me, flashed a toothy grin. Why was she here? Who was she? When I'd seen her at the airport, she'd been unfamiliar. Her father, too. The whole family.

Yet, she was here, and something about her…

Gazing around the cockpit, I saw footprints in the blood-stained floor. Mine and the monster's. Two sets that looked exactly the same.

She wasn't IN HERE, Charlie!

The voice was right. She'd been on the other side of the door, not a care in the world. She wasn't here. She couldn't have been. But I'd seen her for a reason. I knew that, too. I'd noticed them at the airport. They'd been important then.

She was important now.

The luggage.

I fought the urge to ask the voice what he meant, worried the creature would read my thoughts or hear my voice. The luggage? No, I had noticed the passports in his pocket. The way the girl had tugged at her dad's shirt and pointed at me.

Why did she do that? I wondered.

WhY Do YoU care NOW?

That was a good question, too. The better question was: why did she appear to me just as the monster slapped my phone away? Why had it done that?

"You aren't ready," he said, my thoughts as transparent as his body used to be.

"How long until we land?" I asked.

"Not long," he replied.

I swallowed hard. The plane was safe now, but I wasn't safe, and somehow, nothing had changed. Except that I had been given a second chance to tell Aiden I loved him and how sorry I was.

To see him one more time.

That thought was new, and I embraced it. I wanted to see him again. Even if I ended up in prison—where I probably should be after what I'd done to Rachel—I could still have a chance to be with Aiden.

He'd said as much on the phone. He wasn't giving up on me, and now that the plane would land, I had a chance to make things right. If I could only get away from the monster.

"I... uh... I'm going to use the toilet." I feigned a small leg crossing to indicate the need to pee and stood from the co-pilot's chair. My head rushed, and I grabbed the door to steady myself. The monster nodded, cocky and comfortable in the knowledge that I had nowhere to go.

He was right; I couldn't escape. That wasn't what I needed to do right now, though.

I needed to get answers.

And in this plane, kilometres above the ground, there was only one place to get those.

Slipping out of the cockpit, the horizontal angle of the plane steadying my feet, I headed past the toilets and down towards the cargo hold. Last time I'd been in there with Rachel—*No*, I told myself, *I was alone*—I had barely had a chance to look around.

I had no reason to think I'd find answers in there, but as I headed to the cargo hold entry, the girl appeared again. Her eyes were full and human, yet something about her stare told me she was not what she appeared to be.

She waved at me again.

I waved back. "What's your name?"

She giggled and ushered me towards the cargo hold. Pointed down at the door. I lifted it, looking down the ladder into the cold black below.

"Can you tell me your name?" I asked, but she had disappeared.

Breathing hard, I climbed down the ladder, letting the darkness blanket around me, consuming me. My foot hit the floor, and I twisted to squint into the cargo hold. Something clanged in the distance, and my ears perked.

"Hello?"

SHHH, CHARLIE. LISTEN.

I held my breath, eyes wide, and listened as the voice instructed.

Another clang.

SOMEONE IS HERE, CHARLIE.

"That's impossible." Everyone was dead. I knew that. It was just me and the... thing.

SOMEONE IS HERE.

I heard it again, closer this time. Someone was moving around the cargo hold, their feet tapping against the metal flooring.

"Who's there?" I asked, firm and angry.

A STOWAWAY, CHARLIE. A STOWAWAY!

Still holding my breath, I inched forward. My eyes partially adjusted to the light, and I saw shadows stretching in different directions around the hold. Behind a tower of luggage, a lumpy shadow—someone hiding.

"I said, 'Who's there?'" I called, louder this time.

After a moment's pause, a figure emerged from behind the luggage, their tiny fingers clutching the plastic suitcases. A small face, shrouded in shadow, came halfway into view, with a trembling, pink, fleshy bottom lip.

The little girl.

Crouching to one knee, I whispered, "Are you okay?"

She shook her head but stepped further into view. She wiped at her face, bringing wet hands down to her sides. I moved closer, and she lifted her hands to warn me off. They were covered in dark red blood.

"How did you get here?" I asked.

She didn't answer.

"Please," I said. "I want to help you."

The girl looked at me, and I recalled her family. The disinterested parents, the passports. She had a brother, right? A boy was with them. Where was he?

"You never came back," she whispered. "You never... "

I frowned. "What do you mean?"

Her stare pierced me as she said, "You left me to die."

SESSION #11

St Vincent's Hospital, Psych. Ward
5 April 2025
Patient: Charles M. Reed
Referring Psychologist: Dr R Schwarz
Consulting Psychiatrist: Dr J Mathis

KNOWING THE DARK HISTORY of Charlie's family, I wanted to press him to confide in me what had happened the night his parents tried to sacrifice him. They clearly hadn't, but something had occurred that night to scar him—even more than everything else that had happened to him. This session will be dedicated to finding answers. Drawing connections, helping Charlie make peace with the events that led to his delusions.

Below is an account of my session with Charlie, based on my audio recording:

"Can you tell me what happened that night?" I asked.

"I already told you," Charlie said. "Well, the other me told you. I don't like to speak about… that night."

"The sacrifice," I said, nodding. "You said the AFP came out of the woods and saved you from… I have it in my notes from Doctor Schwarz." I flipped through some paper until I saw a highlighted annotation. "Ah, here it is. The Church of Our Fallen Father. Who—or what—did they worship again?"

"Qarin," Charlie mumbled, a tear dripping from his eye. Just one, and I knew he was trying as hard as he could to keep from breaking down entirely.

"This… Qarin," I confirmed. "Your parents tried to sacrifice you to this entity, but you escaped."

Charlie nodded but avoided my eyes.

"Is that all that happened?" I asked. My voice was low and soft, assuring him this was a safe space. I made eye contact with him so he could see my eyes were still human. It was a strategic move, though I admit I was starting to see more and more people with that void in their eyes.

"There was… something else."

I waited for him to continue, but he stopped. The signs of Other Charlie began—the convulsing of the shoulders, the slight shift in how he held himself.

"Can I speak to Charlie, please? The real Charlie?" I asked. I tried to contain my annoyance, but Other Charlie was a keen reader of body language.

Other Charlie smirked. "You get me. Deal with it."

I sighed. "Okay, can you tell me what else happened that night?"

"I could." He frowned. "But you need to stop saying *he* is the real Charlie. I'm real too."

"If you're real, then he's the alter."

"We're both real." Other Charlie shrugged.

"Who experienced the events of the sacrifice in 1994?" I asked.

"We both did." He smirked. "We're always
both here."

I nodded and made a note, the scratch
of the pen sounding louder than my own
heartbeat. "So," I said, "tell me what
Charlie can't say. What really happened?"

Other Charlie leaned back and slung an
arm over the back of the chair. "Well, you
know *most* of it. The folks strung me to
a tree and started some fucked-up ritual.
And the AFP really did come and save me.
What he didn't tell you, and what probably
isn't in those notes of yours, is that I
wasn't alone."

Holding in a gasp, I locked eyes with
Other Charlie, my expression urging him
on.

"I… *We*… had a sister."

I searched the files on my desk for any
mention of a sister. "Charlie, I—"

"Like I said, it ain't in the notes.
Before the cops came, my parents—" Even
Other Charlie bit his lip, making me think

what happened was truly abhorrent. "They offered her to Qarin."

"Offered?"

He glared at me. "I loved my sister. We both did. She was always there with us. In the basement. At the rituals. We were twins, two parts of the one whole. And I couldn't save her."

I noted that Charlie said twins, rather than triplets. Two, not three. There was a nugget there, a tacit acknowledgement of the roots of his dissociative identity. I chose to ignore it in that moment, to focus on the trauma of that night. "You were chained to a tree."

"I should have helped her."

"How could you have helped her, Charlie? You were a child, strapped to a tree, surrounded by… these Qarin worshippers."

"BECAUSE I GOT OUT!" he screamed. Spittle hit my face as he yelled again and again, the muscles in his neck almost tearing from the skin. "I GOT OUT, I GOT OUT, I GOT OUT!"

"Charlie, please," I said, holding a hand up to calm him down. I did some small breathing exercises, and Charlie began to mimic my rhythms.

"One of the chains on my wrist was rusted, and I'd had a previous injury to my hands from one of their… parties. They came at us in their masks, forcing us to drink their wine and to eat their fucking bread. To pray to their god. Qarin, Qarin, our Fallen Father, he will be reborn." His voice trembled. The words were spat out like rancid meat. I put a finger up and guided his eyes toward it to refocus him. "My thumb pops right out of its socket." He shrugged like it was obvious. "I slipped out of the chain and ran."

Nodding, I made more notes about survivor's guilt, which would be useful for a more complete profile of Charlie's psyche. This might have been the piece I was missing.

"She begged me to come back," Other Charlie continued. "As I ran from the horde of cultists, I told her I'd be back. But I… I never went back."

I saw Other Charlie vanish then, and the real Charlie slunk back into his body, sliding down the chair in a mess of tears and regret.

"Charlie," I said, "you were a boy. You were in a terrible, violent situation. Not a child alive would have had the courage to turn back. It's not your fault."

"I never saw her again," he muttered. "Not even afterwards. She's just gone."

He repeated those last words several times until, finally, he stopped talking. He became unresponsive, and I knew the session was over. I'd gotten what I came for—a missing piece of Charlie and his delusions—but it had come at a price.

Charlie had a sister whom he'd abandoned to Qarin worshippers. She'd been sacrificed, which to a child's mind likely meant she was gone forever. No hope of an afterlife or a spirit or anything. It explained why he didn't see her the way he saw his parents. They weren't dead. They were in prison for life. To Charlie's mind, though, the threat they prompted had not ended. They were the last vestige of family that he had, yet they were also gone.

Enter Other Charlie and the obsessions with body thieves. People who might be able to give him a sense of family without the burden of evil—the missing part of the eye is the missing evil.

Charlie is a complex patient, and while today is a breakthrough, there is a lot of work to be done.

<u>Recommendation:</u> Increase anxiety medication and continue therapy as planned.

TWENTY-SEVEN

"You left me to die," she said again.

"I... I'm sorry," I said.

It was true. Somewhere in the back of my mind, I remembered her. I remembered running through the woods, screaming, begging for my life. She'd been chained to a tree, same as me. But an incident with the hammer—Dad punishing me for not finishing my verses—left me able to dislocate my thumb at will.

I hadn't gotten far before a figure clad in black, carrying a semi-automatic weapon, grabbed me from the dirt and pushed me through to a crowd of police officers.

"My sister," I had said, but I was too late.

I never went back for her. I never even tried.

And I was alive. She was dead.

A policewoman had told me not to look when they carried her body, already sagging, wrapped in a body bag, to the ambulance. I had looked, though. I had looked, and I had seen the zipper and the black bag, and I had known she was inside.

I'm here for you, Charlie. The voice was comforting and warm, and I sipped the cocoa someone had given me. Wrapped a police blanket around me until it was as tight as my sister's body bag. I looked up at the cop. Saw the sad smile, the glint in her eye under the moonlight. I couldn't tell then if it was the dim glow of the moon or whether there was a gap in the eye, a void.

"We're going to keep an eye on you, son," the cop said, rubbing my shoulder like a mother comforting her child. "A real good eye on you."

"You left me to die," my sister said, drawing me from the memory.

"I couldn't do anything," I replied. "I was a kid."

"It's okay, Charlie," she said. "I want to help you."

"How?" I asked.

"That thing up there, in the cockpit, wants to take you away. It wants everything that makes you... you." Her eyes drew upwards in the general direction of the cockpit. "You can't let it take you. There have been too many taken already."

"The doppelgängers?" I asked.

She nodded. "Whatever you want to call them, they're here. That thing is yours. It's connected to you. It's been watching you."

SHE'S LYING.

"Shut up!"

SHe Is LyiNG!

"Charlie," my sister said, "it was watching you before you even got on the plane."

"What do you mean?" I asked, conscious that she was in my head, the way Rachel had been. And if she knew more, it meant I did too. But what she said next was like a gut punch.

"It's been watching you for years. Ever since that night."

—————

1994

Trees were always so innocent in the young boy's mind. Greenery swaying in the wind, dancing in the breeze, the crush of leaves like music. He liked to get outside, out of the basement. Anywhere but the basement.

He clasped his sister's hand, feeling her sweaty palms against his own as they were led by the shoulders into the woods behind their house. He and his sister had never been past the tree line, the spot in the yard where the woods began and the dirty grass ended. The boy had chanced a step once, feeling vines and thorns on his bare feet before pulling back with a liberated smile.

"Mummy and Daddy will find out," his sister had whispered. "And they'll take us *both* back to the basement."

The boy had breathed through his nose, all the way into his chest, and his sister had breathed out. Opposite in some ways, the same in so many others. He nodded and reached out a hand. She took it, and it felt like home. It felt like his own hand.

Now, as they were pushed along in white nightgowns, thorny crowns digging into their scalps, her hand still felt like his own. Her heart pulsing in her veins matched the rhythm of his own, and while the tree branches swayed with a hushed silence, the boy thought of being a bird. Thought of flying away, looking down on the world, knowing he didn't have to be with them.

"Just the three of us," he whispered.

His sister eyed him. "Is he here again?"

"You weren't given permission to speak," their father's voice came from above them.

They exchanged glances and focused forward. His sister stepped on a stone and winced, putting a hand over her mouth to stifle the yelp. The boy tightened his grip on her other hand, offering his strength and resolve. It was usually the other way round, and as she limped on, he wished the pain could reside within him instead.

"Walk," their mother spat and pushed them on. "Don't speak, you vile cunts."

"Yes, Mummy," we said together.

She clipped us around the ears, the sting worsened by the thorns latching onto our scalps. "I said don't fucking speak."

Their mother spat again, a wad of thick transparent goo bubbling on the boy's shoulder. He ignored it, used to being spat on.

It was better than what their father did to them, the liquid he'd spat at them. To get them "ready" for the night.

This night.

Neither child knew what was to come, but he could tell the trees knew. They always knew; the way they stopped moving and stood still to watch. Something was brewing, and it was due soon. The boy gulped as they came to a clearing. He wasn't brave enough to look back to see how far from their house they'd travelled. It had felt like the journey was twenty, maybe thirty minutes, but time had a funny way of changing itself when his mood was low. Time always disappeared when he and his sister were having fun. They played games in the shadows and made up stories and different worlds. Worlds where they were happy, where they could see what was beyond the front steps of their home—their prison.

Time often felt too slow, though, like when they were gagged and bound and when Father was naked in front of them. He tried not to think about that as the clearing came into full view. Wooden poles in the ground were alight with an orange flame, sending a glow through the space. They seemed to form a circle around a giant tree.

His sister elbowed him, a subtle, almost imperceptible move. Another game they'd practiced in the dark. The boy focused his eyes so that, even looking forward, his vision was trained to see out of the corners.

"What is that?" The nod of her chin and a half-frown formed the question. It was a code they'd started forming only a week earlier. A slight movement and a facial expression made a short sentence. Different combinations formed a language. The boy wished he could take credit for the idea, but it was *his*. The Other One, who came sometimes when their parents forced off their rags. The Other One, who had ideas of his own. The boy's sister had first told him of his existence when he'd blanked out for a few hours.

"Where do you go?" she'd asked.

"I fell asleep."

She'd shaken her head. "No, you were talking to me. Well, someone with your voice, in your body, but it wasn't you."

"Huh?"

"I can tell the difference because his face is different. It's the same, but... different."

"What's his name?" he'd asked, raising an eyebrow.

She'd shrugged. "He says he's you; he's here to help us. He doesn't chat to me the way you do, though."

"You've met him before?"

"He's always been with us," she'd said. "He told me not to say anything. Not until he was ready." She'd looked at him then, a deep stare into his eyes, searching. "I don't trust him like I trust you."

The boy didn't respond, and when his sister looked away, he closed his eyes to see if he could hear someone else inside him. His sister didn't lie to him. She was all he'd ever had, all he *would* ever have. If she said there was another boy inside his head, she meant it.

From that moment, they called him The Other One.

"What is that?" his sister asked, her chin pointing to the tree in front of them. He wished he knew what kind of tree it was; it was in a book somewhere, he was sure. Maybe one of the books his parents had burned in front of him, citing knowledge as the root of all evil.

He looked at the tree, at the symbol carved deep into the bark.

It was a star, like the ones in the sky, except with five points and lines crossing each other. He'd seen that symbol countless times, drawn onto the floor of the basement during Father's sessions and during the nights when Mother forced them to worship Qarin, letting Him into their souls.

The symbols beneath the star, though, were new. The boy couldn't make them out, not in the dim light. As their parents edged them forward into the middle of the circle, the symbols became clearer. Lines, simple lines, egg-like but split down the middle. Each set of lines was a mirror image of the other, on opposite sides of the star. In each of the half-eggs was a triangle towards the top, a short vertical line halfway, and a vertical line near the bottom. The most striking feature, though, was the squiggly line protruding from the top of the shape—thick at the point where it met the half-egg and thinning out as it collapsed over itself until it reached a fine point.

To the boy, the lines looked like half of a crudely drawn face. He imagined them together, but couldn't figure out what it was supposed to be. He felt a tap on his elbow and focused his eyes on his sister once more.

"The goat," her movements said. "From the magazine we saved. It's a goat's head."

He looked again.

She was right—as always.

He asked her what it meant with a small tug on his left ear—"*What*"—and folding all his fingers bar the middle two—"*Meaning*." She shrugged, taking in the fiery torches surrounding them.

"They should be here," their father mumbled. "Where is everyone?"

"Quiet!" their mother hushed him. Her tone was as venomous to him as it had always been to them.

He obeyed with a solemn, "My queen."

"Our Fallen Father has lain dormant for two thousand years. He can wait another few minutes. In the meantime,"—she spun the children around, her eyes piercing them until they looked away in fright—"get these cunts ready."

They swallowed at the same time, the combined gulp resounding in their ears as their father led them to the tree. He hadn't seen it before, but beneath the star and the strange, halved goat head were two ropes on the ground.

"Get the fuck over there," he spat, pushing them to their knees and forcibly yanking their hands apart. "Finally, we can be free of you."

"Daddy—"

His hand came fast to the boy's cheek before he could utter another syllable. "*Never* speak to me unless I invite it."

The boy looked away, tears stinging his eyes. His sister reached for him, and their father slapped her, too. Her dirty, greasy hair covered the red mark spreading across her cheek, and she stared at the man with hatred. No tears. Just that hate-filled stare.

One of the ways they were different, the boy noted, even in that moment. *She's stronger than me.*

While the boy collected himself, the burn of the slap fading a little, he let his father drag him to the tree, chains in hand. His sister stood, daring to move without being told she was allowed to. The boy blinked fast three times—*NO NO NO*—but she straightened her back and puffed out her chest.

"Leave him alone!"

Their mother laughed, a few feet away, her shrill sound joyless and threatening.

His sister moved closer to their father. The boy could see the terror and rage welling inside her. "Leave him alone!" She pushed her father, and he lost his footing for a moment. His hand came back again, the dull thud reverberating into the trees.

The silent, still trees.

She fell to the ground, casting a long shadow in the orange flames.

"It's okay," he said to her. "It's going to be okay."

She got to her feet again, and while their father tied the boy's hands and feet and wrapped his waist around the tree, he watched their mother calmly walk through the clearing toward his sister. She pushed down on the thorny crown until blood dripped down his sister's face and head. The girl cried and yelled and kicked, but their mother now had her by the hands.

"Fight all you want, cunt. Our Fallen Father is going to rise tonight, and then you'll be sorry you ever existed."

"It's okay," the boy repeated as their parents forced her into her ropes.

"Fuck you!" his sister spat.

He didn't even know where she'd learned that word. Turning to her brother, she said, "Let him out. He can help us."

Their parents stuffed oily rags into their mouths, and the boy had no way of asking how he could let *him* out. The Other One. How could he let him out, and how could he help?

"Ah," their mother said, turning away.

Figures in deep red hooded gowns began to emerge from the trees, a soft hum echoing through the clearing as they came together. Each held their hands just under their chest, one on top of the other, palm up. In their palms, a single wax candle, already lit with a thin thread of smoke snaking into the night air.

"Let us begin," their mother said, once the figures had formed a circle between the fiery torches.

The hoods came back to reveal faces. The children recognised some of the men from their father's parties. They remembered the way their manhood tasted, the way they'd hurt their bodies with glee and desire. Others they didn't know, but the emptiness in their eyes spoke volumes.

"For millennia, Our Fallen Father, Qarin, has lain below, awaiting his disciples—us—to bring him and his legion forth into the world. Into this *filthy* world where spawn like these two"—she spat—"are guided by Christian gods, Catholic gods, the gods of purity and innocence."

The group sneered.

Their father handed out goblets of wine and chunks of stale bread.

"We all know what this leads to," their mother continued. "We've seen it firsthand. The righteous zealots leading humanity into defeat, destruction, and death. Their 'gods' walking on fucking water can't save them; they can't stop the descent into the annihilation of humanity."

"Our Fallen Father, Qarin, offer us salvation," the group chanted, sipping wine and devouring their bread.

"We've seen the death of this planet, we've seen what their gods and their Jesus do—nothing! We've seen war and famine and more and more people on the street living in filth."

"Our Fallen Father, Qarin, offer us salvation."

The children's father emerged from the group, reached under his own gown, and revealed a mask. It, too, was of a goat's face, the star etched into the surface between the eyes. Their mother began the same procedure as she continued, "Qarin has sent us here. He, in His infinite wisdom, has shown me the way to our salvation. He turned me into a vessel, yes, my friends,"—her hands emerged with a mask and a knife—"for these sacrifices. My body was ruined, my penance for following the false god for all those years. Qarin saved me. He made love to me. He offered me his seed for the salvation of humanity."

"Our Fallen Father, Qarin, offer us salvation."

"Yes!" Her eyes connected with the boy, then the girl. "Yes! Qarin devoured my soul when He took me. He showed me the future. He showed me the sacrifices we must make to rebuild the world in His vision. To rebuild humanity for the better."

She walked towards the children, put on her mask, and held the knife out before her.

The boy tried to plead through the rag in his mouth, and he heard his sister do the same. While his eyes were on their mother, hers were on his. She was begging him for something.

Let him out.

That's what she'd said.

He can help us.

The Other One was different, she'd told him. He was someone else, living inside the boy. He could help. His sister had been so sure. Like always, he trusted her. In that moment more than any other, he trusted her.

Their mother shed her gown, a black velvet unlike the others' red, revealing her naked breasts and hairless vagina. The children looked away as she stalked toward them, the goat mask tilted with her head, her eyes black and shiny in the firelight.

"Qarin, oh, Benevolent one. Qarin, merciless devil. We invite you to this world. We invite you to rule, Qarin." She stood before the children, widened her knees, and let the blade fall between her legs, stroking at her thighs.

Their masked father joined their mother while the other figures stripped off their robes. The men were hard already, their flesh throbbing and leaking with excitement. The boy closed his eyes, praying for The Other One to come and save them.

The Other One, who was nowhere to be found.

When he opened his eyes, their father had replaced the long, sleek silver blade of the knife, his head bobbing back and forth between their mother's legs.

"Oh," their mother said, grabbing the hair of their father's head and pushing him deeper. "Qarin, I offer you my pleasure; I offer you the spoils of my cunt so that you may once again walk the earth, residing in the blood and hearts of all humans."

Their father stood now, his naked body glistening with sweat as he rubbed at his cock and inserted himself into their mother with a staggered, "My queen..."

"Qarin, accept my husband as your vessel." Their mother moaned as their father moved inside her. She stared right at her children as her orgasm bubbled under the surface. "Qarin is inside me. Yes, friends, he is coming. I feel him."

The men in the circle moaned with her as they stroked their cocks, some spilling early into the soil but not ceasing the motion. The women rubbed at their clits, knees shaking as they called for Qarin to enter the world; called for his legions to use them as vessels.

"Charlie." The boy heard his name, but he couldn't look away from the scene. He wanted to, but he was too scared. His mother would see him looking away and use that knife on him. His father would see and use his cock on him again.

"Charlie," the voice came again. It was his sister. She'd somehow removed the gag from her mouth. Her eyes pleaded with him when he looked at her. "Dislocate your thumb and run. Get help."

"I—" He was still gagged, but he tried to speak anyway.

"Now isn't the time," she said. "We're going to die unless you—*you*—get us out of here."

SHE'S RIGHT, CHARLIE BOY.

The voice was from inside him, and he trusted it. The Other One. He came!

CALL ME CHARLIE. BUT FIRST—YOUR THUMB.

The boy felt his thumb slip out of its socket. He was conscious of it happening, but wasn't in charge. The Other One—Other Charlie—was doing it.

And he let him.

"Qarin," their mother moaned and cried into the sky, "take me, Lord, make me your vessel once more." She gyrated as their father spasmed against her body, and they fell into the dirt as one. "Qarin... Qarin... you are my Lord. Tell me, O Lord, when to sacrifice these two vessels."

COME ON, CHARLIE BOY.

Her words echoed in the boy's mind, as did the new voice. Sacrifice. He and his sister were a sacrifice.

TIME IS RUNNING OUT!

His thumb was numb, hanging loose next to his fingers, and he slipped free of the bonds around his wrists. They fell to the ground. It was so easy. He smiled, but then there were knots around his waist, his ankles. He tore at the ones around his waist. His sister urged him on, her eyes wide, begging, and hopeful. One knot came loose, and the boy hurried to the next.

"Come on, Charlie!"

He moved faster, scrambling to loosen his ankles.

"Qarin!" their mother cried, white gooey liquid trailing down her thighs as their father spasmed in the dirt. He said something, but the words didn't make sense—they were not in English. "Qarin, I offer you these sacrifices!"

As she moved toward the children, Charlie eased out of the last knot and shook free. He looked to his sister, who shrieked, "RUN!"

He did.

"Come back for me!" Her voice was already in the distance, low under his own screams for help. "Come back for—"

His sister's voice disappeared, replaced by his mother's—"Get the cunt! He can't ruin this for us!"

All he could do was what his sister had demanded: run. And he did. He ran as fast as he could, the dirt and leaves and fallen sticks scratching at the soles of his bare feet. The pain spiked through him, but he ran.

A light pierced his vision, and something grabbed at him.

"Let me go, let me go!" he cried.

Someone in black, no face.

A DEMON, CHARLIE!

"Get away, demon!" he shouted, pummelling the figure's chest.

The figure pulled its mask off, the light atop it falling to the ground to reveal a kind, concerned expression. "I'm with the police, son. Come with me."

The words made sense, but they couldn't be true. The police? Here? Now? Who had called them? Other Charlie? The man took his hand, lifted him into his warm arms, and carried him away from his parents, from the Church of Our Fallen Father, and from—

"My sister... " he said.

As the policeman carried Charlie away from the scene, the boy saw a flash. It lasted only a fraction of a moment, but he knew he saw it. Inside the flash, thousands and thousands of objects.

THEY'RE HERE, Other Charlie said.

"I know," he replied.

"What's that, son?" the policeman asked.

The boy didn't respond. He stared as the objects vanished from sight.

All but one.

<hr>

NOW

"I remember," I whispered, "but why me?" A pause. "How are you here?"

My sister looked at me with a sad smile and wiped her bloodied hands on her torn dress. "Qarin attaches itself to whoever it's connected with," she said. "It's connected to *you*, Charlie."

"Wh—"

"It doesn't matter why," she told me. "Only you can stop it."

"So if I... " Charlie paused. "If I let it inhabit me, this will all be over?"

DO IT, CHARLIE BOY. LET QARIN SHOW US WHAT WE CAN BECOME.

"It's been waiting," my sister continued. Before I could ask, she said, "For you to be ready. That's why our parents did all those things. They needed to break us, to destroy our spirits, so that Qarin could enter you. It can't penetrate people with souls. That's why it could only penetrate certain people on this plane, but it couldn't hold their form because they weren't a match. It can only match permanently with you."

"That's why some people exploded?"

She nodded. "And people with hope, with love in their hearts... they turned to dust."

"No." I shook my head. "It doesn't make sense. Our parents... They were going to kill me like they killed you."

"Charlie, you were never going to be killed. You were to be the new vessel for Qarin. But you interrupted the ritual. You got adopted, you found hope and love, and Aiden. Qarin couldn't enter you. So, He's been waiting. Other doppelgängers found their corresponding bodies. You've seen them, with the gaps in their eyes. Almost perfect replicas, but not quite right."

It was too convenient. All the answers were being given to me on a silver platter. My dead sister was coming for a visit in my most dire hour of need. Telling me to let Qarin take me, telling me I was right all along, that I'm not crazy.

It doesn't make sense.

CHARLIE BOY, the voice teased. *CHAAAARLIE BOOOOY. IT MAKES PERFECT SENSE. YOU SAW THE FLASH OF LIGHT, THE OBJECTS—THINGS—INSIDE IT. THINK ABOUT IT, CHARLIE BOY. THE LIGHTNING ON THIS PLANE WAS EXACTLY THE SAME.*

"How are you here?" I asked.

My sister sucked her top lip inside her bottom one and breathed out while I breathed in. "I'm not."

"Then... "

"You know the answers, Charlie. You, Other Charlie, you've always known. You just needed a push. So... here I am."

I stared at her for a moment, considering. "What happens if I let this thing take me? What happens to me?"

Neither my sister nor Other Charlie answered me. Neither *could.* I was truly and completely alone, like I had been for my entire life.

Until Aiden came along.

"What happens to Aiden?" I asked.

Again, nothing.

"Charlie." The voice came from behind me, from the direction of the cockpit. "It's time. We belong together."

"Can I at least say goodbye to Aiden?" I pressed a hand to my heart, already knowing the answer.

And Qarin walked toward me.

TWENTY-EIGHT

As the creature—Qarin—walked toward me, I reached into my pocket. If I were to be erased, taken by this ancient entity, I could at least say goodbye to my husband.

The phone was slippery in my hand, but I clutched it as Qarin's face began to morph into my own, the bones reshaping with sharp cracks beneath his fleshy skin.

"Please," I said, holding the phone to my ear. "I will let you do whatever you want to me, but I need to say goodbye to Aiden."

Qarin paused, and Other Charlie snickered in my head. *SAY GOODBYE TO EVERYTHING, CHARLIE BOY. SAY GOOD-BYE TO ME, TOO. OH, THIS WILL BE GLORIOUS!*

I never understood that voice, its motivations, hopes, and desires. I never understood when it first appeared—*if* it first appeared or if it had always been there with me. I never understood so many things about myself.

But I understood Aiden.

His smile.

His laugh.

His arms around me.

The way he made me feel.

I pressed his contact picture in my Favourites list, and the phone began to ring. Qarin stared at me with my own eyes now, waiting, letting me have this last request. He licked at newly shaped lips, an intensity in his stare I never knew I was capable of.

"Charlie?" Aiden said. "Thank god, Charlie, I've been worried sick!"

"Aiden, listen to me, I—"

"There was a news story about a plane going down mid-flight. The airline said it was your flight; I thought you were... I thought... Oh, Charlie, are you okay? What's happening up there?"

"Aiden, listen to me." I choked back a tear as I looked at Qarin, stepping towards me again. He held out a finger and circled it in the air—*Hurry up, Charlie.*

"What's happening, Charlie? Why are you going to Perth? It's not a good idea to go back there!"

But I needed to go back; Schwarz had told me so. I had tried to get away, but it was all following me. The only way forward was to go home and face what happened to me. I tried to tell Aiden that, I tried to speak, but even though Other Charlie was silent—*Why is he silent now?*—I felt the pressure in my head. Sweat slicked my hands, and anxiety pulsed through me as Aiden repeated his question.

He sounded distant and far away, and I realised I'd dropped the phone to reach for my pills. Pills that were no longer there.

"You'll never need them again, Charlie," Qarin said, stepping closer again. "Not once we're joined."

Joined. Taken. Erased.

I grabbed the phone and pressed it to my ear. "Aiden, I love you."

He said something back, but I pressed the red phone icon, and the call disconnected.

"Will you erase me?" I asked.

Qarin took my hand in His.

"Will it hurt?" I asked.

Qarin breathed in, his chest filling with the scent of my sweat, tears, and the blood of the other passengers.

"What will I become?"

My heart pulsed; my body shook. Qarin clutched at my hands and drew me in, and I felt an incredible warmth as He, with arms like my own, embraced me.

CHARLIE BOY, Other Charlie broke his silence, *THIS IS JUST THE BEGINNING. WE'VE COME HOME.*

Home.

The way he said it, like Qarin was everything I'd ever wanted and needed, everything I had longed for, sent chills down my spine. I didn't want Him, didn't long for Him. I wanted Aiden, the warmth of *his* arms around me. The subtle smell of the ocean from his cologne as I breathed him in. The tickle of his beard on my neck as the space between us vanished.

WHEN WE JOIN WITH QARIN, WE'LL HAVE THE WORLD.

The world? And I remembered what Qarin had said earlier: "I want everything. I want the world, Charlie. And I will have it."

It wasn't about me at all. My sister was right—I was a vessel. Not once had I stopped to question what would happen to everyone else if Qarin were able to take me. Not once had I asked the most important question: What would Qarin do with the world? Regardless of the answer, it would not be good.

"You can't have it," I whispered.

"Charlie?" Qarin asked.

I pulled away from Him, whose eyes were blank. The irises hadn't formed properly, and the light was missing.

"Fuck you!" I slipped from his grasp, Qarin grabbing at me but catching only the fabric of my shirt. "I won't let you take it!"

NO CHARLIE! WE CaN HavE THe WHolE WORLD!

I slapped myself in the face to silence Other Charlie and raced for the stairs to exit the cargo hold. It was only me and Qarin, and I had to get away.

"Charlie," He called after me, "it doesn't have to be this way."

I was tempted to let Him take me, to let Him erase all the pain I carried with me. I almost gave in, almost let Qarin finish what my parents had started all those years earlier. As I gripped the metal stairs and forced myself up, back into the passenger section, I cried. Emotions were usually my enemy, sending me into fits and hallucinations, but now they were friends.

The anxiety warned me; the pit of my stomach dropping told me to get the fuck out of there, not to give up, and not to let Qarin or Other Charlie—or anything else—erase me.

Qarin's hand was on my ankle, pulling at me with a strength I'd seen but not felt until that moment. I kicked and kicked and spun onto my backside to kick again. I heaved the metal grille that led to the cargo hold with both hands and slammed it down onto Qarin's hand.

"Let me go!" I cried.

His grip loosened, and I squeezed free, crawling a few feet and grabbing at the seats to help me stand. On my feet, I searched for a way out. My mind went straight to the cockpit, but it offered no exit. I wasn't a pilot, and I couldn't land the plane.

Even if you did, I thought, *Qarin would land with you.*

"Charlie!" Qarin called after me, now in the passenger section.

We were face to face, the open emergency exit a few feet behind me. I turned to it and saw my sister standing by the edge, looking down. Her hair flailed and whipped at her face, but she was smiling.

"Charlie!" Qarin called again, His hand extended towards me.

He can't take me, I thought, *not permanently. Not unless I let Him.*

My sister reached out her hand, and I moved toward her. Took it. She felt like home, like all those years ago. We exchanged a look, the same look we had always given each other in the basement.

With a flick of her right index finger and a nod of the chin, she spoke to me in a language I'd almost forgotten. Our language.

"Okay," I said, and I stepped to the edge alongside her.

"Don't, Charlie," Qarin said.

I looked back at Him and smiled. "You're as powerless as I've always been," I said. "You can't take me. You can't finish the ritual. I will always have hope and love, and there's nothing you can do about that."

Qarin shifted back to his original form.

"You're not a god," I continued. "You're nothing without me."

My sister nodded her chin again—*Let's go.*

"And you will *never* have me."

Like all those years earlier at the edge of the woods, we held hands and stepped over the breach.

TWENTY-NINE

To die was preferable.

Despite everyone hating me and treating me like I'm crazy and dangerous—*YOU ARE A MURDERER, CHARLIE BOY*—to save everyone was the right thing. After what I'd done to Rachel, after what I'd sat by and watched Qarin do to every single person on the plane, I owed them. I owed everyone.

To die was preferable to letting Qarin take the world.

With my sister at my side—a manifestation or otherwise—was how I'd dreamed of dying since I was young. Every time my father held a party and ripped me apart, I dreamed of dying. Dreamed, fantasised, hoped.

Yet I'd lived, and I shouldn't have. I'd done too much damage. To Rachel. To April. To Aiden, who only hours earlier had wanted a divorce.

The wind was like a hurricane, rushing at my face until the skin was stretched and numb from the cold. My sister looked at me with that same smile she'd always given me, the smile that told me I'd be okay.

Sound disappeared, and I felt peace, watching the world beneath me grow bigger and bigger.

Even as the ground rushed up at me, I felt peace.

Even as Other Charlie screamed at me that I'd made a mistake, I felt peace. If he thought it was a mistake, it was definitely the right thing.

To die, to make sure Qarin could not use me as a vessel. That was the right thing to do. It should have happened a long time ago. I knew that deep down.

This is the best thing.

For me.

For the world.

My sister's grip vanished from my hand, and as I looked to where she had been, falling beside me, was Qarin.

"You thought it would be that easy?" He smirked.

Qarin was not falling. He didn't fall; he floated.

The peace I felt disappeared, and Qarin floated closer to me, embracing me the way he had on the plane.

"You can't have me!" I screamed.

His smirk remained as His face morphed into mine once more, His body melting into mine until I couldn't tell where I ended and he began.

"You can't take me," I said, my lips like melted wax as Qarin merged more and more into me.

"Not permanently," He replied. "But I can hold you long enough to get you to the ground."

"No!" I wanted to fight, wanted to punch and kick and get Qarin off me, but he was inside me now, swirling through my veins and my organs, finding the empty spaces between the synapses in my mind and settling there.

Pushing me aside until I was a passenger. Until I was a stowaway in my own body. In my own mind.

The ground rushed up, and I tried to close my eyes to brace for impact, but I couldn't. Qarin was in charge now, more in charge than Other Charlie had ever been. More than I had ever been. He wanted to see. He wanted to feel the impact of my bones against the earth, to feel the snapping of my limbs as we pummelled through the trees, breaching the canopy.

"Ready, Charlie?" Qarin asked.

READY, CHARLIE BOY?

The trees beneath grew larger and larger, and I was powerless to bring my hands to my face. I screamed and screamed, the noise only echoing through the corner of my mind that I now occupied. Even though I was not in charge, Qarin somehow let me feel.

I felt the branches as my body slammed into them, cracking my ribs, stabbing into my arms and legs; a wooden spike slicing my neck and tearing my stomach apart.

Thudding against another branch, tumbling through the tree towards the ground, my spine cracked and twisted, and as the ground rushed at my face, I felt something slam into my knee, sending a spike of pain through my legs and up my severed spine.

Finally, the ground smacked into my face, the force sending shockwaves through me and a resounding *CRACK* tearing at my skull and nose.

For a moment, I thought I was dead.

The pain told me I had, somehow, survived.

Qarin had made sure I would.

Lying there, on the ground, my body twisted and broken, I managed to breathe. It wasn't me, though. It was Qarin, sucking in lungfuls of air. It came in short bursts, tasting like blood. Parts of me I didn't know I had throbbed and swelled and ached and bled.

I'm dying, I told Qarin.

"No, Charlie," He said, coughing up blood again. "This was merely a punishment."

You can heal me?

"I can heal *us*." Qarin closed our eyes, and I begged him not to heal me. I begged him to let me die, like I should have died all those years earlier in the woods.

Woods not unlike these.

My bones began to crack back into place, and Qarin let me feel that, too. It was a punishment, like He'd said, designed to show me the extent of his control. Of his power. To reinforce that I was his vessel.

I felt the skin around my broken bones moulding around freshly healed joints; torn veins reconnecting, untwisting, and growing thick with new blood.

I want to die, I told him. *I don't want to be here anymore, not like this.*

"Poor, poor Charlie," Qarin said, as we stared up at the trees swaying in the soft breeze. "You know I can't let that happen."

Most of me was healed now, but residual pain lingered in my left shoulder, and there were some bruises and scratches on my face and arms. My clothes, drenched in blood—both my own now and the dead passengers'—were wet and sticky.

My toes wiggled in my shoes, and I realised I had done that. Qarin's hold was slipping, and I wondered if he had used his energy to heal me, if that had shortened his ability to stay inside me.

"You will... never... have me." And I was the one who'd said it. Despite my body shuddering in pain, I smiled. All I had to do was die. Find one way to kill myself, to reunite with my sister.

In the distance, I heard a crash. I didn't need a newscaster to tell me what it was. Without a pilot, the plane had gone down anyway, and I hoped it hadn't crashed in a populated area. From my spot on the ground, I could see thick plumes of black smoke and knew it was close.

But I am alive.

WE WILL ALWAYS SURVIVE, CHARLIE. Other Charlie was back.

"Where do you go?" I asked him.

QARIN DIDN'T SILENCE ONLY YOU, he told me. *I WAS THERE, BUT I...*

He didn't finish the sentence, and I didn't know what he could have said that would make any sense. He was what? Repressed? Asleep? Had I been the way he was when I was in charge, looking out through my own eyes like a passenger in my own life?

I THOUGHT QARIN WOULD MAKE US BETTER, he said. *THE WAY OUR SISTER DID. BUT... I WAS WRONG.*

"Can we die now, then?" I asked him.

YOU SAID WE.

"Well, can we?"

WE CAN, CHARLIE BOY. WE CAN DIE NOW. WE CAN REST.

I closed my eyes, hoping my internal organs were still failing. The silence was encouraging, with nothing but a slight breeze and the rustling of trees. Last time I'd heard that rustle, I was tied to a tree watching my parents fuck each other to begin a sacrificial ritual. Now, it was a sign that I was alive—that I was okay.

That I was okay to die.

LOOK, CHARLIE BOY.

I opened my eyes, a new sound overpowering the rustle and the breeze.

Footsteps.

Fast, hurried.

"Oh shit," a voice said. "Shane, over here! I found one!" A second voice came closer, calling for Manny—whoever that was—and yelling, "I'm coming!"

"Is that... Are they... " I figured Shane was the one stumbling on his words.

A figure in black, with his face visible under the visor of a cap, knelt beside me, taking in my damaged body. We looked at each other, his expression full of disbelief. "He's alive," the man whispered. Then, to Shane, "We have a survivor! Get the medics out here!"

"Leave me," I said, and grabbed at his shirt collar. "Please, let me die."

The man shook his head. "He's in shock."

Shane approached, a radio in his hand, shouting the code to order a medic and giving their location. I didn't recognise the name of where we were. It didn't matter.

"Sir," the first man said. "Sir, can you hear me?"

I closed my eyes again and wished them away. Wished them to let me lie there and die. To reunite with my sister. Even if I had to stay there until I starved to death, I didn't care. I'd be doing the world a favour.

"The paramedics will be here in five," Shane said, kneeling beside me, opposite the other man, Manny. "How the fuck does someone survive a plane crash like that? And he's all the way over here."

"Must have jumped. He's pretty banged up."

Shane scoffed. "Dude. He's got scrapes and bruises. No fucking way. There's just *no fucking way.*"

The next few minutes were a blur with the paramedics shining lights in my eyes, lifting me onto a gurney, and pumping IV fluids into my arms. They fired questions at me, and I didn't have the will to answer. I didn't want to answer.

As they rushed me into the ambulance, I saw my sister standing by a tree. When I blinked, she was gone, now standing beside me in the ambulance. She breathed out. I breathed in. We held hands until I fell asleep.

———

I didn't think I'd ever see the world again. Staring out from my hospital bed at the television, I saw it now. Footage of the plane crash, reporters asking where the passengers were and where all the bodies were. Search parties for kilometres around the crash site, into the ocean, following the flight path.

"Reports came in earlier that there is one survivor, who has been identified. We've been asked to keep his name private for now while investigations continue, but what I can tell you is that, miraculously, the survivor has escaped with only mild injuries. This person is currently being treated—"

I turned the sound off, and the reporter on the screen continued talking about me.

There was a silver lining to being rescued. I was in the hospital, surrounded by all manner of drugs. Qarin was still around; I knew he was. We were connected and would be forever until I took my own life.

"It's the only way," I muttered to myself.

WE GOTTA DIE, CHARLIE BOY. WE GOTTA DIE!

He was excited, and I felt a twinge of adrenaline pulse through my newly healed veins. Maybe I was excited, too. Excited to die—wasn't that part of my condition?

No, CHARLIE! YOU don't HAVE A CONDITION!

"Whether Qarin is real or not," I told him, "I do have a condition. That's what he's been relying on. He can't take me now because I have a purpose. Even if that purpose is to die."

I don't know how I made the connection. It was some innocuous thing Qarin had said, I was sure. I couldn't pinpoint it, but in my heart, I knew. My mental illness was his gateway. My spiral, me hurting Rachel—that's what had led to His actions on the plane. A final push to destroy my hope. To destroy my spirit so He could finish the ritual and take me. It hadn't worked, though. I still had Aiden.

The curtain separating me from the other patients was ripped back, and I jumped in my bed.

"Sorry, Charlie," the nurse said with a small frown. "I didn't mean to scare you. I know you must be scared enough as it is, but"—she motioned over her shoulder—"there are some police officers here to ask you some questions."

To TaKE uS AWaY!

"I can talk to them," I said, trying to ignore Other Charlie.

The nurse ushered two officers in, a man and a woman.

"How are you feeling, Charlie?" the woman asked. "I'm Senior Detective Mitchell. Do you mind if we ask you a few questions?"

DOn'T TalK To THeM, CHARLIE BOY. DO NOT TALK TO THEM!

I nodded, unsure why Other Charlie was freaking out. "Sure."

"You're married to Aiden Reed?" Mitchell asked.

I nodded. "Is he here? I want to see him before... "

"Before what?" Mitchell asked.

Shrugging, I said, "Doesn't matter." I was searching for drugs with my eyes, though. Anything would do. Enough of anything would get it done.

The detectives exchanged concerned glances, and Mitchell cleared her throat. "Where were you at approximately eight pm last night?"

"I was—" I stopped, and Other Charlie whistled so loudly in my head I couldn't hear myself think. "I was—" I put a hand to my temple and tried to focus.

"We have reason to believe you are responsible for the murder of Doctor Rachel Schwarz. We al—"

"I confess," I said hurriedly. "I did it." I held my breath for a moment, taking in the sound of my voice admitting to murder, and the knowledge that I was capable of such a thing. I'd known it; I'd been confronted with it on the plane, but it hadn't sunk in. I hadn't had time to let it sink in.

"You admit it?" Mitchell raised an eyebrow and reached for her handcuffs.

"I'm not a bad guy," I said, my voice breaking. "I'm sorry. I'm so sorry for what I did."

She placed the handcuffs around my wrist, and I saw my sister behind them, putting her hands to her ears. *Don't listen.* She was saying the same thing. Other Charlie was still screaming at me.

"Charles Reed, you are under arrest for the murders of Rachel Schwarz and Aiden Reed." The handcuffs clicked, and I stared at her.

"What did you say?" I held my breath.

"Anything you say can and will be used against you in a court of law."

NO, CHARLIE. CLOSE YOUR EARS!

"What did you say?" I cried. "Aiden? Where's Aiden?!" I tried to breathe, tried to listen to Mitchell reading me my rights, tried to understand the words.

...for the murders of Rachel Schwarz and Aiden Reed.

"No, no, no. Aiden isn't dead. I saw him this afternoon. I've been talking to him on the plane."

The world was shrinking, and my sister was signing to me that it would be okay; everything would be okay. Other Charlie was laughing and crying and screaming and screaming and—

"I WAS TALKING TO HIM ON THE PLANE!" I shouted.

"Mr Reed—"

"No!" I pulled away from Mitchell and her companion, the cuffs tight around my wrists. The cops raced to me, but I grabbed the IV machine and launched it at the male cop. Mitchell came around the bed, and I shoulder-barged her as hard as I could. Ripples of pain eked through my own shoulder, and I stumbled but ran.

"You're making this worse for yourself!" Mitchell called after me as she recovered and gave chase.

People, everyone, stared at me, cowered, and got out of the way of the crazy person fleeing the police. I didn't kill Aiden, I could never kill Aiden or hurt him—

—the wine stem was so sharp—

—or do anything but love him.

Down a hallway, an elevator door was sliding shut. I raced to it, slipped in as it closed, and pressed the first button my finger touched. The cuffs were tight, but I could escape. Like in the woods as a kid, I dislocated my thumb with a sharp pop and slipped my hand free. The cuffs hung loose from my other wrist as I pulled my thumb back into its socket.

I needed to find a phone to call Aiden and prove to them he wasn't dead. There'd been a mistake. It had to be a mistake.

"It's going to be okay, Charlie," my sister said. She pulled me to the corner of the elevator, where we sat together. "It's all going to be okay."

"They made a mistake," I said. "I... I did a horrible thing, I know. I did kill Doctor Schwarz. But Aiden? No"—I shook my head furiously—"no no no."

Before she could say anything else, the elevator doors dinged, and I was in the lobby. The street was through the nearby automatic sliding doors, so I was almost free. I could get home and see Aiden again. Tell him to his face that I love him, that I need him, that I'll take all the pills in the world if he will stay with me because we belong together forever, and I'll do whatever I need to do to prove that to him and—

The air was warm against my skin as I raced into the street, my hospital gown flowing in the morning air. The sun was well into the sky, a brand new day to usher out the waste of the recent past. I looked up, and behind me. Mitchell ordered me to freeze.

I spun around, searching her eyes. She was human.

"I didn't do it," I said.

Mitchell had a gun trained at my chest. "On your knees. Now!"

I collapsed to my knees. My sister did the same next to me.

"You are under arrest—"

"I didn't kill my husband." Tears muffled my words, and I repeated them until I was sure Mitchell had heard.

She was behind me again, using zip ties around my wrists instead of cuffs, so I couldn't get free. My hands behind my back this time, I sobbed while she read me my rights.

"I spoke to him on the plane," I whispered.

"Mr. Reed," Mitchell said, "no calls have been placed from your phone since early this afternoon."

THIRTY

11 HOURS EARLIER

THE CHEESE MELTED IN my mouth, the saltiness of the cracker offset by the sweetness of the cheese. I sipped at the wine again—alcohol-free shit for the crazy guy—and nodded to Aiden to show I liked it.

The lounge felt too small for us in that moment, too. He wanted to be close, and his thighs rubbed against mine. I loved his thighs, how thick and hairy they were. But in that moment, I fucking hated them being on me, scraping and scratching and tickling at me, even through my jeans.

I moved away and saw him sizing me up.

"What's up?" I asked.

HE KNOWS! MURDER! MURDER!

Aiden took a deep breath, sipped long on his wine, and cleared his throat. Putting his glass on the coffee table, he pushed his plate of cheese and crackers aside and held his arms across his torso. He was folding in on himself, the way he did when he had bad news.

"This doesn't look good," I said with a shy laugh.

"Charlie," Aiden began, "I love you more than anything."

"Uh oh," I said, the laugh fading into the heavy silence.

After a few moments, Aiden spoke again. "I want you to know that despite what I'm about to tell you, I do love you. It's just... ." His eyes darted to the next room, and I half expected another man to come waltzing out with his cock on display—*WE'RE IN LOVE NOW, CHARLIE, AIDEN HAS MOVED ON!*

I was being silly. Aiden was not a cheater.

"It's exhausting being with you."

"I'm sorry?" My eyebrows perked up, and my grip tightened around my wine glass.

"I hate myself for saying this," he said, "but there's only so much support one person can give. And I'm all out. The tank is empty."

I sat in silence, staring, daring him to say the words.

"I've filed for a divorce."

THeRe IT Issss, CHARLIE BOY. HE HATES YOU!

"You... what?" I asked.

He looked down. "I can't do this anymore. I love you, but being with you... I'm always walking on eggshells. I'm always wondering if I'm saying the wrong thing or *being* the wrong thing."

"Being the wrong thing? What does that even mean?" I stood up and paced back and forth, sculling the wine down.

"Am I happy enough, am I sad enough, am I being supportive enough or doing the right thing... I never know how to *be* when I'm with you."

HE HATES YOU. HE'S ONE OF THEM.

I searched his eyes. The light was faded, but it was there. He was human. He was human, and he was saying these things. The voice was right. Other Charlie had been right, as always. My husband hated me. He wasn't one of *them*, but he was like everyone else. Everyone else who hated me and treated me like a monster.

"You don't love me," I said.

Aiden jumped to his feet. "I have stayed with you through so much, Charlie. I have stayed with you through how many stays in the psych unit? Don't you dare say I don't love you."

"But your tank is empty," I said, moving close to him. My chest was heavy and tight, and my fist closed around the empty wine glass. "*Your* tank is empty? Try having my fucking tank. Try having the voice in my fucking head telling you what to do all the time. THAT'S EXHAUSTING! You don't have a FUCKING CLUE!"

I tried to stop, but Other Charlie seeped into my words. He was there, in every syllable, and I couldn't stop him.

"Charlie," Aiden raised a hand and pushed me back. It was a soft thing to get some distance between us, so my angry spit wasn't propelled onto his face. "Don't speak to me like that. I'm telling you how I feel."

HE PusHeD US, CHARLIE BOY. ThaT FUcKInG guY PUSHED US.

"I know he did," I said.

"Who are you talking to?" Aiden asked.

"Why are you leaving me now?" I ignored him.

"I've had the papers for a while. Since you were admitted this time round." Aiden turned away, heading to the next room. The home office. "I've signed them already."

HE KNOWS, CHARLIE. HE KNOWS!

"You know, don't you?" I could feel the wine glass cracking in my hand, felt shards dig into my palm. "You saw me?"

Aiden paused. "What?"

"That's why you're leaving me."

He ignored me with a dismissive wave and left the room. I heard him shuffling around in the home office, and I couldn't move. Couldn't breathe. Aiden was leaving me. My Aiden. My world. My life.

Leaving me.

Aiden came back holding a bunch of papers. Little yellow tags stuck out from the sides, and he flipped to the first one. "You just need to sign where I've already signed."

He stepped closer.

I felt the wine glass come apart in my hand.

Closer. Looking down at the papers, avoiding my eyes.

The stem cracked in half.

I dropped the rest of the shattered glass on the carpet.

Closer.

"Aiden?" I said.

He looked up.

I thrust the broken stem into his neck and stepped away as Aiden dropped the papers—like leaves rustling to the floor—and stumbled backwards into the wall. His eyes were on me now, the light still faded, but there. Something else was in them now.

Fear.

Confusion.

Moving towards him, he held one hand out to keep me away, the other clasped around the jagged glass in his neck. Blood spurted from the wound, ran down his skin, and through his clothes. I could see he wanted to scream and yell, but the shock had taken over.

"I'm sorry," I said as I pushed his hand away, and he slid down the wall. "I didn't mean to."

He gulped hard, a choked sound echoing through the room.

"Let me help." I guided his hand away from the stem, his wide, terrified eyes stuck on me. Pulling at the stem, I worked it free and dodged the geyser of blood that spurted from his neck.

DO IT, CHARLIE!

The voice was right.

I had to do it.

"I'm going to help you," I said.

Aiden held a hand over the wound and opened his mouth to speak. Blood leaked out, but he managed a small, "Please... "

"Shhh," I said, and I leaned in for a kiss. He tasted like wine and cheese and blood, and it melted in my mouth. As my tongue searched for his, I gripped the stem once more and thrust it into his chest.

Aiden gurgled, and I came off his face to see the light in his eyes go out.

YOU'VE DONE IT, CHARLIE BOY. YOU'VE FINALLY DONE IT!

"I..."

I let go of the stem, the glass sticking an inch out of Aiden's chest, right in his heart. I fell away from him and stared at what I'd done.

"I... "

There was nothing to say. Aiden was dead, his empty eyes looking back at me.

WHAT SHOULD WE DO NOW, CHARLIE?

It was a good question, but I didn't want to hear it. I didn't have an answer anyway. My husband was dead. I had killed him. His blood was on my hands, my clothes, my face. I could taste it, had swallowed it.

"This isn't real," I whispered. "I didn't really do this."

YOU DID.

"No, I didn't."

From the corner of my eye, I saw something shift within the shadows of the living room. A bright light sparked behind me somewhere and then vanished. It didn't matter. All that mattered was Aiden.

Moving him from the wall, I positioned him so he was lying with his head in my lap, and I stroked his beard and face until the sun had disappeared. He was sleeping; that was all.

"I didn't do this," I said. "I didn't do this."

Other Charlie was gone, silenced somehow, but I heard something else. A whispering from some dark corner of the house. I couldn't make out all the words, only: "*Fallen Father.*"

The memory of that night in the woods was always with me, but in that moment, the whispering brought that night into the present. It wasn't *with* me; it *was* me. It was real, it was in that room with me, it defined my actions, it had made me... hurt... Aiden.

"I have to get out of here," I said to Aiden. "I'm going home. I'll call you from the airport."

He'll be awake by then, I told myself. *He'll be awake, and he'll feel much better.*

Kissing him on the forehead and resting his head on the carpet, I grabbed my pills, wallet, and car keys—my phone was still in my pocket—and headed for the door.

Pausing for a moment, I looked back at Aiden and said, "We can fix our marriage. I love you."

NOW

The memory rushed back to me, and I doubled over, wailing into the street underneath me.

"Aiden!" I called his name, begging the memory not to be true but knowing it was. Knowing that I had stabbed him and fled, leaving him there alone to rot.

Mitchell forced me to my feet and dragged me to a nearby police car. Her male companion opened the door and muttered, "Watch your head."

They slammed the door, and the sound reverberated in my brain.

My sister was beside me again, but she didn't say anything. She sat there, looking at me with those sad eyes. She wore the clothes she'd had on during the ritual, complete with the crown of thorns digging into her skull.

She was gone.

Aiden was gone.

I was a killer.

There was nothing left.

No hope. No reason to fight anymore.

I wept in the back of the car as the detectives took their respective seats. Mitchell grabbed the radio and clicked the button on the side. "We're bringing in the suspect."

I looked at my sister, and while she breathed out, I breathed in. It was what we did. Nothing could ever change that, even if she wasn't really there. I smiled at our synchronicity, at how we were still the same.

She touched a pinky to her nose and then rubbed the back of her right hand with a thumb. *Look right.*

I did.

Qarin was outside the car.

"No," I mumbled. "Let me die. I can't live without Aiden."

As the engine started, He slipped inside the car as though the metal door didn't even exist.

"It truly is time now," He said to me.

The detectives turned around.

"Who are you talking—"

"What the fuck—"

Qarin was taking me, melting into me, making me his vessel. And I couldn't stop him.

Without Aiden, I was nothing. The moment I stabbed him had sealed not only my fate, but also the fate of the entire world. The knowledge that I had destroyed my husband was the last lost shred of hope Qarin needed to enter me forever.

I cried and looked at my sister, who was telling me it was going to be okay. She'd said that all those times in the basement, too, and it was never okay then. It wouldn't be okay now, either, but it didn't even matter.

As Qarin's body melted around me, inside me, his thoughts pushing mine into the dark corners of my mind, there was nothing I could do about it.

"Mmmm," Qarin moaned as he raped me almost out of existence. "You feel so good."

"Just get it over with," I said.

GET OUT GET OUT GET OUT! Other Charlie screamed. He'd never said where he went last time, but he'd seemed scared. I didn't know who I'd be without Other Charlie, or with Qarin using me to destroy the world.

Will I become one of them? I wondered.

"No, Charlie," Qarin said, as the detectives watched our bodies merge into one. "You are something new. I'm not just any doppelgänger. I'm the fucking God of them. And now,"—he smirked—"my legions can begin remaking the Earth."

"What the fuck is happening?" Mitchell asked, reaching for her weapon again.

Qarin ignored her, focusing on finishing what He'd started. I felt His presence inside me, reaching into my veins, arteries, and muscles—planting Himself deep inside my mind again. It felt different than last time. He felt stronger but also gentler.

Please let me die, I begged Him. *You can take my body. I just want to die.*

"Oh no, Charlie," Qarin said. "You will live. You will live forever with what you've done, and you will bear witness to the rebirth of the world."

NO!

"Oh yes, Charlie. You will see it all."

Mitchell and her partner climbed out of the car, the guy chattering to someone on his radio, calling for assistance. Mitchell pried open the rear car door and pointed her weapon at me—at Qarin.

"Get the fuck out of the car. Now!" she yelled, but her voice quavered.

Through my eyes, a small void forming, Qarin gazed at her.

"I said, get out!" she cried.

Qarin did as He was ordered, and I moved further into the recesses of my own mind. I didn't want to see this—I didn't want to see any of it. Whatever Qarin was up to, whatever He was going to do, I didn't want to be here for it.

Standing next to the police car now, Qarin stepped towards Mitchell. Her hands shook as the last of Qarin's body disappeared beneath the surface of my own. He had complete control, and though I existed somewhere in my own brain, he owned my body.

"Put the weapon down, detective," Qarin said.

Don't hurt her, please, I begged.

Mitchell's hands were still shaking, but the gun did not lower. She scanned for help until her eyes rested on something behind me. I felt the butt of a gun on the back of my head and heard Qarin laugh through my mouth.

"You think that's going to stop me from getting what I want?" Qarin asked and spun fast. His arm—my arm—thrust forward into the detective's chest and ripped out his heart. He fell to the road, his eyes still open, and Qarin looked at the organ with interest as Mitchell shot Him three times in the head.

"Wh... What do you... w-w-want?" Mitchell asked when Qarin didn't even blink.

He raised a finger to His lips and shushed her. "Do you hear that?"

She looked around, unsure what was happening. A crowd of people was descending upon the hospital, their eyes all missing a tiny spot. Their feet fell in sync, and they hummed with a noise that slowly became a chant: "Hail, Our Fallen Father."

Qarin walked to Mitchell—

Don't! I begged. *Spare her!*

—and with one movement tore off her head. He held it up to His face for a moment before tossing it aside, letting it roll on the road next to her fallen body.

"I'm here, my children," Qarin said. "After all this time, I'm here."

"Hail, Our Fallen Father." The chant rose. The footfalls came closer.

NO, NO, NO! I cried, banging on the walls of my own mind.

"I want the world, my children. And I will have it."

Acknowledgements

I'd like to shout out to Chisto Healy in particular; a dear friend, and a wonderful editor. His comments on my book helped to shape you've read, and the book is much better off having his thoughts added.

Marc Ruvolo read an early draft of this book, back when it was titled *Stowaway* and his feedback was impressive and helpful. Stephanie Sanders-Jacob was also instrumental in the production of this book, particularly in workshopping character traits and testing the twists. Finally, I need to thank L. Andrew Cooper for all his help surrounding medications and the diagnosis that appears in the book. His generosity knows no bounds, and I'm incredibly grateful and honoured to have people in the horror community who I can call on, and whom I count as true friends.

This book is incredibly important to me. It deals with mental health and the isolation, stigma, and fear living with severe mental health can have. My own battle with depression, anxiety, and Borderline Personality Disorder informed much of the character of Charlie, and many of the passengers on the plane. It feels wrong to not acknowledge everyone who is also currently dealing with severe mental health.

This book is for us.

For all of us.

About the Author

David-Jack Fletcher is a gay Australian horror author, publisher, and editor, specialising in work that emphasises the everydayness of LGBTQIA+ individuals.

He is the Aurealis-nominated author of *The Count*, a vampiric novel centred on the evil that lurks within the earth itself. His other titles include the award-winning *Raven's Creek*, *The Haunting of Harry Peck* (Lethe Press), *Hell is Other People: Stories* (Lethe Press), and *Indentured* (Truborn Press).

David-Jack is also the founder of Slashic Horror Press, an queer indie press focused on promoting under-represented voices—and stories—in horror and dark fiction. Since beginning in June '23, Slashic Horror Press has released over 20 titles. For more details, visit the website here: https//:www.slashichorrorpress.com/titlesandstore

Content Warning

This book contains depictions of severe mental health conditions, abuse of medication and alcohol, suicidal ideation, implied child abuse, and spousal abuse. These depictions are not *representative* of mental health and I do not intend to imply the actions undertaken in this book are those perpetrated by anyone with mental health diagnoses/conditions; the book is a work of fiction and should be read in the spirit of horror.